Praise for the novels of Beth Albright

"Albright good-naturedly displays her inner redneck while steering this giddy Dixie romp with ease—leaving lots of room at the happy ending for another adventure starring these steel magnolias."
—*Publishers Weekly* on *The Sassy Belles*

"*The Sassy Belles* reminded me that the South is like no other place on earth. Kudos to Beth Albright for capturing its spirit so perfectly in this lighthearted debut novel."
—Celia Rivenbark, *New York Times* bestselling author of *We're Just Like You, Only Prettier*

"Dripping with southern charm and colloquialisms, the novel once again proves Albright's firsthand knowledge of southern culture. The women in Albright's novels are especially well written—happy to challenge the status quo when necessary but also aware of that old adage: 'You catch more flies with honey.' This delightfully campy and romantic read will satisfy fans of Mary Kay Andrews, Alexandra Potter, and Lisa Jewell."
—*Booklist* on *Wedding Belles*

"The Sassy Belles are back and sassier than ever!... With clever dialogue and richly drawn characters, Albright shows once again she's a natural-born storyteller who knows how to pen a charming tale. Regardless of game-day colors worn, this sexy and fun Southern series will have readers coming back for more!"
—*RT magazine* on *Wedding Belles*

"Readers will find some sexy, Southern fun for Christmas with the Sassy Belles."
—*Library Journal* on *Sleigh Belles*

Also by Beth Albright

WEDDING BELLES
SLEIGH BELLES

BETH ALBRIGHT

the Sassy Belles

HARLEQUIN® MIRA®

Recycling programs
for this product may
not exist in your area.

ISBN-13: 978-0-7783-1640-4

THE SASSY BELLES

For questions and comments about the quality of this book, please contact us at CustomerService@Harlequin.com.

Printed in U.S.A.

For my mother, Betty, the original Sassy Belle, who pushed me to keep writing, who believed in me no matter what I was trying to do. A little piece of you is in every one of these women. They are smart and funny. Motivating and warm, strong and wise, beautiful and stubborn, they are the heart of all I admired in you. And you were the heart of my childhood. Not only my mother, but my very best friend, you loved me into my potential. I am so grateful. You are the wind beneath my wings. I love you more than any words can say. This is all for you.

For Brooks and Ted, my universe.

1

My name is Blake O'Hara Heart and, boy, do I have a story to tell! It wouldn't be such a story if Vivi, my best friend since forever, hadn't done what she did. You have to understand that women in the South, women of Southern blood, just don't partake in scandalous adventures—and when we do, it's in a discreet manner. We have reputations to consider, after all. But since Vivi's trouble became headline news, our lives became anything but discreet. I'm an attorney, and even *I* wasn't sure I could get her out of this one.

When I met Vivi in the third grade, we were silly nine-year-olds in ponytails and Catholic school uniforms. She was exciting and confident. I loved her immediately. I was new to St. Catherine's, Tuscaloosa's Catholic academy, and didn't know a soul. Vivi made a beeline across the room, her pale and freckled arm outstretched. "Hi," she said. "My name is Vivi Ann McFadden. I'll take care of you today and make sure you don't get lost. This is my fourth year here including kindergarten. So, I'm an expert." I loved her self-assurance, outspokenness and all that crazy, wild red hair, which she was constantly pushing from her face.

She took care of me that day, it's true. But from eight o'clock the very next morning I have been taking care of her. I always want to protect her, but she makes that difficult. Her huge messes are almost always of her own making. Luckily for both of us, I've always known how to get her out of jail, so to speak. But this particular instance, on this particular day—well, let's just say she must think I'm a miracle worker.

See, the problem is, in Alabama, women are most definitely…women. Vivi—well, some would call her opinionated. Others would say, "Bless her heart, that girl is just a redneck!" That's a little secret of the South: you can say awful and insulting things about anyone, and as long as you start with "Bless her heart" you're not really gossiping. Like, "Bless her heart, that girl looks like a pregnant heifer in that dress." See? That makes it look like we're so sad for her, when you know we really think otherwise. Women from Alabama are strong—well, stubborn—and, above all, we are beautiful. There's nothing in the world a little spackle and Aqua Net won't fix. We are trained by way of the beauty pageant system. In the Deep South, pageants aren't just fun, they're a way of life. With the heavy doll makeup applied to perfection, the big hair jacked up to Jesus and the princess-cut, bedazzled gowns with full crinoline and sometimes even a hoop skirt underneath—we are brought up to walk the runway. And a proper Southern girl *always* has a strand of pearls around her neck. That way, if anyone ever needs to be strangled, we have the perfect tool. Just remove and use.

But Vivi never quite fit into the *fru fru* of it all. Her frizzy, wiry Irish curls and endless sea of freckles made her a standout for all the wrong reasons. Her skin was so white she was almost blue. But I thought she was beautiful. She had a wonderfully infectious smile, straight, pearly white teeth, ruby-red lips that never needed lipstick and I thought her green eyes were just perfect. Vivi was a real Southern blue blood, too. She came from sugar cane. Really! An actual plantation was part of her family history. And that made what Vivi did seem like the end of the world. Someone from the "uppa crust" wouldn't dare be involved in such activities. But Vivi wasn't quite as "uppa crust" as the rest of her family. I mean, how could a blue blood be a redneck? That's exactly what made me love her. She was different. Unexpected. Surprising. What she did was a surprise, all right, but not the kind you hope for on Christmas morning....

Harry, my husband and my law partner, was in the lobby of the old Tutwiler Hotel when the news came. He was waiting to meet me. It was our tenth anniversary and we were meeting for lunch. We did this every year; same table, same bourbon-n-peach cobbler. I wasn't looking as forward to this lunch as I had been on other anniversaries, though. Harry and I had been having some problems. Well, unless you don't consider silence a problem. We had been growing apart as he grew ever closer to his political dreams. With every step toward his coveted Senate seat, he stepped farther away from me. My plan was to talk to him during our lunch, to tell him that I'd had enough of his absentee husband routine. I spent all morning gearing up to tell him that I was through with being second to his career and his political dreams—it was time to focus on our marriage, or I wanted a separation. Of course, I'd been a nervous wreck since I'd opened my eyes that morning. But, lucky for me, I was saved by the belle…a belle named Vivi.

I was running late that morning, which was basically on par for me. I was stuck at the law school in an alumni meeting that was reaching into an eternity. I was sure Harry stood patiently waiting, checking his pocket watch at least once every 23 seconds, then glancing into the nearest mirror to check his gorgeous hair. If there was a mirror within 20 yards, you'd find Harry looking at himself—usually in admiration—but checking, always checking, for perfection. Every thick strand of hair in place, gold cuff links hitting just at the hem of his suit sleeves—down to the last detail, Harry liked to be in control. His cell phone rang in his vest pocket. It was Vivi.

"Harry, where are you?" she said.

Now, Harry is rock-solid by anyone's standards, by far the most patient soul. His emotions are buried deep, like down near the Earth's core. But, as even-keeled as he is, Vivi could almost always manage to rattle his cage. This phone call would shake Harry to his soul.

"I'm in the Tutwiler waiting on Blake," he answered.

"Shit! I forgot it's your anniversary," she said. "Harry, forgive me for this. I need Blake."

"She's at the university, Vivi. You okay?" Harry asked.

"Harry, I'm drivin' and I don't have a destination," Vivi said in her thick-as-molasses Southern voice. This wasn't the typical Vivi call for help.

"Vivi, where are you?" he said.

"I don't know. I'm just drivin'. When can I talk to Blake? When will she be there?"

Harry was having trouble making sense of her words between her frantic nonsense and the god-awful cell reception.

"Vivi, just tell me where you are and Blake and I will meet you," Harry said.

There was no response.

"Vivi! Vivi! Can you hear me?" Harry shouted. By this time, he'd stepped outside onto the courtyard for a little more privacy once he realized everyone in the lobby was staring at him for all the wrong reasons.

Vivi answered slow and sober. "Harry…I think I've just killed Lewis."

Silence followed.

"Harry? Did you hear me? Lewis is layin' dead in the bed, buck naked and blue, at the Fountain Mist on I20!" Vivi screamed.

Harry Heart came from a long line of legal counsel—defense attorneys to be exact. Generations upon generations of Hearts were all University of Alabama Law School graduates.

All except for Lewis. Lewis was Harry's younger brother. He was the wayward son who wound up on the radio. He was the play-by-play announcer for the University of Alabama Crimson Tide; a partygoer so popular with the women, he never married—never had to. All of his needs were met nightly by the groupies, from cheerleaders to professors to coach's wives. Lewis Heart was at your service, so to speak.

Harry stood among the gardenia blossoms in the Tutwiler courtyard, dumbfounded, wanting to utter something, but unable to make a sound. Finally, he managed to ask, "Vivi, are you talkin' 'bout *my* Lewis?"

"Yes, dammit, Harry," Vivi said. "Who the hell else? Oh, my God, he's dead. He's dead, Harry! And I've killed him, I know it!"

"Stop, Vivi. Slow down," Harry said. "Okay. Let me get Blake. We'll meet you at Mother's."

"I'm sittin' in front of her house right now, Harry. I didn't know where else to go."

Meredith Blakely Fletcher is my maternal grandmother and the matriarch of everything. She is known affectionately as "Mother" to everyone who knows her. Her house has always been the command center. At one time or another it had been home to all of us, both friends and family alike. It became known as "Mother's" decades before I was even born.

Mother has a real rags-to-riches story. A young woman during World War Two, she was born in the mud of the Mississippi Delta, surrounded by money and old plantations, but never quite able to grasp it herself. She was absolutely gorgeous, a movie-star type of beauty with dark, wavy hair and eyes as blue-green as the Gulf. She worked at a five-and-dime during the war as a cosmetic salesperson. One day a handsome young law student by the name of Frank Fletcher came into the store and approached the lunch counter. Her Southern beauty caught his Yankee eye and they were together for 41 years, until his death twenty-one years ago. My New York–born grandfather always bragged that he found a million-dollar baby in the five-and ten-cent store, just like the song says.

Frank gave Meridee, as he affectionately called her,

everything: a big Southern home and the exciting life of a wealthy lawyer's wife in the late forties and fifties. Frank set up his practice and Meridee gave birth to three children. She entertained with lavish parties for Frank's clients and two maids helped her care for her home and children. Meridee was the epitome of a Southern blue blood, even though her blood had originally run plain ole red.

Eventually, after much success on his own, Frank Fletcher and Hank Heart set up practice together. Yes, Hank is my Harry's grandfather and, no, mine was not an arranged marriage. They were affectionately known in Tuscaloosa as Hank-n-Frank, Attorneys-at-Law. Go ahead and laugh now and get that out of the way.

I remember as a child, Mother's house was my favorite place to be. Her bedroom was so full of the thick scent of perfumes that I can't think of her and not recall those fragrances. Her dressing table was a place of pure fascination to a little girl. The French pink glass bottles and the powder she had custom mixed to match her delicate skin tone made that table an island of enchantment to me. And the silver makeup brushes were the wands of magical transformations. Meridee wore black transparent stockings with seams running up the back. Her long nails were always perfectly manicured and always matched her endless array of bloodred lipsticks. I wanted to grow up to be just like her.

Mother's was a stone's throw from the law school, so it made for a very convenient hangout. Frank was a huge success as an attorney, but on Saturdays in the fall, you'd find him in the broadcast booth of the Alabama Crimson Tide. Frank was the play-by-play announcer for the famous football team. He was so proud of that. Our blood runs perfectly Crimson in *my* family. Their house was a place for everyone, and Meridee made sure that all felt welcome. All my life, in any moment of crisis or excitement, we always wound up at Mother's. No surprise, it's where we all wound up on that day.

Harry drove like a bat out of hell over to Mother's. He later told me he knew it would be bad for his Senatorial run if he had gotten a speeding ticket, but for once he didn't think about the political dreams first. Amazing.

When Harry got to Mother's, he found Vivi sitting in her car, gripping the steering wheel and staring straight ahead in a dazed stupor.

Harry had called me as he was driving to Mother's. When I found the ringing cell in my red leather Gucci bag and saw the caller ID announcing it was Harry, I don't know why, but I instantly suspected something awful. Harry never sounds hurried or breathless. He is the consummate lawyer, always in control. So when I answered the phone and heard his voice, I knew it *was* something awful.

"Blake!" Harry sounded like he had been jogging. "Meet me at Mother's—now!"

"Harry, what's wrong?" I asked.

"Blake, just come now." A silence. Then, "Lewis might be dead and Vivi's involved."

"*What?* I'm on my way." He explained all the details as I sped through town.

I don't remember the drive over there. I don't think I breathed even once in the five minutes it took me to arrive at the familiar cracked driveway. You had to angle your car just right to get in and out of it so as not to bottom out. I wasn't thinking of any angling as

I ripped right in behind Harry's Mercedes and Vivi's powder-blue convertible Thunderbird. Harry was standing beside her car. The shock of what I'd just heard was stealing my breath, but I knew they both needed me. I opened my car door and turned and touched my high heels to the cement.

"Tell me again—what the hell happened?" I heard Harry say to Vivi. "Go slow this time. I need every detail."

The consummate lawyer. Even when his own brother could be dead, Harry was in full lawyer mode.

"For God's sake, Harry, you aren't takin' a freakin' deposition are you?" Vivi reacted in pure Vivi form. "Your damn brother, my lover, is dead, Harry! Dead! Dead! Dead!"

Vivi is a tactless wonder. "I did it, but it was an accident! I thought he was enjoying it. He was yellin' and moanin' and…Harry, he just stopped," she said. "I don't know if I suffocated him or what, but oh, my God, he's dead!" She was crying and trembling, pushing the red, wiry frizz away from her eyes.

By now, Harry was visibly shaken. He pulled off his wire-framed glasses and dragged his long fingers through his thick salt-and-pepper hair. He was in his late thirties, but if you keep yourself so bottled up all the time you go gray before you know it. Harry was bottled *and* corked.

"Vivi," he said slow and steady, "is Lewis still at the Fountain Mist?"

"Well, Harry," Vivi answered with as much sarcasm as she could muster, "unless you believe in the walkin' dead, he's still right there where I left him, buck naked."

"Vivi, if Lewis is actually dead, you need an attorney," I interjected. "My God, we need to call an ambulance! The police."

"Well, y'all," Vivi said, "aren't I lookin' at two lawyers right now?"

Harry and I stood, looking dumb and stupid, first at each other, then at Vivi. Still, Harry looked the most confused. The most disoriented. I could tell he was trying to process how this little development might impact that precious blossoming political career.

He and his brother, Lewis, had never been close and Harry had spent a lifetime bailing Lewis out of one mess after the next. Lewis was the baby of the family. He was good-looking, but in a *Field and Stream* sort of way. He was the polar opposite of Harry. Harry was prep-school gorgeous. Straight out of *GQ*. Lewis was two years younger, with a loud, center-of-attention boom of a voice that could really get irritating. Actually, overall, Lewis *was* quite irritating. Why in the world Vivi would shack up with him was beyond me. I looked at her and, despite her mascara-stained eyes, her sheet-white skin and runny nose, well—honestly, my thought was that Vivi could do better than Lewis. But what I loved in Vivi was her wild streak. She was one of the few people who really lived in the moment. Hell, Vivi lived *for* the moment. And I was sure that's what attracted Lewis.

After a long, awkward silence in the warmth of the late morning sun, Vivi spoke. "Well," she said, as if she had been picked last to play kickball, "since I don't really have a turkey wishbone handy for y'all, somebody be my damn lawyer already! Do we need to play eeny meeny miny moe or what?"

Harry answered first. "No matter what, not report-

ing a death in a timely manner is a real crime, so if
we don't call the police and an ambulance, we will all
need lawyers."

I took out my cell.

"Here, honey, let's get this over with. You need to
call the ambulance first, even if you think he's dead."

I handed the phone to her as I rubbed her shoulder
and then looked over at Harry. He had turned around
and was leaning against Vivi's car, running his fingers
through his hair over and over—his nervous tic. He
looked lost in thought—as though floods of terrible
memories were coming back, like waves crashing a
shoreline. I wanted to say something, but had no good
words at the moment. My thoughts turned back to Vivi.
She was waiting for the 911 operator to answer.

Vivi had been through this before. No, she hadn't
ever killed anyone, but short, steamy love affairs were
basically on par for her. At one point, she'd been married
to a congressman who lived full-time in Washington.
He was twenty years older than Vivi and totally unat-
tractive, but another blue blood just the same. The marriage didn't last too long, though no one ever thought it
would. Vivi would never leave the South. That would be
like asking cotton to grow up North. Vivi just couldn't
be planted anywhere else. But the congressman had to
live in D.C. With all that time apart everyone knew it
would just grow stale. And it did after just a few short
years. Besides, Vivi loved to be…well, let's call it social. Yes, *social* was a perfect word for Vivi Ann Mc-
Fadden. I'm not saying that she was a party girl, but
she loved, thrived actually, on social interaction. Okay,
Vivi was a party girl. She was an only child of wealth

and privilege and most of the time she took the privilege part too far.

She never gave anything much thought. She just flew by the seat of her pants, or anyone else's pants. Her free spirit was enviable. She swore like a sailor, even during high school, and had the reputation as a bit of the wild child of Tuscaloosa. She was popular and, no, not just with the men. Everyone loved her because she was so damn funny. The only little problem was that if Vivi thought it, it popped right out of her mouth before it ever stopped to register at her brain. Vivi never learned that some things should be *thought* but not actually *said*. Sometimes that got her into trouble. But she had such a hilarious personality she stayed at the center of the most sought-after social circles.

As I listened to her choke out her story to the 911 operator, I could tell that this event with Lewis would change her.

Harry and I left Mother's with Vivi to go to the police station. I suggested to Harry that he could go on to the Fountain Mist and meet the ambulance, but he insisted he would prefer to stay with us. He didn't seem to want to see Lewis, dead or alive. I tried my best to persuade him, but he wouldn't budge. After all the years that had gone by, six, I think, since he and Lewis had even spoken, Harry just didn't want to be the one to ID the body. If he got there first, it would be just him and poor, dead Lewis. And Harry didn't want that, not after the way things had been between them. So he led the way to the police station downtown. After that we would all go together to the motel.

My emotions were in overdrive. Vivi was my best

friend since third grade, my sister in every way, and Harry was my husband, my college sweetheart, though we had had our share of troubles. Between these relationships, the fact that Lewis was dead and the fact that I'm an attorney, too, well, I've never felt so stuck in such a messy fix as this. I didn't know which feeling to feel, never mind knowing the right thing to say or who to say it to. We were all in shock for different reasons, and the trip to the police station was a silent one.

We arrived at the station in minutes. That's the good thing about Tuscaloosa—everything is only minutes away. We got out of our cars and walked into the little building. It was on the corner of the street that faced the Warrior River. We stepped inside and I stood next to Vivi and held her hand as she talked to the police. Harry stood on her other side, trying with every fiber in his being to hold it together, to cover his emotions. Luckily for him, it was something he'd being training himself to do for ages now—even with me. A politician should be stoic, composed, unruffled—and I can tell you, he was great at that.

The little balding officer sat in front of us, diligently taking down Vivi's half sentences and descriptive details of her last breathless moments with Lewis. When she finished, the pudgy officer looked up with his mouth open and eyes bugging through his tiny square glasses and eventually spoke. "Ahem. Anything else, ma'am?"

Officer Dooley knew Vivi. He used to work detail for her mother at the gate of the famous McFadden plantation and had known the family for years. Tuscaloosa is a small college town, where everyone knows everyone and has probably slept with their best friend's brother. Believe me, I know that one for sure.

This scene at the station reminded me of the principal's office in the fourth grade. Standing there together with Vivi and Officer Dooley and all his questions took me back. Vivi and I were in Catholic school together and were in Sister Pauline's class—and she was the meanest old nun in the entire school. One day, Vivi brought a big roll of clear packing tape to school and we carefully devised the plan. At recess we practiced. Sister Pauline went out of class at 1:30 every day to meet with Father Mike about the religion lesson.

On the big day, we waited until she'd left for her meeting, and then Vivi rolled the clear tape all over the back of her chair. When Sister P. came back she sat down in her chair, snapping her ruler sharply on the desk and ordered us into silence. I remember the look Vivi and I passed each other. We were full of the devil, you could say—typical schoolgirls, at least most of the ones I knew.

"Here it comes," said Vivi with a huge smile on her freckled face.

"Oh, my goodness, I gotta think of something in case we're busted," I said. I was always a lawyer. Even in the fourth grade.

As Sister P. got up to go to the board, a loud ripping noise tore through the silent class. In a split second, the veil full of curly brown hair fell from her head, flopping there over the back of the chair, sliding down into a puddle as Sister Pauline moved toward the chalkboard.

The classroom erupted with laughter and it could be heard all the way to the principal's office, which is where, of course, we ended up—standing together at the principal's desk, holding hands just like we were right now.

I was snapped abruptly back to the present when Officer Dooley launched another question at Vivi. "Where's the body?"

"Shit!" Vivi said.

That was actually Vivi's favorite word. She used it whether she was happy or sad, surprised or bored. However, this time it was more like an *Oh, shit* as she began to utter those next few words.

"I left the body…"

"Stop, Vivi," Harry jumped in. "As your lawyer, I'm advising you not to discuss these details further, not without consultation."

"Wait, are you my lawyer?" Vivi asked with an excited mix of relief and worry. "Harry, I hate to remind you, but your brother is the…um, dead guy."

"Well, Vivi, I know you didn't do anything but screw his brains out," Harry said, rolling his eyes. It was a familiar tactic—covering up emotion with sarcasm. "Of course, I'll help you. Besides, there is no case if Lewis died 'cause you wore him out. That's not murder. For God's sake, it's a death pure and simple. But if you were the last one with him when he died, you will still need counsel."

That vision will remain branded on my brain for all eternity.

Harry helping Vivi. She needed him and, while Harry wasn't the most cuddly, affectionate guy anymore, he seemed a little like his old self at that moment. Ever since the big family breakup with Lewis years ago, and now even more as he pushed to climb the political ladder, Harry had learned to turn off the emotion and the feeling and keep the business hat on at all times. Even with me—especially with me.

But he was softer with Vivi for the moment. I could see a small glimpse of him, the old Harry, there with Vivi in the musty police station.

Maybe it was because Lewis, for whom he had shown such absolute disdain, could actually be dead. Harry hadn't always been this cold, but over the past couple of years I had certainly become quite lonely for affection and good conversation. We never talked about anything but work and politics and career climbing. I was lonely, but as I noticed a shadow of the old Harry there in the little room, I began to hope that maybe this drama with his brother might bring the real Harry back. My Harry was at least there in the police station for the moment. And it was good to see him.

Harry and I had a good beginning. Watching him there in that moment took me back to the very first time we met. I had been attracted to him immediately.

We met in law school, but not at a party or the library like most college sweethearts. Harry and I met in New York City in line at the half-price tickets booth in the middle of Times Square. We were in line for a little-known Broadway show called *Baby*. I had gone to NYC for an internship at Columbia, and Harry was there that summer, working in the city.

I felt him getting close behind me as I stood in line. I was listening to him talk to a buddy and I knew I detected an unmistakable Southern lilt in his deep, sexy voice. I liked feeling him close to me. I could smell his aftershave and then…my turn at the ticket window.

"Two for *Baby*, please." I was picking up tickets for me and my roommate, Alexa, for that evening's show

"Last two for today ma'am, good timing."

"Noooo," Harry groaned from behind me.

In a split second, I thought, *What do I do?* Little did I know my entire future lay in these next few seconds and how I chose to handle this deliciously terrible, heart-pounding, awkward situation. I hesitated only for a breath, then something else took over. This "something else" spoke for me.

"Oh, I have one extra." My alter ego sounded just like me. Evidentially the other me decided in that split second, *Oh, the hell with Alexa. Alexa who?*

"But what about…" Harry was motioning to the spot where his buddy had been standing seconds ago and saw that he was halfway across the street walking backward and nodding with two thumbs up. I giggled and he said, "Are you sure?"

"Sure am."

He smiled at me.

Harry, ever the curious attorney, furrowed his brow and asked, "Weren't you originally asking for two tickets?"

"Yes," I said, feeling cross-examined.

"Well, who was the other ticket for?"

"Alex, my *female* roommate from New Jersey."

"Oh," he said, smiling. "But won't she be expecting her ticket tonight?"

"Oh, my goodness," I said in an overanimated Southern accent. "Didn't you hear? They just sold out." A smile crept across his preppy boy face and I knew I was in for something wonderful.

Behind his desk, Officer Dooley cleared his throat, dragging my thoughts away from the once-romantic Harry and back to the police station.

"Where is the body?" he asked again, trying to get an answer.

"I left him when he began turnin' blue," Vivi said. "I slapped him a few times. Well, I had slapped him before, but that was durin' our—well anyway—he asked me to. But after he stopped movin', I slapped him really hard and when he still didn't budge an inch, I ran for help."

"Did you call an ambulance?" The chubby officer continued.

"When he stopped breathin', I panicked and ran for Blake."

Vivi looked lost, like Little Orphan Annie. Harry looked exasperated, but there was something else hiding behind his frustration. At that moment, Vivi picked up on it, too. Then, "Oh, Harry! Are you thinkin' he could have still been alive?"

"My client did not call an ambulance right away," Harry answered officer Dooley. "Instead, she called my wife, Blake O'Hara Heart."

Oh, shit, I thought to myself, now using Vivi's vocabulary. With his statement, I knew that I would definitely be dragged into the investigation. I also knew that I would never forget my tenth anniversary.

I turned to Officer Dooley. "Yes, Vivi was trying to call me. But my husband, Harry Heart, was the first to speak with her."

"One moment, Officer Dooley, would you, please? All of this is so sudden that we haven't had a chance to speak with each other," Harry said.

While Dooley crossed his arms impatiently, we moved to the back of the little office and I leaned in and whispered to Vivi to keep quiet for a second. That would take a miracle all its own! I then looked at Harry and discreetly said, "You remember that you were in fact the first one to speak to our client after the fact? Remember? I was still at the school."

"Yes," he said. Well, Vivi tends to rub off on people, and I was sure Harry was the one thinking *Oh, shit* in his own head now.

Clearly, we were all still in a mumbo-jumbo state of shock. We continued to whisper while we watched Vivi fidget.

"But I'm her attorney," he said, looking at me in desperation.

"But you weren't at the time," I reminded him.

"It doesn't look good, Blake." Harry's voice had become firm. He didn't get angry often, but you knew it when it happened. Harry was feeling trapped.

I heard Officer Dooley tapping his pen pointedly against the desk. So did Harry, who didn't want this next bit to be overheard.

"Excuse us, Officer Dooley, for one moment. I need to confer with my co-counsel," Harry said.

"Why don't I just put my pen down for a second," Officer Dooley said.

Harry took me by the hand and pulled me just outside the door of the musty little office. Vivi stayed up front with Officer Dooley, still fidgeting uncomfortably, shifting from side to side, crossing then uncrossing her legs.

"Blake," Harry began, "first and foremost, I am Lewis's brother. Second, I am now Vivi's attorney. That, in and of itself, is strange, considering my connection to them both. But the idea that, after the…deed…I'm the first one she calls? Me, of all people, who has the worst possible relationship with Lewis? This screams conspiracy! It shouts premeditation if we have a dead body over there. It further implicates her and jeopardizes her. And when it comes out that I haven't spoken to Lewis in over six years, it begins to implicate me! Blake, this could put my career in question. My eventual run for the Senate will be shrouded in this controversy."

Harry stopped abruptly. The depth of the situation had overtaken him.

"Harry, snap out of it!" I said, squeezing his arm. "Lewis had been charged with investment fraud and you distanced yourself from him. There's no crime in that—it just proves how respectable you are, not wanting to associate with such a person, brother or not. But your cell phone will register the call from Vivi and what time it came in. All of her missed calls to me will register, as well, with the times they were missed. The truth will be easy to prove, so there's just no point trying to cover it up. Now, I have been her best friend since third grade. Harry, we both know she didn't do anything. This was all just a terrible, unfortunate accident if anything—and, well, a bit disgusting."

Harry's face softened and he gave me a little nod. We both hurriedly returned to Vivi's side.

Harry cleared his throat and began more calmly, "Vivi McFadden did not call an ambulance right away. She tried to call my wife and co-counsel, Blake O'Hara Heart, and when she couldn't get her, she called me."

"Well," Officer Dooley said, "then I go back to my original question: Where is the body?" Officer Dooley pushed his tiny glasses up his tiny nose and looked pointedly at Vivi.

"I left the body at the Fountain Mist motel and that was the last time I saw Lewis. Dead on the bed."

"An ambulance was called once we'd managed to talk to Vivi and find out what had happened. It should be there right now," Harry said.

Officer Dooley looked relieved. "Well, now. That wasn't so hard, was it? I'll send an officer and squad cars over now." Vivi collapsed back into a chair.

I sat with Vivi, holding her hand and looking around at the old room we were in, thinking back to my days as a child and visiting my grandfather in his office just down the block. Nothing changes much in Tuscaloosa. It's a town that thrives on its rich history. And I loved that. I noticed that the decor at the station hadn't changed since probably 1945. Cracked leather chairs with cotton seeping from their seats were scattered around the office. Slow-moving, black ceiling fans whirred around the musty, damp air. The large windows were just slightly open and the fragrant late Southern spring floated inside, like slow deep breathing. The room became still. Officer Dooley called in the incident.

"Which room, Ms. McFadden?" he asked.

"Room 106," Vivi answered. "It was…our room." The impact of the moment suddenly strangled her and her voice weakened. Harry squatted down on one knee to face Vivi eye to eye.

I walked over to the old water fountain and grabbed one of those pointy paper cups. I filled three, one for each of us, and walked to Vivi and Harry and handed them the water.

"Shouldn't we head over there?" I said.

"Yes and no," Harry said. "Yes, Vivi will need to

be there for statements, but no, I'd rather her not talk. But…we don't have a choice about that."

We all took a swig of the water as if it were bourbon in a shot glass, throwing it back like it would stop this nightmare.

"C'mon, honey," I said to Vivi. "I'll be right there next to you."

"Okay," she said. "Let's get this over with."

She grabbed my hand and pushed her red mass of curls from her eyes. I could see Vivi breaking, tears coming quickly now. I squeezed her hand and helped her up.

"It's okay, honey," I said. "We all know you did nothing wrong. You are going to be fine. Besides, you've got the two best attorneys in the state."

And I was sure hoping I was right.

2

"Vivi and I will go in my car," I said.

"Okay," Harry agreed. "I'll take mine in case I have to leave." We heard the sirens of the police and emergency vehicles racing ahead of us as we walked to the parking lot behind the station.

The warmth of the late-spring sun hit my face in the street. God, I so loved this time of year. With the magnolias in full blossom, the smell of the coming Southern summer was overwhelming and transporting. A sweet, pungent aroma lingered in the breeze, reminding me that summer and good watermelon were just around the river bend.

As though a time portal were drawing me in, I was suddenly eight years old and on my grandmother's screened front porch. I could smell her roses and honeysuckle and the huge magnolia trees in the front yard. I watched the bees on her camellias. I loved Mother's, every corner of it. I took in a deep whiff and pulled in as much of the fragrance as I could, held my best friend's hand and put her into the Navigator.

As I walked around to get into the driver's seat, I felt so protective of Vivi. People could call her a lot of things, but they certainly could never call her a murderer.

As I slid onto the warm leather seat and put my key into the ignition, Vivi looked over at me with her wet green eyes full of insecurity. "Am I goin' to jail, Blake?"

I answered her without hesitation. "Not on my life, sweetie. Not on my life."

"Blake," she said. "Thank you."

"For what, honey?"

"For always being my Swiss Army knife."

I smiled at her. I knew what she meant. I also knew how much she was counting on me to get her out of any mess that lay just on the other side of the river.

Vivi would be a person of interest simply because she was the last person to see Lewis alive. She wasn't guilty of a thing. They were just screwing, for God's sake. But Vivi is a reactionary. She will think the absolute worst and in the most dramatic way possible. It's just part of being Vivi. Regardless, I was bound and determined to make sure she would never be charged with anything.

Vivi broke the conversation in my head. "I'm a nervous wreck, Blake."

"Why, honey?"

"It's just that, well…uh, we had a little friend with us in the motel room."

"What? You were in a threesome?"

"Oh, my good God, no, honey. I meant—you know… a sex toy. I named him Deputy Dick."

"Oh, for heaven's sake…I thought you were fixin' to

really shock me. I know you and Lewis can be a bit on the kinky side, no big deal."

"I just don't want the police to discover him. It. I will just die of embarrassment. But I have no idea where he got to. I was in such a panic when I ran for help."

"Don't worry, I'm sure you aren't the only woman in the world to play with toys in the bedroom. I'm sure he will turn up." I tried to get my thoughts together as we drove, and wondered if Vivi had any other interesting details she needed to divulge.

Though we rode in silence, I never let go of her hand. The emotions were stuck in our mouths. Vivi and I have never really needed words. In moments we had crossed the bridge over the Warrior River to the Fountain Mist motel. We drove in and parked as Harry made his way over to us. He opened Vivi's door and helped her out.

The Fountain Mist was one of those old, side-of-the-highway kinds of motels. The kind that could charge by the hour. It had a red neon sign out front and a lighted fountain, like one of those old silver Christmas trees from the sixties that had the colored lights spinning underneath. The fountain changed colors and definitely helped to cheapen the motel's appearance. Inside the lobby, the green carpet was threadbare and fading. The entire place needed painting. And sanitization.

Harry had his legal pad in hand and was standing with the police and the paramedics outside room 106. Everyone was in a panic, and Harry looked like he'd gone into shock.

"Where's the body?" a paramedic yelled out at us as we approached. "There's no body here!" Vivi and I walked over to the door at a clip. The dust from the gravel parking lot swirled in the air.

A frenetic chaos filled the room. The motel manager was standing on the dusty carpet, answering questions while a police officer took notes. I couldn't see for the glare as the sun bounced from the mirror of the cheap dresser. Two officers and two paramedics had turned the room upside down. The frustrated sounds came again from the first paramedic. "Where the hell's the body? We got a call from someone saying that her boyfriend had stopped breathing."

"I left him right there, dead on the bed, buck naked and blue as blue blazes," Vivi said with fear and panic in her eyes. I looked at Harry and he looked at Vivi.

"Vivi!" Harry said. "Where the hell is Lewis?"

In a split second, a breathless silence fell over the room and Vivi fell over backward right onto me. I caught her just as she slumped sideways, and a paramedic rushed to her while a policeman radioed the station.

No body, I thought. *Is Lewis possibly alive? Or is someone hiding evidence?* I held Vivi up till the paramedics got hold of her.

I looked at my stoic Harry. I knew he was thinking of his public image and trying not to show any emotion. At the same time, I knew he was trying to process and manage this unbelievable situation. But this was typical Harry. Sometimes so closed off he became his own worst enemy. He locked everyone out to make sure his image was so perfect it was almost not even human. It was robotic, with all the right responses, always so prepared with just the right answers. Sometimes he was just exasperating. *Feel,* I thought. *Let me see you.* Though he would say that I feel too much. I *overfeel,* he had said once. Too happy, too sad, too angry.

What was happening to us was much like the story of Scarlett and Rhett. You don't show me any emotion, so I won't show you any. Both of us would be independent, spirited people, strong and stubborn, who just didn't need anyone but ourselves.

And so it had gone for about six years now. Lots of work, lots of career building and even lots of sex. But not much lovemaking.

I wanted him to really *see* me again. But he was not about to let me see him. In that moment I just felt sad for both of us.

We were still all crowded inside room 106 with the bright sun streaming in like a laser beam through the open door. It made it difficult to see anyone except in silhouette. But the next image I saw coming through that door was a shape that I knew well. At six foot three, he looked ominous in the shadows, even with his slender frame. Shadows or not—I knew that body all too well. I'd know that man anywhere.

Sonny Bartholomew had been all mine at one time. From my first year of high school to my first year of college, Sonny was my on-again, off-again love. Over those years we went from harmless exploration to seriously discussing forever. And now, on the rare occasion that Harry and I had a heated conversation, Harry would say, "Why don't you just go look up your cop? I'm sure you should have just married him anyway."

This was my cop. My detective, actually.

Sonny Bartholomew. Homicide Investigations.

I fell in love with him back when he was the yearbook photographer during our freshman year of high school. Back then, he was sort of a misfit like me. Sonny had the cutest smile I had ever seen. He would cock his head to one side as he grinned at me. That's all it took. His smile turned up at both corners of his mouth. He was precious, with his sandy hair and oversize feet and it all came together to make him even cuter. And he sure grew into those feet.

At fifteen we were just the right age for the beginning of the end of our innocence. But we never did go all the way. I was the good girl—at least in that respect. Though, somehow, I have always wished I hadn't been so good back then. He should have been my first.

It felt really good—and really odd—to see him standing there in the doorway of the motel room. It had been a long time since I had run into him last, at a Bama game a few years back. It was a fall football Saturday, with bright blue skies and a bite in the air. We were in line for a beer at one of the bars along the strip. I'd asked him about his life and prodded him for information about his wife, a wallflower of a girl, Laura Logan. She'd gone to Catholic school with me and Vivi. She was so quiet and certainly was never involved in any of our infamous pranks. Laura was so shy and good that we believed she might actually become a nun.

Obviously, she did not.

Sonny had seemed uncomfortable during our chance encounter in the beer line. I told him I was married.

"I know," he said. "I saw it in the paper."

At that moment, standing in line on that football Saturday, I suddenly couldn't imagine a life without Sonny. *We should be friends,* I'd thought. At least friends.

I had loved him for as long as I could remember and so I'd grabbed his hand in mine and said, "Look, we're both married now. Can't we all get together sometime, all four of us? For a cookout? I know Laura, for heaven's sake. She was at my birthday parties growin' up. We made our first communion together. Whatdaya say? I really miss you, Sonny."

Sonny still had a face full of freckles and the darkest brown eyes. They could always see right through me. And I could still see that fifteen-year-old in him. As he paid for his beer, he looked at me with that smile and his famous one eyebrow up, cocked his head and said, "Blake, we run in different circles now. You're all elite with your law school buddies and your near-blue-blood husband. My friends are good ol' boys, rednecks, ya know? On the weekends we got longnecks in one hand and a remote in the other. And I always said, Blake, if I can't have you in every way, I can't bear seeing you, knowing somebody else is lovin' you."

I had been lost in his words and that curled-up smile when the beer lady's shrill voice had shattered the moment. "Honey, you want yer change 'er what? C'mon now."

Sonny tipped his baseball cap to her and shoved his change into his too-tight jeans. He'd looked back at me, leaned in and kissed my cheek. "It was good to see ya, Blake. Hi to Harry."

With that I had felt a sudden chill in the October air. I'd watched him walk away for only a second, then I turned to the lady with the shrill voice. "I'll have one of those longnecks, please."

Room 106 was now filling to capacity. Nobody knew if it was really a crime scene or what. The police took a few notes and never even cordoned off the scene. No one seemed to know how to classify it. Vivi, now revived, sat on the side of the bed sipping water from one of those little square glasses from the motel bathroom.

Harry moved toward her and Sonny stepped fully inside the room.

"Hey, Blake. How are ya?" Sonny greeted me with a quick kiss on the cheek. He sounded happy with his deep baritone, honey-dripping, slow Southern drawl. Seriously, he had me at "Hey."

I swallowed instead of speaking and smiled at him. But I couldn't stop myself. I stood.

"Hey, Sonny!" I stepped in closer and gave him a hug. That's how Southerners say hello. We hug everyone, all the time, both hello and goodbye. It's bad manners not to. In fact, it's downright hurtful. I heard the heavy Southern drawl in my hello. When I've had a few drinks or I'm feeling a little flirtatious, my accent seems to intensify. And Sonny, well, I guess he just brought out a tinge of my inner redneck. We all have some. Inner redneck, I mean. There's someone in everyone's family that's a teeny bit red. Think about it. For me, it came from my dad's side. Way back in his line were the moonshiners. Yep. I know. Unreal, huh? My mom's family is a bunch of lawyers. One story has the moonshiners on my dad's side being defended by the lawyers on my mom's side. And of course, if you think about it, you can imagine what the payoff was— yep, fresh whisky, right from the backyard! I'm not from stupid lawyers!

As I stood, Harry caught Sonny's reflection in the mirror. He left Vivi and came over with his hand extended. Harry's not a hugger anyway, but he would *never* hug Sonny. This was my *cop,* remember?

"Hey, Sonny. Thanks for coming." Over the years, these two men I loved had come to an understanding through work. This was not the first case they had worked on together and I'm sure it would not be the last. Harry and Sonny stepped outside into the late afternoon sun and I sat down on the bed next to Vivi.

"You okay, hon?"

"Oh, I'm just fine, but you're lookin' a little red," she teased.

"Oh, stop it," I said.

"He does it to you, doesn't he?" She scooted back on the bed to make room, but kept one eyebrow cocked.

"He who?" I shot back as if shocked at the insinuation.

"You know, there was a time I thought you'd marry that boy." She looked at me, seeing right into my soul as only Vivi could.

"I'm taking the Fifth," I said, grabbing her water and taking a swig. I decided to get the conversation back on track. We needed to talk about the body, or lack thereof. This was no time to be gossiping about my love life.

Just then, in walked Bonita Baldwin, the newest investigator on Sonny's team. She was African-American, plus-sized and drop-dead gorgeous. Sonny had just hired her from Mobile and it was in all the papers that she'd be joining the force. The daughter of Tuskegee professors, this apple sure didn't fall far from the tree. She'd graduated top of her class and her loud, opinionated mouth had all of our attention, as did her designer shoes. She could size things up in seconds, and she wasn't afraid to tell it like it was. That's why Sonny hired her.

"Hey, Blake, how are you?" She leaned in and gave me a hug. I had met her at a function at City Hall for the police benefit the month before. "We've got us a squirrelly little situation here, I see," she said as she quickly took in the room.

"I know," I said. "Vivi is just a mess because of it."

"Well, look here, Vivi, not to fret. We'll get to the bottom of this before long. Just trust me and Sonny. We got this, okay?" she said as she snapped on her latex gloves. And with that, she bent over and began looking all around the bed, lifting the bed skirt until…

"Oh, my good God in heaven above. What in all hell is this?" And up she came with Deputy Dick in her hand, holding it like it was the Olympic Torch.

"Vivi, you recognize this nasty thang?"

Vivi turned ten shades of crimson, threw back the last sip of her water and choked.

"We're gonna need us a big ole' plastic bag for this. Just somebody get over here quick and take this disgusting thing from me!" She was holding it by two fingers, her face contorted somewhere between fear and nausea, turning in circles in the tiny motel room looking for *anyone* to take the rubbery blue dildo from her perfectly manicured, and thankfully gloved, hand. "Ooh, Lawd have mercy, I need to have my hands sanitized after this!"

Vivi leaned into me and said, "That's Deputy Dick."

"Well," I said, "I am so happy to finally meet him in person. He is certainly a lovely shade of blue." Vivi smiled and that relieved her embarrassment, but only for a second. Another officer came in with a bag and Bonita dropped the "deputy" into it.

"Have mercy, I ain't never seen such a big ugly thing as that. It's gonna give me nightmares…." She went to the sink, tossed her gloves and washed her hands, muttering to herself as she primped in the mirror. Her makeup was a thing of perfection. She looked like a doll with the most beautiful hair and all of it in place, all the time. She, too, was a former pageant queen and knew how to carry herself, plus size and all. Her weight never seemed to matter—if anything, Bonita gave curves a good name. All anyone ever noticed was her beauty and her spunk. As a detective, she was able to avoid the uniform—which was a good thing, since her sense of fashion would never stretch to black polyester. Today, she was wearing one of her many Chanel suits, cream and trimmed in black. She was stunning to the eye.

Vivi had gathered herself and was wiping her face with the wet cloth Bonita had handed her when she finally spoke.

"Uh, yes, to answer your question, Bonita, I do recognize that, um, item. It is mine and I had it with me here in the room." Vivi let out a huge breath as if she had just admitted she knew the secrets of the Vatican.

Bonita finished cleaning and primping herself and came over to Vivi. "Now don't you go worrying yourself over this, Vivi. All of us got our kinky little secrets." She winked at her.

Vivi smiled up at her from where she was still sitting on the bed.

"Certainly this one is a good bit…shall we say…*bigger* than most, but it'll all be okay."

Sonny and Bonita stepped to the doorway and planned their next steps. Vivi was too out of sorts to notice them chatting, but I strained to listen.

"Sonny, what do you make of this?" Bonita asked.

"Well, at the moment, none of this is gonna make any sense till we talk to Miss Vivi. Maybe she saw something out of the ordinary, or maybe we can jog her memory when we talk to her."

"Do you need me to question her or do you wanna do those honors?" she asked sarcastically. It was clear Bonita would rather hear *any* story other than the one Vivi would be telling.

"No, you go on. I'll talk to her. I've known her a long time and she can be, shall we say, difficult. She enjoys being difficult. I'll handle her." Sonny kept thinking and talking. "I think you ought to check the usual spots—the hospitals, coroner's office. Maybe someone already moved the body and this is all just a problem of mis-communication. But just in case, maybe get together a list of Lewis's coworkers at the university that we can talk to. Somebody's bound to know somethin'."

"No problem, Sonny. I swear, this may be the craziest case I've ever worked on and we're just getting started. That Vivi, she is sure somethin' else. I don't believe I've ever bagged evidence quite like that little blue friend I found." They both laughed and shook their heads.

"Okay, I'll keep ya posted. Have fun talkin' to Vivi. Almost wish I could be a fly on the wall for that one, but I'm already gonna have nightmares after meeting the little blue man in there." She laughed.

Bonita was a good soul, even if she did talk too much. She did one last mirror check of her lipstick, then hugged me and Vivi and headed outside. I heard her car start and drive away.

"Vivi, do you have any ideas at all about where Lewis could be?" I looked at her as I took the cloth from her and wiped her cheeks.

She began to tear up. "I swear, Blake. With God as my witness, I do not know where he is or where he went.

He was laying right there on this bed, dead and stiff and naked. He was stiff and naked before, but I swear…" She paused and looked at me in the eyes. "You believe me, don't you?"

"Of course I do. Of course." I pulled her frizzy red head under my chin and held her. "You know you will have to go into all the details with Sonny? He's the chief investigator for the police department. You need to tell him everything. I still can't believe Sonny married Laura Logan." I couldn't help it from blurting out. I knew now was not the time to be gossiping, but seeing Sonny again had stirred something up inside me.

"Oh, my God! Laura Plain and Tall?" Vivi recalled Laura's elementary school moniker. "I haven't thought about her in ten years. I guess the whole convent thing really didn't pan out for her."

We both let out a laugh. It relieved the heaviness of the situation. It felt good to almost forget where we were, even for just a moment.

Harry pushed back through the little room and touched me on the shoulder.

"Blake, is Vivi able to talk to Officer Bartholomew?"

"Yes, she's much better. Let's go outside."

We stepped out into the warm afternoon air. The police inside kept up their search for anything that might lead us to Lewis, and the evidence was stored in plastic bags—including the big blue rubber penis. I saw the wrecker pull out from behind the motel with Lewis's red Corvette attached. They would take it to the police station and hold it until it had been fully searched and swiped for evidence.

I hesitated on the sidewalk as Harry, Vivi and Sonny walked through the dusty parking lot over to Sonny's truck. I knew every hair, fiber and drop of semen could be used against Vivi if they ever found Lewis's body. For a moment my eyes began to fill with tears, but then anger took over and I thought, *No! Over my dead body.* Then I thought, *There* is *no dead body.* And with no dead body, there was no murder. Only a missing person. I sniffed and wiped my eyes, then put my lawyer face on. I felt transformed into a heroine for all Southern women: Scarlett O'Hara and a Steel Magnolia all in one. I joined the group already gathered at the truck. However, my bravado may have faltered a bit as I stumbled in the parking lot, realizing that high heels were definitely not the appropriate foot fashion for gravel. As I approached them I overheard Vivi.

"Harry, I just cannot discuss this."

"Vivi, you have to. You have no choice. You were the last one with Lewis and you reported him dead—although his body is, well, not where you left it. You are still at the center of this investigation. And Officer Bartholomew is the chief investigator. You have to tell us the details of the day as you remember it."

"This will help us find Lewis," I explained to Vivi. "Harry, I think we better move this discussion elsewhere if you want all of this from Vivi. This is the scene of the…well…whatever it is, and Vivi has already fainted once. Let me help you with her and we'll get all we need."

I turned to talk to Vivi.

"It's okay, honey. I'll be right there with you. What do you need?"

"Oh, Blake, I can't possibly discuss this tête-à-tête in mixed company. I'll die of total embarrassment."

"Sweetie, you don't have a choice." We all stood

there in silence waiting for Vivi to tell us what would make this easier for her. It was an awkward moment. We knew what we were asking her to do. We knew what we would be hearing. The very last dirty details of the sexual escapades of Lewis and Vivi. It was a lot to ask for any of us to sit through *that!* But everyone stood there, the hot sun baking the long minutes that dripped by like molasses from a hot spoon. Then finally—

"Well, okay," Vivi said, letting out a deep breath. "About five Long Island iced teas might do it."

"What, honey?" I asked.

"You asked me what I need, right? So I'm tellin' you. I've got to have a drink or three or this story will, through no fault of my own, stay locked in my head. It's just not somethin' I can discuss without lots of help, from Jack or Jim…. As in Daniel's and Beam—drinks I mean, not more men!"

"Okay," Sonny said, "let's run over to the Tutwiler. It's close by and the bar opens at four, and that's right about now."

Harry and I looked at each other and nodded our heads in agreement.

"Fine," Harry said.

So, we would go to the Tutwiler and sit and watch Vivi get stone drunk while listening to her recount her last day with Harry's estranged baby brother, Lewis, screwing his brains out till he was dead, while my former lover sat across from us taking notes. Yes, it looked like Harry and I would have our anniversary date at the Tutwiler, after all.

3

We got in our cars and headed back across the bridge to the Tutwiler, looking for all the world like some sort of procession. Driving across the Warrior River to downtown, I looked over at Vivi. She sat motionless, white-knuckling the door handle as we rode to the old historic hotel.

"I can't do it." The words shook loose from her mouth. "Blake, I just cannot tell all this to Sonny. You can't tell me they need to know *everything*."

"What do you mean?" I asked.

"Why in the world do they need to know that Lewis was a licker?"

"What?" I said, in utter confusion at what I thought she said.

"You know. A licker. He wasn't much of a kisser but, God, he sure loved to lick. Can you tell me just why Sonny needs to know that?"

I started feeling drops of perspiration dripping down between my breasts, and my breath had left me. But I grabbed Vivi by the arm and explained, "We are trying to clear all of this up so we can find Lewis."

"And by learnin' all about Lewis lickin' me from my knees to my neck, I'm a free woman?"

I slammed on my brakes, realizing we had reached our destination and I was about to jump the curb getting into a parking space. Vivi and I looked at each other.

"Maybe we can leave that little detail out." I was already feeling nauseous. "It'll be fine," I said, hoping I was right. "Let's go." I parked and we got out.

The Tutwiler was so elegant. It was a regal 1920s hotel with most of its original architecture still intact. Dapples of yellow and cream splashed the walls, shadows of the afternoon sun dancing and darting up and down the curving banisters and sprinkling light across the 20-foot ceilings. Sunlight peeked through the palms planted in oversize ceramic pots scattered throughout the lobby. White ceiling fans whirred slowly, just enough to stir the jasmine-scented air and cause the palms to wave in their breeze. The large French doors around the lobby opened onto the courtyard at every corner, and the three-layer fountain stood in the center offering a watery lullaby to the early evening. Every sense was stirred here. It was intoxicating.

Harry and Sonny had arrived first, and I could see them in the shadows of the bar off the lobby. Sonny was propped up on a bar stool, his long legs stretched out in front of him, and Harry was talking to the bartender. Harry motioned to us. I wanted to linger a little longer.

The courtyard beckoned, and I was swept back ten years earlier when Harry, fresh out of law school, stood in the spring sun in the middle of the Tutwiler courtyard. He had a martini in one hand and a peach-colored rose in the other. God, he was gorgeous. Dressed in navy dress pants and a heavily starched, crisp white shirt, silver wire frames and his wavy mass of dark hair, he looked straight out of a magazine. His cuff links glistened in the sunlight.

I loved that Harry wore cuff links. I'd never known anyone who wore cuff links. They made him seem elegant and refined, classic. They were a symbol to me of who Harry was. Eccentric and his own man in every respect. He was unexpected. The cuff links were unexpected. They made you notice that he was confident, but not in a flashy sort of way.

That evening in the courtyard was about a month after we'd graduated from law school and I was meeting him for drinks. Harry had had a job interview with the most prestigious firm in Tuscaloosa that day. They had offices in Atlanta and Birmingham and Harry had wanted to work for them ever since I had first met him. When he called to invite me to drinks, I thought, *Oh, he got the job! He wants to celebrate!* I had hurriedly dressed in my favorite suit, covered myself in my perfumed body cream from my hot-pink toenails to my tan shoulders, slid my favorite pink lipstick over my lips and flew out the door.

When I met Harry at the Tutwiler, I expected to hear all the nitty gritty details of the interview. I spotted him in the courtyard and raced across the lobby and out through the French doors, throwing my arms around him once I'd reached him.

"Hey, honey! How'd it go?"

"Great! They told me they were hoping the next Heart out of law school would choose their firm. My name is my reputation," he said proudly.

"Oh, baby, that's great!" I said, but I sensed something else. "Harry, what's wrong?"

He cocked his eyebrow up.

"Oh, no, they're not sending you to Atlanta, are they?"

"Blake. Sweet, sweet, Blake," Harry whispered as he pulled me closer. "No, darlin', I'll be here in Tuscaloosa, 'cause I told them I couldn't leave at the moment. They'll hand me my first file next Monday."

I continued holding him tight. "Oh, thank God. I don't think I'm cut out for long-distance."

"Sweetie, they're looking for one more fresh-faced attorney."

"You mean…me?" I blurted out.

"Well, I took the liberty of suggesting you and they'd like to talk to you in the morning."

"Harry! This is our dream coming true! To practice together until we can open our own firm. I can't believe it's really happening." My eyes had filled with happy tears and I felt Harry move his hand from behind my waist just as a waiter in a crisp white serving jacket and a black bow tie approached. He had a sterling silver tray with a round silver dome over it.

"Your order, Mr. Heart." Harry reached into his front pocket and handed the man a tip.

By this time, I was thinking, *Okay, time for a champagne toast.* Harry told the waiter to set the tray down on a nearby table. He slid his fingers through mine and looked down at me and smiled in a way I had never seen. As if he had a secret.

He led me over to the table and said, "Time for a toast!" He lifted the tray top, revealing two champagne flutes full of amber bubbly.

Handing me a glass, he said, "To us, and our future."

On the tray next to the glasses was an antique china plate covered in pink and white and peach-colored rose petals. In the center was one large pink blossom.

"For my Southern beauty," he said.

As I picked up the large center rose, and lifted it to my nose to breathe in its sweet fragrance, underneath it I saw lying on the rose petals an amazing, large, square-cut diamond ring. The sunlight flickered in its brilliance.

"Oh, my God," I said for about the ninetieth time that day. "Oh, my God, Harry!"

He knelt down before me, slipping my fingers through his and said, "Blake O'Hara, I love you and want to share every breath with you. You are the sweetest, most beautiful girl in the world. I love every little thing about you—the way you smell and the way your hair frizzes at the slightest bit of humidity. I love it that when you sing you continually change keys. You are my very best friend, and I can't imagine my life without you. I promise to take the best care of you that I can. I promise your happiness will be what I strive for every day. I promise I will keep you in legal pads for the rest of your life. Will you please do me the honor of a lifetime and be my wife and partner?"

I lost all sense of time and space and was down on my knees before I knew it. I could barely speak. I looked into his blue-gray eyes and put my hands on his clean-shaven face and pulled him to my mouth, kissing him before I answered.

"Harry, I love you more than life itself and I will never be able to have joy without you. Yes, baby! Yes!" Between every yes I kissed him on the lips, then the cheeks, then the lips. "Yes! Yes! Yes! I'll marry you! Yes!"

There we were. In the courtyard of the Tutwiler. Both on our knees. Both crying and holding each other, my tears mixed with his. In that moment, the whole world went away and there was only us. The bees were buzzing, the dandelions floated by, the jasmine and magnolia filled the May air. I was in Harry's arms, in the bosom of my hometown, and it was the single best moment of my life.

I was shaken away from that memory by Vivi. Literally shaken when she grabbed my shoulder.

"Blake, honey, you home? I'm talkin' to ya. Your eyes are somewhere else."

"Yes, Vivi. I'm here. "

"Oh, damn," Vivi murmured under her breath. "I get it, honey. You and Harry. Today, it's…"

I interrupted, "It's okay."

"No, dammit. It's not okay. You and Harry should be kicking up your heels. Oh, my God, and this is your spot. Oh, Blake, this is so awful!"

"No, no, Vivi, this was all beyond your control today. Let's go on to the bar and get this over with." She knew Harry and I had been in a slow-motion free fall for a while now, but I had not even discussed with Vivi my plans to talk to Harry during our lunch date earlier today.

I am by no means a needy person. But I am all female and I do like to be pursued. Romanced. Fussed over. Maybe even the center of attention. Harry's attention had been elsewhere for so long and every attempt to talk to him ended with him saying, "Well, what do you want from me, Blake? You knew this was the life I wanted when you said you'd be my partner." Little did Vivi know, she probably saved me from asking Harry for a separation today. But I couldn't decide which was worse—being at the Tutwiler to discuss a divorce, or being there to discuss a missing brother-in-law! I took Vivi by the arm and we headed into the abyss.

The bar in the Tutwiler was massive, made of deep, rich mahogany wood with intricate carvings. The ceilings were at least twenty feet high and the moldings had the same beautiful etchings. There was a huge mirror over the bar that reflected everything and everyone. It was all done in dark mahogany. The hardwood floors were a throwback to the 1920s. Just entering the bar was an event. You went through time to the elegant era of Bugsy Segal and flapper dancers and it always felt like you needed a long strand of pearls to twirl. They even had music from the 1920s playing, usually by a live band over in the corner. Maybe this location would help to ease the tension of the moment.

Though Harry and Sonny were both waiting at the bar, neither of them was drinking. Sonny was on duty so he had his usual, a Dr Pepper. Harry had club soda. We all knew this was going to be very uncomfortable, so there was an agitated, prickly uneasiness in the air. Like trying to swallow hot peppers with a whisky chaser followed by dill pickle juice. It was just too much at one time for the tongue.

Vivi and I stepped up and slid onto our stools. I ordered a seltzer water with lime, and Vivi ordered a Jack Daniel's straight.

"Ms. McFadden," Sonny began, "I'm going to be recording this and taking a few handwritten notes. You are not at this time a suspect of anything. There is no crime at the moment. We are treating this as a missing person case, and we will until such time as it becomes something else. Any details you can provide may go a long way in helping us locate Mr. Heart. But this is informal, so please feel relaxed and try your best to remember everything. Even some things you don't think are important might become just the details we need later on. You were the last one to see Mr. Lewis Heart. Can you please describe your encounter with him?"

Oh, Lord, I thought. *Here we go.*

"Okay." Vivi looked over Sonny's shoulder to where I had positioned myself next to Harry. She grabbed her shot glass and threw her Jack Daniel's back in one swig, her mop of orange frizz flying.

"Lewis called me this mornin'. I was out at the Big House." (That's what Vivi called her family's plantation.) "I had been tendin' the rose gardens with Arthur, my gardener. I love it when I can get my hands in the soil and feel the earth damp and squishy in my palms. Know what I mean, Mr. Sonny?"

"Yes, ma'am," Sonny answered. "But, please, can we jump on over to when you met up with Lewis?"

"I'm gettin' there, Mr. Sonny. Another JD straight up, please," Vivi said to the bartender. "Make it a double. Anyway, when the phone rang, I told Arthur I'd be right back. I ran in the house and grabbed the receiver. It was Lewis.

"He said, 'Hey, Red.' Only Lewis calls me Red.

"'Hey, baby,' I said. 'Whatcha need?'

"'You, baby. Lots of you,' he said. Lewis sounded, uhh...needy.

"'Okay, sweetie. You name the place and I'll be there,' I told him.

"'Fountain Mist,' he said. 'Our room.' I knew that meant 106—it's where we always met."

"Miss Vivi, you said you always met Mr. Heart there," Sonny said. "How many times would you say and over what period of time? Were these encounters going on for a while?"

Vivi stopped him. "What do you mean by *a while?*" Vivi was being difficult and by this time I had ordered a strong drink. I'm usually a margarita kinda girl but I drink those when I'm celebrating something, not when I'm trying to spring my best friend in a missing persons case. When the bartender served me my Bloody Mary, I looked over my left shoulder at Harry who had ordered his usual dirty martini by now. It was our anniversary, after all. He cocked his eyebrow and toasted me silently. We took a simultaneous "Yeah and happy anniversary" swig, then turned our attention back to Sonny and Vivi. Sonny was explaining what he meant by "a while."

"Miss Vivi, how long have your 'meetings' with Mr. Heart been going on?"

"A couple of years," Vivi answered.

Harry rolled his eyes and shook his head and I choked on my celery stalk.

"And when you had these, um, meetings…was it always at the Fountain Mist?" Sonny kept a straight face and dove head-on into the questioning.

"No," answered Vivi. "Sometimes we 'conferenced' in his car. And sometimes we had meetings at the Big House since we moved Mama to that fancy retirement center last year."

"Would you say that the Fountain Mist was the main place for your conferences?" Sonny asked.

"Oh, without a doubt. Room 106 every time."

Sonny kept writing. "Okay, back to the events that led up to the disappearance of Mr. Heart."

"Well, I said goodbye to Lewis and hung up the phone. Then I went upstairs and sprayed my entire body with rose water and told Arthur Mama needed me at the center and I'd be back in a jiffy. He said, 'Okay, Miss Vivi, you tell her I say hello.' I put the top down on my car and flew to my meetin' with Lewis. When I got there, Lewis's red '72 Corvette was parked outside in the back. He had already gone inside. I pulled in next to him. We always parked in the back 'cause both our cars are a dead giveaway. Anyway, I walked to our room about halfway down the sidewalk. When I got there I stopped for a second to catch my breath and straighten my dress. When I reached for the door handle, I realized it was already open."

"What time of day was this?" Sonny asked, swigging his Dr Pepper slowly.

"It was at eleven o'clock this mornin'." Vivi had obviously returned body and spirit to room 106. Her demeanor had changed. The alcohol had subdued her normally frenetic pace.

"Go on. What happened next?" Sonny kept up the questioning.

"Well, my God!" Vivi yelped. "You know what the hell happened next. Dammit, Sonny, just use your imagination!"

"Miss Vivi," Sonny said, slow and steady, "we have no choice. The details here are important. It could lead us to Lewis."

"Vivi, remember," I said, "the details are what will

clear all of this up and maybe lead us to what happened to Lewis. That has to be your focus."

"Okay," she said. "Lewis was already waitin' for me in bed. I kicked the door closed and he revealed himself to me. He was deep into a fantasy."

"What do you mean?" Sonny said.

"He had a gun holster on," Vivi answered directly.

"He had a gun?" Sonny shot back.

"No, no!" she said. "He had on a *holster*. He had no gun. But he did have a little surprise for me where the gun goes."

"What was that?" said Sonny.

"A toy," Vivi answered, swigging her drink a little faster.

"What kind of toy?" Sonny was dead serious as he continued taking notes.

"A sex toy, you idiot! A ginormous blue penis! We named it Deputy Dick."

I threw back the rest of my Bloody Mary in one gulp.

"I'll have a double scotch on the rocks," Harry announced once he'd flagged down the cute bartender.

"It had fiber optic rainbow lighting," Vivi explained. "Lewis told me to grab it, so I slipped out of my shoes and pulled up my dress. I had no panties on and my thighs were still moist from workin' in the rose garden. I began to perspire on my neck and the water rolled around and down under my breasts. I unbuttoned my dress just enough so he could see I had no bra on either."

Sonny had a bewildered look on his face. He'd asked for the details, but by no means was he expecting a play-by-play account of their sexual escapade. He looked at me helplessly, and I tried to think of a way to get Vivi to shut up without embarrassing her. But before

I'd come up with anything, Vivi continued to reveal her dirty little story.

"Lewis looked hungrier than ever. He said, 'Hey, Red, save a horse, ride a cowboy.' You know like that song says? So I thought, *What the hell*. I slung my leg over and sat straddling him with Deputy Dick in my hand. 'Ride it first,' he said, so I did. Did you know that with each little movement that damn thing turned a different color?"

"Vivi!" I said with my eyebrows up. There was no time to be polite—I needed to stop her before it got any worse. "Stop! That's enough. I think that will do. You've said plenty." I was talking with my eyes bugging out, trying desperately to make her stop, but Vivi being Vivi and after a few drinks, she just kept right on talkin'.

"Lewis threw me over on my back and crawled under the covers to the end of the bed and started suckin' my toes and lickin' my calves. His body was to die for—he had bulked up a little lately, trimmed down some. He was in amazing shape, and those great big shoulders and that thick black hair… God, I was so into him."

"Can't you stop her?" Harry mumbled to me as he took a big swig of his scotch. "I don't think she'll ever get to the finish line. And this is making me queasy."

"Miss Vivi, please. That'll be all for this part. Can we try to skip to the place where he stopped breathin'. Please?" Sonny tried to redirect her, but Vivi didn't hear anything, she was lost in the story, unfortunately reliving it for all of us like it was a sick skin flick. With all that had happened to her today, none of us felt ready to be harsh with her. There was nothing to do but keep right on listening.

"Lewis kept licking—all the way up to my thighs,

then I felt his mouth on my abdomen, sliding his tongue below my navel. Just as he was on arrival, he slipped the toy out of my hand and flipped me back over on top of him, and said, 'How 'bout a ride on the real horse, Red? Let's go for a trot.' He was full of the devil! And I loved it. I positioned myself just right. He was primed and ready. He started buckin' like a wild bronco. I was bouncin' up and down when…when it happened."

We all sat up, backs straight on our bar stools, bugeyed, mouths dropped open. I was afraid to ask, but someone had to do it. "When what happened, honey?"

"When suddenly, I felt him stop," Vivi continued. "No sounds. No movement. No nothin'." Vivi stopped talking. Her face dropped. She took a minute and we were all sitting still in the hushed silence.

Then she added, "I looked down at him, and he looked a little purple. But his eyes were open. So I… dismounted."

By this time we could tell she was feeling her alcohol.

"I called his name out. 'Lewis, Lewis!' I got louder and louder but he just turned bluer and bluer. I slapped his face and nothin'. So I jumped up, and buttoned my dress and kept shoutin' and shoutin' the entire time. I shook him and still he didn't budge. So I reached across his chest to the chair, grabbed my purse and fumbled for my cell phone and called Blake while running out of the room to my car. I just started driving aimlessly. Not sure where I was headed—I just knew I needed to be doin' something. When I couldn't get a hold of Blake, I called Harry."

"Vivi? You okay?" I said. She looked at me, her eyes drooping. She heaved a big sigh. We all sat quietly. We had been through all of the emotions. No one spoke. I could hear the noise of the bar, but the mood had dropped. We all stared at Vivi. Sadness was hanging in the air like a wet drape. It was a crushing heaviness suffocating us.

"Okay, Miss Vivi, is that your statement?" Sonny was trying to remain professional, but I could see even he was shaken. "Would you like to add anything else?"

I motioned to Vivi to say no, but she couldn't focus anymore. With all the Jack Daniel's she had, she felt she needed to jabber.

"Mr. Sonny," Vivi said, her eyes brimming with tears, "I never meant to hurt Lewis. He is my dear friend. I love him. Please find him. He may be out there confused. Maybe he had a seizure and when he came to, I wasn't there. Or he could have forgotten who he is. Please…" Tears now spilling down her cheeks, she was like a child that needed to be held through the night after a nightmare.

Harry shoved a hundred-dollar bill at the bartender, stood up and straightened his tie. "Okay," he announced. "I think my client's done all she can and, personally, I don't think she's physically able to do much more." He stood up and touched my shoulder. "We need to get her home."

Harry said he would drive both me and Vivi in my car. We'd leave his vehicle at the Tutwiler. He shook Sonny's hand and helped Vivi down from the stool.

"Thank you, Miss Vivi, you've been very helpful. We'll be in touch," Sonny said.

I balanced Vivi on my left side and Sonny leaned down and kissed my cheek. "Good seein' you, Blake. Take care of yourself. I'll be in touch." He turned to walk away and his cell phone began ringing. He kept walking as he answered.

"Officer Bartholomew."

Silence. Then, "Okay. I'm there in ten."

He hung up and abruptly turned and looked at all three of us in the twilight of the Tutwiler lobby.

Sonny cleared his throat and looked Vivi in the eyes as he announced, "We've got a body."

4

The chandelier in the Tutwiler lobby could have dropped and none of us would have moved. We were frozen. I looked immediately at Harry. This was possibly his baby brother. And though he and Lewis had not spoken in years, I could see he was visibly shaken.

"Where is it?" Harry said.

"Washed up at the Cypress Inn out at the river," Sonny answered. "Some girl discovered it while taking a walk at the restaurant."

The Cypress Inn was a longtime Tuscaloosa mainstay. It was built up high on the banks of the Warrior River, and it had a beautiful walking path that led down from the restaurant to the water.

Vivi started to cry at Sonny's announcement. I held her still with my arm tightly around her shoulder.

"No, no, no… It isn't true, is it? It's not Lewis, is it? I don't know what could have happened to him. Oh, I think I'm gonna throw up. Am I gonna be charged with murder now, Blake?"

She was breaking down now and crying hard. I held her a little closer and told her we weren't even sure who the body was. She was shaking and going into shock.

"Vivi." Harry was trying to help her get hold of herself. "The body has to be identified and the cause of death has to be determined, too. Nothing is gonna happen until we do the ID. Let's get over to the Cypress Inn and see if we can get some answers. I'll drive."

Harry had a way of doing that. Taking charge. He was good at it, especially in a crisis. He could turn off the feelings and purely think—quite easily, actually. Sometimes I hated that.

We rode back over the bridge, back to the river for the third time that day and headed to the restaurant. The drive was a total blur, but ten minutes later we were all in the parking lot of the Cypress Inn.

Dusk is beautiful at the river. The reflection of the sun shimmering on the water can take your breath away. Flaming pinks and soothing turquoise draw blurry patterns across the indigo water. A liquid sunset. The expanse of the river is wide and the bank is thick with trees and snaky roots and kudzu vines that creep and crawl all the way down to the muddy water.

It's a fast-flowing river, full of waves and ripples. It's thick with underbrush and debris, making it notoriously one of the hardest areas for police divers to find anything. Or anyone. The Warrior is used for transportation. Time here is marked by the occasional slow-moving barge pushing coal up and down the river. Every so often, a speedboat races past, causing heavy waves to lap against the banks. A beautiful old riverboat called the *Bama Belle* would paddle down past the restaurant till sunset, when service would stop on the old vessel.

The *Bama Belle* was a sweet part of the fabric of the river. It was just for show. Tourists and out-of-town family loved it and kept it in business. But it was one of the main reasons I loved to eat at the Cypress Inn, especially at dusk. It was beautiful to see the boat in all her original glory just meandering along the curve of the river, on her way home, straight toward the setting sun, with her paddle wheel churning the muddy, ink-colored water below.

The Cypress Inn is built hanging off the hillside. All glass and old driftwood, it looks like it has been there forever. Two stories and facing the river, it's built in a triangle shape so everyone can watch the river while they eat their catfish and hush puppies.

Hanging baskets of azalea and begonias drip blossoms over the outdoor porch. And the trees are thick with magnolia blooms big enough to hold the spoonfuls of occasional afternoon rainwater that was a daily, almost unnoticeable part of Southern springtime.

It was this gorgeous scene that we all stepped out of the car to see, though the beauty of it was muddied by the dark reason we were all gathered there. Harry left us as he jogged ahead to catch up with Sonny. I knew he needed to see the body for himself. I also knew he wasn't fully embracing the possibility of what might actually be waiting for him at the bottom of that path. But I was.

Vivi was mumbling to herself, "See what horny can do? You see? If Lewis and I weren't always so horny, I'd have beautiful roses on my supper table tonight and Lewis would still be here." She kept walking and mumbling and looking at her feet as she stumbled to the path. She looked up at me. "Okay, I know it's not possible for us not to be who we really are, but I just cannot believe that my last vision of Lewis alive will be with that holster on and Deputy Dick in his hand."

Vivi and I linked arms like two old women and walked down the curvy stone walkway to the riverbanks. The footlights along the daffodil-strewn path twinkled in the encroaching darkness. It led us, roaming, down the hill and delivered us to the wooden planked bridge that guided us to the gazebo.

I heard the sounds of the sirens coming in the distance.

We located Sonny and found a small huddle of people standing east of the gazebo and, at the center of the group, with bare shoulders shaking, stood young Mandy Morrison, Tuscaloosa's Miss Everything. She was head cheerleader, Miss Tuscaloosa High School, Miss West Alabama Fair Queen…. She had plans of moving to New York and launching herself on Broadway.

Seeing how distraught she was, I had a feeling this event might slow things up a little.

Mandy, her mom, dad and younger brother were all at the Cypress Inn celebrating her high school graduation and acceptance into a small liberal arts college in New York when Mandy and her dad went for a little father-daughter stroll along the river. They had stopped to smell the wandering vines of honeysuckle when Mandy spotted the body—well, part of the body.

Right there, bobbing against the bank, was someone's leg and the lower half of their torso.

Vivi and I pushed into the little crowd of people just as Mandy was recounting her unfortunate vision.

"I was just giving my dad a hug and, like, I looked

over his shoulder and I saw a leg! At first I thought it was, like, a log.…"

Mandy kept talking…enjoying the attention even though she was somewhat "grossed out." As she kept up the frenetic, breathless encounter of her graduation dinner surprise, Sonny took notes and the officers collected the evidence.

Vivi and I peeked over the crowd of people now gathering at the banks.

"For God's sake!" she hollered. "It's not even the whole entire body! But *this* is the half I know best. No. No way is this my Lewis." Vivi could not keep it to herself.

Harry jumped in immediately. "This is not a good time to share your opinions unless someone asks, okay?" He was clearly on edge.

Vivi looked up at me with her half-drunk eyes. She was purely exhausted and it was showing. She pulled me down the bank away from Mandy and the crowd and headed toward the river. "C'mon, Blake, I've got to get a better look."

"Vivi, say nothing unless it is in a whisper directly to me. The last thing we want is to get you any more involved than you need to be. This is critical."

"I've got it, Blake. But if there's a chance in hell this is my Lewis, don't you think I ought to at least try to identify the half of the body that just washed up?"

"Honey," I said, "I'm right behind you." My curiosity had taken over, too. I just had to see it, not that *I* would recognize the half that just washed up. But down to the muddy riverbank we went. I knew that with Sonny nearby, he would make sure we were able to slip through the crowd without a problem.

We reached the edge of the river and there it was. Big and hairy, it was definitely the leg of a man. Sonny joined us. We were on the slope, and he was above us in the crest of the bank. At six-three he was a big presence anyway. But up on that riverbank he loomed like a superhero there to save us all. Vivi moved a little closer to him and leaned in as if in secret.

"Sonny, it's only half a body," she said quietly.

"Yes, Miss Vivi, we've got that part figured out."

Vivi stood between us, her head moving from side to side in slow motion, in disbelief. Silence fell over us. The three of us stood there on the banks of the muddy Warrior River under a darkening Southern sky.

Vivi broke the silence. "Well, thank God this is the half I know best, huh? This is not my Lewis."

She leaned in and squeezed Sonny's arm and tears rolled down her cheeks. We stood on the bank and watched the river roll. I looked at Sonny and noticed his face had softened in the moment. He looked at me full on and gave a little grin. I knew with his help we would all be okay.

Harry walked toward us in his determined, deliberate way. He looked exhausted but still pulled together. His white oxford shirt still looked as starched as it had been that morning, the silver wire frames sitting on his nose sparkled along with the silver hairs sprinkled throughout his dark hair.

"Well, the body part is already causing a problem."

"Why, Harry?" Vivi asked. "'Cause there's no dental record for you?" Vivi smirked.

Harry then told us the police would perform the DNA tests in the morning, and would try to match what they swiped at the motel room. He wanted to talk to me alone. Then Vivi said she wanted to talk to both of us alone.

"Well, I know when I'm a third wheel," Sonny said and winked at me.

"Do you have anything else for us?" I asked Sonny before he walked off. I didn't realize it, at first, but I was touching his arm.

"No, Blake, I'll get in touch with you in the morning," he said. Something came over me. I squeezed his wrist and, I don't know, but a feeling of comfort swept in and it made me feel warm and calm. I looked up at him and he was looking right through me. I let go and looked forward to the morning.

"Okay, ya'll. Listen to me," Vivi began after Sonny headed back up the banks. "That is not Lewis's lower half. There is no way in hell. I would bet my life on it."

Harry and I were silent and looking at each other.

"Dammit! I *know* him. This is not him! Believe me…that little thing would have *never* kept me coming back!"

5

It was a quiet drive back to the McFadden place. The crystal-clear night sky was ablaze with starlight. The moon hung over the tall pines and dodged in and out of sight, like a thief following us.

I sat in back with Vivi, her head on my shoulder. The quiet felt good. No radio. No conversation. We had all been through a tremendous amount of emotions and it was a relief to take a minute and let everything digest.

I stared out the window at the cloudless night sky. As the city baked in moonlight, slow-motion movie scenes flickered like a Super 8 film in my head. Scenes of my life with Vivi.

It had always been just like this. I've always taken care of her. I think we both liked it this way. I'm older than Vivi by only three months, but Vivi's the kind of girl who always needed a caretaker. I'm a little stronger, a little more able to focus. I am on a perpetual schedule. I like things neat and orderly…and predictable. Meanwhile, Vivi is full of adventure. She always loved a spontaneous road trip, though for me, that meant I had no time to pick out all the shoes I would need for the journey. But Vivi could just jump in her Thunderbird with no luggage, saying, "Oh, hell, we can get what we need when we get there." Oh, I still jumped in the car with her, but immediately I'd get out my notebook and pen and start making a list. The more I thought about it, the more I realized we balanced each other out. She may have needed me to take care of her, to organize her life and keep her on the right track, but I needed Vivi to remind me of my wild side. To remind me to really live in the moment. As I sat in the car reflecting on the days I'd been living lately, playing second fiddle to my husband's burgeoning political career, trying to forget what true love and romance really felt like, I realized that maybe I needed to be reminded of everything Vivi was. Maybe I was the one who needed Vivi right now, not just the other way around.

Vivi was an only child, and her parents were quite a bit older than the rest of ours. Her society-bred mother was always somewhat sickly, and her father was a loud-mouthed, hard-drinking, gambling partygoer who loved women—often several at a time. They lived on a massive plantation, and though she was surrounded by wealth, no one was ever really there to care for Vivi aside from her nanny, Corabelle, and the gardener, Arthur. She loved those two people like *they* were her parents. And truly, they were. In all the most important ways.

Vivi ran the whole place now. It was certainly not a plantation anymore; it had been decades since it was even active, and little by little, acre by oak tree, it has been sold off to developers. There was about a hundred acres left of it, and Vivi and Arthur were the only ones who lived there anymore since they had moved Vivi's mother to that fancy retirement center.

After we finished high school, Vivi had gone to the University of Alabama and gotten her journalism degree. Now she did freelance work, writing articles for magazines and newspapers on subjects that were dear to her heart, such as women's rights, gardening, home and friends.

Vivi was deeper than she let most people see, and her energy and wild streak made her seem crazier than she actually was. But she was just fine running the place all by herself. "Plus, I have Arthur," she'd always say. And she did.

She loved that man maybe more than she'd ever loved anyone. They were family as far as she was concerned. He loved taking care of her and took such pains around the place to keep it feeling like home.

Arthur had his own room in the house, and it had been appointed with the finest things. He was family since the beginning. Interestingly, he was actually born there, on the plantation, nearly fifty-five years ago when both of his parents had worked for the McFaddens. When Vivi's father died when she was young, Arthur just moved in and took on the responsibility of caring for her and her mother.

Corabelle, Vivi's nanny, died a few years back when she was nearly seventy-five. Arthur and Vivi took it pretty hard, but you could just see that they would get through it with each other to lean on.

Harry was always asking me why I kept rescuing her. Was it because I'm really all she's got? Was it because that's the way it'd always been and I love being needed? Well, maybe a bit of both. And I knew it would always be this way with us.

As I held her in the moonlight, she fell asleep on my shoulder, trusting me, as always, to keep her safe. And I would, even if I didn't know quite how at that moment. I knew I would figure something out. She was counting on me. I was her Swiss Army knife.

We arrived at the plantation at almost nine that evening. Harry pulled the car around the circular gravel drive. A fountain spilled over its edges creating peaceful, soft splashes under the moonlight. Vivi's home was something special. A true Southern plantation, the main house was huge and stately, typical antebellum Greek Revival architecture. Wide, white, round columns surrounded a wraparound front porch, and floor-to-ceiling windows doubled as doorways much of the year. The upper level held a sweeping veranda, hugging the columns with a whitewashed wooden rail. Rocking chairs were scattered around every few feet. Hanging baskets were full to brimming and dripping with ferns, English ivy and petunias, while bell-shaped purple-and-pink verbena hung at every window and spilled over the sides of the containers. The gravel drive was long and shaded on either side by huge oak and magnolia trees that reached across the road and lay gently upon each other, branch intertwined in branch, forming a fragrant flowering tree tunnel all the way to the front of the house. The side yards were full of pecan trees and tall pines. Just as you reached the porch, the left side yard held a huge rose garden with every colorful variety imaginable growing and blooming. The fragrance surrounding the main house was mesmerizing on a hot summer night with a breeze drifting in the humid air.

Located on the right and to the far back of the main property was Arthur's new BBQ place. It had its own entryway down from the main road and would eventually be a takeout BBQ spot for pickup. He was busy working on it much of the time to get it ready for football season and the tailgating orders that came with it. The Moonwinx was what he called it and he planned to just serve good, sweet Southern BBQ. The whole plantation was regal and lovely and had been Vivi's home her whole life, and her father's place before her, going back for generations.

Harry got out and opened the back door of the car to help Vivi out. We all walked up the four gray-painted steps of the porch.

A note from Arthur was waiting on the door. *G'nite, Miss Vivi. Hope you had fun visitin' with your Mama. Tomorrow I think we should get those hydrangea bushes lookin' good. Arthur.*

Exhausted, Vivi went directly upstairs and into the large master suite, and I followed her up to say goodnight. She had taken the room over after her 71-year-old mother went to the Center. Vivi had had the suite redone in her favorite colors and fabrics, and the bedroom was spectacular, covered in periwinkle silk and taffeta. Drapes fell into a pale blue puddle on the wood floor, framing the old floor-to-ceiling windows. The night air drifted in through the open windows and the fragrance of roses and honeysuckle blanketed the room. I gave her a hug, but didn't say a thing. We didn't need words right now, just the knowledge that we were there for each other was enough.

Back downstairs, Harry was waiting in the hallway, the moonlight bouncing off his glasses. "Let's go," he said, and leaned over and kissed my cheek.

His face was rough with evening whiskers, and I was shocked at the closeness. He had let me in for a brief moment and I wanted to stay there, pressed up against him a little longer, feeling his skin and smelling his end-of-the-day cologne. He pressed his hand into mine and we turned and left the house. He held on to me as if he would lose his way in the darkness if he let go. We stopped at the bottom of the porch and Harry pulled me into him and said, "Blake, I need to talk to you."

I remembered it was our anniversary, but I could tell he was not thinking of that. I pulled away from him. I knew this tone and I didn't like it.

"What is it, Harry?"

"I don't know…I just have a strange feeling."

"About what?"

"About Lewis," he said.

We sat down on the step, moonlight drenching the hydrangea bushes that bloomed on either side, framing the entrance. The humid night air kissed my skin and I took a deep breath. Lightning bugs dotted the darkness. I remembered Vivi and me as children, chasing the glowing amber fireflies every late spring evening when I spent the night there. We call them lightning bugs down South. They go hand in hand with sultry warm Southern nights when the damp humidity descends, the sun sets and the twilight sparkles with the flying magical insects. We'd catch them in old Mason jars and bring them inside and sit in the dark, telling ghost stories around the glowing jar, then we'd let them go. I listened to Harry but lingered in the safe memory of my childhood for another minute.

"I don't think that was Lewis tonight, do you?" he asked.

I said no and asked him what he was thinking. He was rubbing his fingers through his hair and saying he didn't know, but he just knew something was not quite right.

"It's just not clicking," he said.

"Harry, we're both tired and we haven't eaten. This day has been about as crazy as it could possibly be. Let's just put this to bed for tonight, okay?" I was so exhausted all I could think of was a long, hot bath and my down-filled comforter. But Harry needed to talk and so he did.

"I don't think that was Lewis," he said.

"I know, honey, that's what Vivi said."

"I know, Blake…but that's just it. If that's not Lewis, then where the hell is he?"

Harry did not look exhausted like me. He looked wide awake. He had that look in his eye that he always had when he was pursuing a case.

"Harry, what are you thinking?" I asked. "That Lewis isn't dead?" I waited for a response but Harry was in another place in his head now. I could see it.

He looked straight up into my eyes. "Dead men don't just up and walk away. Lewis isn't dead, Blake. I know him and this is typical Lewis. He's done so many things in the past and then come running to me for a bailout. I'm sick of saving his ass. Not this time. He's up to something again. I'm sure of it. Somebody must know where he is. And I'm gonna find out who."

6

The next morning, a ringing woke me from the depths of sleep. It was one of those heavy slumbers that, when you wake, it takes you a few seconds to realize where you are and what's going on, and the night before is still clinging to you and leaving its essence in all the wrong places. The tired was still stinging all over.

It took another second for me to figure out that the ringing was the phone and not the alarm clock. With my eyes still closed, I moved to reach across Harry and answer when I realized that he wasn't there.

The digital clocked glowed 6:47 a.m. in the dim morning light.

"Blake?" It was Vivi.

"Vivi? Hi, honey."

"I am just crazy." She thought I needed a phone call to confirm this? She continued, "Oh, my God. I am so sorry about last night." An apology bathed in embarrassment. "I was so tired I don't even remember getting up the stairs."

"Don't you worry, it was a long day for all of us. Are you okay this morning?"

"Oh, yeah, honey, I'm always okay…you know, just nervous as a long-tailed cat in a room full of rockin' chairs, that's all. I don't know what to do next. Just pacing everywhere…waitin' for the other shoe to drop. Any word?"

I was still on my stomach with the phone tucked under me, pushed into my pillow, eyes still closed.

"No word yet. I'm going to get up and I'll meet you at Mother's at eight-thirty. Okay?"

"Is Harry there?" she asked.

"No, he must've left early."

"Oh…do you think there might be some news?"

"He would let us know right away if there was. Try not to worry. I'll see you in a few."

We hung up and I lay there, clutching the phone to my chest and breathing in the morning air. I tried to exhale, pushing away the events that were about to play out.

I turned over in my bed and stared at the double crown molding. I loved this old house. It was built in the 1800s. You know…one of those huge old Southern homes with the sweeping, wraparound front porch. The ceiling fans turned in slow motion all the time. I never turned them off. Slow-turning ceiling fans were so inviting. To me they meant someone was home, cooking something, the down pillows were all fluffed and waiting for you to rest your weary head, iced tea and fresh chocolate cake were waiting somewhere in the kitchen. The fans welcomed me home every night, even if the house was empty. Somehow I believed they made the place feel full, awake and alive.

Harry and I bought this house five years ago as a gift to each other. It was for our fifth anniversary. We had lived in a little town house near the campus up until then. We both loved this house from the minute we found it that evening in November. It needed a little love, but it felt like home the second we walked in the door. Harry and I didn't say a word to each other...just a glance and we knew. We could love this house into our home. Of course we walked the whole house, holding hands, almost giddy with the rush of the future and all it held tingling between us.

There was a sweeping, curved front staircase, a wide and airy front hall, two large parlors on each side, creaking wood floors and brick fireplaces in nearly every room creating a fairy-tale ambience that I had never felt anywhere before. Sleeping many nights with the dance of the firelight on the walls was a comfort that is indescribable.

Many a spring night we slept with the windows open. I loved the seasons in that house. Each one has its own indelible fingerprint on my memories of living there. I had hoped the house would be a new beginning for us. The year before we moved in, when things had just started to become cold between us around the time of the awful disintegration of Harry's relationship with Lewis, I still had a lot of hope for us. The house symbolized a new start. It never really became that for us, but even lying in bed the morning after Lewis went missing, I still loved it there. It was home for me.

As I made my way to the shower, I decided to call Harry.

"Hey, sorry about running off this morning. I didn't want to wake you," Harry said. He sounded breathless.

"What is it?" I asked.

"Seems like Lewis's clothes, or *someone's* clothes, washed up at the river last night…about fifty yards up from the Cypress Inn."

"Have the clothes been tested yet?" I asked.

"They are actually on their way to the lab, but we were thinking maybe Vivi could ID them. We need to know if these were the clothes Lewis was wearing when she was with him at the Fountain Mist. We're still waiting on the DNA results of the washed-up body parts, but this could definitely get things moving."

"I talked to her this morning. She's meeting me at Mother's at 8:30."

"Sonny and the police are all already involved," Harry said. "I'll meet you there, too. We should let Vivi know what's going on. That way we can warn her before she has to look at the clothes. There's going to be a press conference at noon."

I figured that would be next. Since Lewis was the play-by-play…*is* the play-by-play announcer for the Alabama Crimson Tide, the news of his disappearance would have the media in a frenzy. See, Tuscaloosa is not just any football town. There are plenty of college towns with good teams. But in Tuscaloosa, football *is* the town. Everyone there, whether they went to Bama or didn't even go to college, is a fan. There are only two seasons here—football and *waiting* for football. As soon as the season ends, usually with us in the national championships, the town goes into what you could almost consider a mourning period, then a depression and then the countdown calendars come out with "Only ____ days till kickoff...." We think, eat, sleep and breathe football—365 days a year, every single year.

Tuscaloosa on game day is especially a treat. The quad is literally covered in tents for one humungous tailgate party. The air is thick with excitement and the sweet smell of meat on the grill. Everyone cooking and drinking—they even clip satellites to their tents for their big-screen TVs. My very favorite moment of the entire season is when I'm standing in that stadium when the song "Sweet Home Alabama" by Lynyrd Skynyrd begins.

So for Lewis to be missing from the Bama pulpit in Tuscaloosa—well, it was like the Pope missing from the Vatican. I knew the entire population would show up for his press conference, as well as every reporter for college football from all over the country.

The gravity of the situation stole my breath for a minute, but Harry's voice brought me back.

"Hell, the entire South Eastern Conference will be sending their reporters to swarm Tuscaloosa, especially since we're the national champions," Harry said.

While the reason for the press conference was a bit depressing, the thought of being on camera excited me and I suddenly felt much better.

"Where's it gonna be?" I asked.

"Denny Chimes."

I began to picture the fiasco that was about to blow into town...and how Vivi would be in front of the mic, flanked by me and Harry on one side and Sonny on the other. As Vivi's attorneys and Lewis's most immediate family, Harry or I would have to be the spokesperson.

"Vivi cannot speak on camera!" Harry was stern. "Those reporters will have a field day with her. And

God only knows what she would say. Part of her would love this attention, and the other half of her will be scared to death. She'd be completely uncontrollable."

"Okay, I'll take care of it. I'll see you at Mother's," I said, but he had already hung up.

I laid the phone down on the marble vanity and turned on the shower. The steam began to fog the mirrors. I stepped inside. The hot, pulsating water felt good. I didn't want to get out. I knew what this day was going to look like and I had barely been awake fifteen minutes.

I wanted to let the water rain over me all day. I turned a couple of tired steps so the water could hit my face. I knew the day would be nearly unbearable, and none of it would feel as good as this moment. Even the thought of being on camera started to make me feel anxious, so I stood still, on purpose, avoiding the day that lay ahead.

Then I heard it in my head. Harry's words from last night.

Lewis is alive. And someone knows where he is.

The words jerked me right out of my serenity. What is he thinking? All of the scenarios from the ridiculous to the haunting invaded my peaceful shower. I rinsed my hair and turned off the water, leaving my oasis behind. I lost the last of my tranquility in my next thought: *Does Vivi know anything about Lewis and his life that could lead us to him?*

7

Vivi was already at Mother's when I pulled into the driveway. Out of years of habit, I rolled directly under the old tattered basketball net, now just hanging by a thread. The redbrick back steps invited me in and the screen door creaked and slammed behind me. My heels clicked on the red-painted concrete floor of the cluttered back porch. Stacks of old newspapers and magazines were everywhere. An antique 1940s refrigerator stood in the corner. It was always filled with plenty of Coca-Cola. The minute anyone arrived, the first thing Meridee did was offer you a Coke.

The smell of coffee drifted through the kitchen, which had butter-colored walls and a yellow-and-green vinyl floor. The 1950s yellow laminate table was already full of people, just the way Meridee liked it. This place relaxed me like an instant sedative.

Vivi was sitting comfortably with both of her hands wrapped securely around her cup to warm them. Meridee was in her chair at the spot near the stove, holding her lipstick-stained cup with one hand while dipping a doughnut into the coffee with the other.

Next to her was what we liked to call the "snack corner." The snack corner was a treasure trove of deliciousness, brimming with scrumptious concoctions, mostly from the Keebler Elves and Krispy Kreme. It was my absolute most favorite place as a child and, let's be honest, as an adult, too. But today my favorite spot was already occupied.

"Hey, Blake, sweetie. Come give your mama a hug."

Yes, that was my mother, Katherine Meredith Fletcher O'Hara Sandoval Sugarman—or Kitty, as she was known to all…and, believe me, she was known to all. She could never make up her mind which man she loved, so, in true Kitty fashion she eventually married them all. Kitty was by far the loudest, bluntest and rowdiest of all the clan. Hell, she was the loudest person I knew, period. And *that* is saying something since Vivi and Lewis are in the group!

Kitty looked up from her ice-cold glass of Dr Pepper and her chocolate grahams when I walked in.

"How you doin', baby?"

I walked over and hugged her. Truthfully, Kitty and I are nothing alike. I keep most of my nasty thoughts to myself. Kitty must get them out in the open for all to hear the very minute she feels them. "It clears the air and lets people know the truth," she says. "And nothing's better than the truth."

"Unless it hurts people's feelings," I would counter, but to deaf ears.

Kitty was an original, a one of a kind, and most who knew her would say, thank heavens. I remember when I was a teenager, Meridee would get me aside and say,

"Blake, your mother is crazy. Always remember that. Whatever she says, never forget that." And I didn't. And Meridee was right.

"Hey, Mama," I said. "What are you doing here?"

"Well, I just thought I'd stop by to check in on Mother and looky who I found here…Vivi Ann McFadden. Can you believe it?"

I gave Vivi a questioning look. I didn't want to start spreading the news about Lewis without her approval, so I wasn't sure what to say to Kitty. All Vivi offered was a dirty look framed by dark circles and her halo of red wiry hair.

Without stopping for an answer, Kitty continued, "So, sugar, tell me what y'all are doing here."

Vivi and I spoke at once, nervously overlapping our explanations.

"Well, Mama, Vivi and I just thought we needed to catch up," I said and Vivi continued.

"So, we thought we would meet here for coffee."

And just as Vivi said that, Harry walked in fast and furious.

"Sorry I'm late," he said, brushing the water from the arms of his suit coat. "It's raining like—" He stopped midsentence as his gaze caught Kitty in the corner. "Hey, Kitty," he said with a confused look on his face.

"Well, hey there, Harry, darlin'," she said with sugar dripping from each syllable. She stepped from the corner and gave Harry a hug.

"Oh, honey, look, now I'm all wet, too." That woman just could not help herself. She flirted with every male who crossed her path, and she always had a double entendre going.

Kitty loved men. And men loved her back. She was,

in her time, a leggy, busty debutante. All I inherited from Kitty was her boobs, not her legs. I'm only five-three, while Kitty is a lucky five foot seven. I definitely look more like Meridee—a former beauty queen herself, but only five-one, she was a tiny blue-eyed, brunette spitfire. I have Meridee's dark hair and blue-green eyes, deep dimples like my dad and a sassy attitude just like my Meridee. I was proud of that…that I was like her. Plus, she is awfully cute. I figure if I can look that sweet and sassy in my old age, that's something to be pretty thankful for.

Harry came around to me and gave me a hug and whispered in my ear, "What's she doing here?"

I raised my eyebrows, responding with an "I have no idea" look.

"Well, isn't this quite the morning get-together?" Kitty announced. "Let's all go get Egg McMuffins!"

Meridee jumped up.

"No, no, no," she said. "Y'all sit right back down! I never get to cook for anybody. I'll have eggs and sausage and grits and biscuits up here in a jiffy." Meridee had such a look of joy on her face as she smiled, pushing Kitty out of the corner and humming "Rock of Ages" as she gathered her ingredients.

As we all sat around the yellow table where I had spent hours and hours of my childhood, the pressure started to build. Harry, Vivi and I knew we needed to get to work on the facts. I ran things over in my mind. Best-case scenario, Lewis was only missing, and at worst dead, but none of us wanted to say anything with Kitty there.

Clothes had washed up early this morning at the Cypress Inn and all hell was about to break loose at this press conference, which was now only three hours away. Meeting at Mother's now seemed like the worst plan we could have made—there was no way we'd be able to discuss Lewis and the case with loudmouth Kitty ready to hear all the juicy details. The whole state would know about Lewis's disappearance by lunchtime.

We were awkwardly quiet, Kitty sitting at the head of the table where my grandfather used to sit, staring at all three of us with a "cat that ate the canary" grin.

"Okay, what'er y'all up to?" she said, finally breaking the silence. "Oh, my God! Are y'all planning my birthday? Lord! Y'all are so good! It's still over a month away. No wonder y'all are so uptight. How in the world can y'all do any plannin' with me sittin' here?" With that, she stood from the table. "Mother, none for me. I'll be off now, my sugars, and y'all can keep up your whispering and your hush-hush…and I'll just pretend I heard nothing." She finished in a whisper as if she were keeping the secret. She kissed Meridee's cheek and grabbed her polka-dot Kate Spade bag.

"I guess I'll get my Egg McMuffin, after all!" The back door slammed and she was gone. We all let out a sigh of relief, but this meeting wasn't fixin' to get any easier since Harry and I were mustering up the courage to tell Vivi about those clothes soaked in river water.

I dropped my head to the table like a schoolgirl in trouble. "Sorry, y'all, I had no idea she would be here." Meridee kept singing and cooking, and for once I was so happy she couldn't hear very well anymore.

Vivi spoke first. "Harry, what are you doing here? Blake didn't tell me you were coming."

I chimed in before Harry could speak. "I talked to

Harry after you called. We have some new evidence and Harry wanted to talk to you."

"Oh, no," she said, the caffeine kicking in. "Not another body part?"

"No, nothing like that," Harry said. "But…clothes. And we don't even know if they're his. That's where we thought you could help us. Do you remember what he was wearing when you last saw him?"

"Harry, I thought we had already had this conversation," Vivi said. "Lewis wasn't wearing *anything* the last time I saw him!"

Although none of us felt like eating, we all managed to look interested in the mountain of food that Meridee laid before us. We couldn't refuse, so we set the table and picked at the breakfast. I needed to add a little kick to my coffee, but it was too early. But hey, as my favorite humorist, Celia Rivenbark, says, "You can't drink all day if you don't start in the mornin'." Sounded like a plan for today.

Thirty minutes later, after cleaning things up, Harry said, "Meridee, that was delicious. Now, I hate to be a devil and eat and run, but I've got to get these girls over to the office. They promised to look over my campaign poster designs before I send them off to the printers."

"Don't you worry, Harry. You do whatever you need to. I want to see you win this thing and then I want to see you on TV."

We walked outside and, with Vivi and me in my car and Harry in his, we all headed over to the police station.

The police station was across the street from the bank and where one of my favorite Tuscaloosa relics stood on the corner. The old turn-of-the-century clock was the centerpiece of downtown, black iron framed with a round white face and black hands. It had witnessed the history of Tuscaloosa unfold around it. From my earliest memories of three or four years old, I remembered the old clock standing right there, watching over all of us.

Sometimes we'd go on big outings downtown—which consisted of two whole streets back then—to see my grandmother peddle her cosmetics at Lewis Weasel's department store, the most expensive shop in town. Then we'd cross the street to Kress's and eat lunch at their lunch counter. As I enjoyed the delicacy of grilled cheese and fries, I would sit looking at all the busy people rushing to somewhere important. I studied the women and their Southern way of dressing, cotton dresses billowing behind them. I couldn't wait to be old enough to dress just like them. And to wear the pearls. All the women wore pearls. After lunch, we'd head back across the street to the bank. That's where the clock stood, like an old sweet guard watching over the rush of cars and people.

If only now the clock could speak. It saw everything for the last hundred years. It always knew the truth. As I glanced over at it in the morning sprinkling of rain, I saw the old relic as a source of comfort.

Mine and Harry's law office was just next door to the bank, so I dipped in to check with Wanda Jo, our secretary. Now, that woman is cranky even on her best days, but she sure knows how to run a law office. She was a good bit older than me and Harry and had known us both since we were children. She was sharp and organized but spoke like a redneck sailor on shore leave.

Wanda Jo was a former majorette when she went to Alabama State, aeons ago. She was always a little heavy and a good bit too loud, but I liked her. She tried to mother us and we just let her.

"Hey, Wanda Jo, any messages?" I asked as Vivi and I stepped inside. "I'm only here for a sec, meeting Harry and Sonny across the street on some business."

"Hell, yeah, you've got messages! This damn phone's been ringing off the hook all mornin'. I've just been tellin' everybody you'd call back this afternoon, so you better keep my word." She laughed and took a drag of her cigarette. "Hey there, Vivi," she added with a wink.

"Now you know you can't smoke in here," I reminded her. She put the cigarette out, opened the window behind her desk and answered the ringing phone. "Heart and Heart Attorneys. How can we be of service?" she said into the receiver. "Uh-huh... Uh-huh..." She was writing. "Okay. I will pass it along but don't hold your breath, honey. They are actually working on something important today." And she hung up, smiling. "I swear, some people in this town are just pure ol' lunatics." She looked up at me. "Now what are you doing still standin' there starin' at me? You can see I've got things under control, so git on outta here and go over to Sonny's. You gotta lot of calls to return this afternoon. Tell Mr. Heart he has his fair share, too."

"Okay, Wanda Jo, let me know if something pressing comes in. I'm expecting that package on the Myrna case."

"I know it. I'll sign for it, as usual. Now go on."

Wanda Jo had come to work for us when we first opened. She had been a law office manager most of her life, and at one point had worked for my grandfather. She'd found the Lord and lost him nearly as quick: she'd become a preacher's wife until she decided she didn't like the pressure of trying to be holy for the congregation. Wanda Jo had been known to throw back a few and she loved to dance and cuss. Reverend Mayes was always embarrassed by her behavior and lack of culinary skills and eventually they divorced. I mean a preacher's wife who can't bake a pound cake for the family of the departed was nearly useless in the South. Wanda Jo never remarried. Kitty says she looks like she's been "rode hard and put up wet," meaning she's lived a hard (wild) life and it showed on her face. And she does look a bit worse for the wear. Her two kids live in Florida and work for one of the horse tracks in Tampa. She's a good soul. And I trust her. At the end of the day, that's what counts.

I grabbed Vivi by the hand and gave it a squeeze. We walked out the door and headed across the street.

"That Wanda Jo is a sight," Vivi said as we crossed the downtown street to the police station. "She never changes."

Sonny was waiting outside the station. The rain had turned to a sprinkle and he stood in the hazy mist drinking a Mountain Dew. At the sight of him, Vivi started to shake. "Oh, Blake, he's waitin' for me. This is it," Vivi said.

"No, sweetie, he's just gonna show you what was found, that's all. Now let's go."

"Hey," Sonny announced in his baritone Southern drawl as we approached the old wooden and glass door. "Y'all come on in. Mornin', Vivi." Sonny extended his hand and ushered her inside. As he took her hand and then let go, his skin brushed mine. He looked at me, right in my eyes. I smiled at him and immediately felt my cheeks flame.

"Mornin', Blake," he said, all businesslike to break up the awkwardness of the moment.

Harry had pulled in right behind me and was just getting out of his Mercedes. I heard his door slam. Vivi and I were inside when Harry arrived at the door, Sonny shaking hands with him quickly and patting his back as though they were golf buddies.

"Y'all have a seat," Sonny began, just as Bonita entered the room with her hands full of a delicious-smelling little box.

"Hey, y'all. Sorry to interrupt—" she began, but Vivi cut her off.

"What in the world is that scrumptious smell? My stomach just rumbled so loud you could hear it across town. All this mess with Lewis has me so worked up, I don't think I've remembered to eat much."

"Well, here, honey, have a rib! They're from Arthur's new place. I told him I would pass samples around the neighborhood for him. We want the whole town talkin' 'bout these so everybody is excited when we—uh, when *he* has the grand opening. They are so good…" she said, opening the container and passing them around.

"You and Arthur seem to be spendin' a lotta time together since y'all met at church last month," Vivi said, taking a rib from the box.

"Yeah, he is a sight and, man, can he cook up some sweet, saucy ribs. He is just so talented in the kitchen."

"Uh-huh, and maybe elsewhere…." Count on Vivi to say the thing we were all thinking. She just couldn't keep even a single thought to herself.

"Now, Vivi, you know me and you know I don't fool

around, but I do love spendin' time with Arthur. He is quite the gentleman…and quite the chef. Blake, have a rib, honey…it'll just melt in your mouth." I took one, looking at Sonny with my eyebrows up. Was Bonita investigating cases, ribs or Arthur these days?

"Well, I better get goin' before I don't have any ribs to pass out. See y'all later," Bonita said with a smile as she covered the ribs and turned toward the door. "I got me a list of places to visit with these little delicacies. I just know the courthouse would love a rib or two. And, Sonny, I'm on my lunch break so don't be thinkin' I'm shirkin' my work. You know nothing's more important to me than this department." And with a swish of her curvy hips, she stepped outside and shut the old wooden door with a bang.

"Yeah, nothing except Arthur and his new BBQ business. I do believe he may have himself a new business partner 'fore this is over with," Vivi said.

We all chewed our saucy ribs and Sonny grabbed some napkins from his desk drawer. Vivi began to tap her fingers on the table anxiously. You could just tell she'd reached her limit for waiting, and she was quickly running out of patience.

"Can I get anyone a drink?" Sonny offered as he handed out the napkins.

"No!" Vivi said, full of exasperation. "For God's sake! Let's just get this over with. I swear, if I smoked, I'd be settin' new records. Besides, I drank enough coffee at Mother's to be wound up tighter than a Bessie bug for a month of Sundays! So, please, just show me the damn clothes!"

"We're fixin' to get right to it." Sonny motioned to Deputy Officer Dooley with a raised eyebrow and a quick flick of his head to retrieve the evidence. The little officer made his way down the wood-planked floor to a small room at the end of the hallway. We wiped our mouths as Officer Dooley returned with a large plastic Ziploc bag. Sonny passed around a little garbage can and we all dropped the rib bones inside. Vivi sat up in the wooden barrel-backed chair and scooted to the edge of her seat. She removed her oversize round black sunglasses that she used more to hide her worried eyes than shield any sun on this gray morning.

Sonny stood and pulled on latex gloves from behind the desk and slowly removed each garment from the bag, holding them between his thumb and index finger. The clothes were so muddy, I could barely make out any color or texture. Vivi stood and moved forward one step toward the desk. Her hand was outstretched toward the wet bag but Sonny yanked it back.

"No, Miss Vivi. You cannot touch this. It's classified evidence now. Do you recognize anything?" He continued to lay the garments out across the plastic sheeting that covered the desk. He pulled out the trademark khaki polo pants, torn and muddy. And then the sherbet-orange polo shirt. It was almost unrecognizable, the color so destroyed by the rush of the river and all the mud. But Vivi started to shake.

"Oh, shit. Oh, shit," she muttered.

Harry and I stood up slowly. I put my arm on Vivi's shoulder and glanced at Harry in the sudden sharp silence. For a split second, only the whir and beat of those old overhead fans filled the air. Thump. Thump. Thump.

"Miss Vivi," Sonny broke in, "do you care to, uh, elaborate?"

Vivi only continued to mutter, her hands trembling.

She was shaking her head back and forth as if in disbelief.

"Okay, Vivi," I said. "'Oh, shit' is not an identification or an elaboration. You've got to give us something else."

I glanced back over her shoulders at Harry. He looked chalky white. "Harry," I whispered, "are you okay?"

He knew he couldn't identify the clothes, but he obviously recognized Lewis's style in that wet muddy bag. He squinted, swallowed hard and brushed his hand across his brow. I knew he was not okay. He swallowed hard again, as if trying to suppress the words he had shoved deep down along with his emotions. Several years of wanting to speak to Lewis seemed to regurgitate in his throat. Several years of wishing things hadn't happened like they did. I felt for him in that moment there in the little office. But Harry had never handled Lewis very well. Watching him now took me back to that awful night six years ago when they'd last spoken.

I will never forget the way it all unraveled. Nearly seven years ago Harry's dad died suddenly. He was sixty-two years old and had a stroke in his sleep. He had just quit the law practice his own father had started. He lasted barely six months into retirement when Julia, Harry's mother, found him cold in the bed one Friday morning over the Fourth of July weekend. She called Harry first and he gathered the rest of the family.

After the funeral Harry was named executor, as his mother had to go on medication. She became much too fragile to handle the estate. Most of it certainly was going to Harry in any case.

Shortly after, Lewis and Harry got together to discuss what to do with their widowed mother and that's when the trouble began. Harry wanted to make sure Julia stayed in her own house. He wanted to take the money they'd inherited, and there was a lot of it, and hire 'round-the-clock care for Julia—a cook, a housekeeper, a driver—all so that Julia could stay in the house she had called home for over forty years.

Lewis, however, did not want to donate his share of the inheritance for that purpose. Instead, he wanted to invest it, turn it around quickly to make millions and then take Julia to live with him, to finally be the son he had never quite been able to be. He told Harry his investment was a sure thing. It would make them even richer.

This was typical Lewis. His heart was huge, and it was almost always in the right place. He just didn't have Harry's knack for thinking things through. Harry was the tortoise and Lewis was the hare, running fast and furious, throwing caution to the wind, wanting to fill up every second of life *with* life. His epitaph would probably read: "I never wasted a minute. I never took the safe path. I risked it all and loved every second."

Harry was quite the opposite. Slow and steady. He knew what he wanted and he only took the sure bet, the low risk path, trodden by many a Heart man before him.

Clearly, he and Lewis clashed. Harry needed Lewis's part of the estate to care for Julia in the way he intended, in the grandest style and opulence. But Lewis refused. They argued for weeks. Then one day, Lewis burst into our house and announced he had done it. Some college buddies of his in Birmingham had a sure thing going. Lewis invested in their new business as a partner. He was so excited. "Full turnaround with massive interest," he had said, "is guaranteed in six months."

Harry and Lewis did more than argue this time. You could've heard their shouting two blocks away.

"I'm sick of you always making all the decisions for this family," Lewis had hollered. "Dad only ever believed in you because you're just like him. Always walking the straight and narrow, even when it means losing out on the chance of a lifetime! He always thought I was a joke 'cause I wouldn't even consider law school." Lewis paused and shook his head in disgust. "The predictability of it all makes me sick. Another Heart goes to law school. Oh, that's original. I'd rather die than be another Heart in law school."

"Oh, and what have you gone and done instead? Talk on the radio? Selfish, as usual. You know, I have had just about enough of your shit. I'll take care of Mother my way till the money runs out. And you can go straight to hell."

"*I'll* be caring for Mother," Lewis shouted, "and won't that be just a shock to everyone. You'll see, Harry. In six months. I guarantee you!" And with that, Lewis slammed the door to the house on his way out.

"God, he is absolutely ridiculous," I remember Harry saying after he left. It was true, what Lewis had said, though. Harry always thought of Lewis as a joke.

Six months passed and Julia was getting better every week. Harry cared for her with an entourage of help and kept her in her Southern mansion on the southeastern edge of town. We didn't hear from Lewis at all for the entire six months.

Then, late one soggy November afternoon, Lewis showed up at our door. Soaking wet and reeking of alcohol, he looked as though he hadn't showered in a week.

"Lewis! My God, get in here!" Harry said, pulling his brother inside from the storm.

"Lewis, what happened?" I asked.

"It's gone." He was dripping rainwater all over the wood floor and trying hard to hold himself together. He looked so lost and helpless, it broke my heart. Harry, however, had no pity. He was full of rage.

"How much did you lose?" he asked, his voice as cold as ice.

"All of it."

"Oh, dear God." Harry sank down on the couch. "I knew it," he muttered. "What happened?"

Lewis explained this new mess he was in. Harry and I had been married about four years at the time, and this was at least the sixth time that I'd seen Lewis in trouble.

"The investment didn't work."

Harry and I looked at each other as if to say, "Duh."

"We got that part," I said. "What happened?"

"I'm in trouble." He kept his head down.

"What now?" Harry said.

"This time it's really bad."

"Lewis, what the hell happened?" Harry pushed.

"The company was illegal."

"What?" Harry stepped closer to him. "What company? What do you mean illegal?"

"It was all fake, Harry, a money-laundering scheme."

"How much of it is gone?" Harry asked.

"All five million. All of mine plus some of Mother's."

Something seemed to break for Harry at that moment. His practiced stoicism, his perfectly calm and always unruffled demeanor suddenly cracked. He grabbed Lewis by the front of his shirt. "Tell me everything, you sorry bastard! Now!"

"I invested part of Mother's money and all of mine into a new radio franchise. A new national network." Lewis was shaking, his usually clear voice nearly inaudible.

"We sold all of this advertising. They were out of Baltimore. All of the money was coming out of Birmingham. They told us we were on the satellite and soon every station in the country doing talk would be carrying us so we sold the advertising."

"You sold advertising on a phony network?" Harry broke in.

"Now the Baltimore group has shut down and disappeared. No station, no advertising, no money."

"That's an FCC violation, you idiot!"

"I know, Harry, but eventually the network was going to carry the advertising. We were sold a bill of goods. But now there's no network and all five of us from the Birmingham group will go to jail. Harry, you've got to get us off."

"You knew you were selling ads on something that didn't exist yet," Harry shouted, infuriated. He was in shock. We all were. Lewis had outdone himself. This was by far his biggest mess.

"Yes, but we'd have millions as soon as we turned on the satellite. It would be instant. Tuscaloosa would be carrying the new network, too," Lewis continued, his voice high and shaky—clearly he was living a nightmare.

"Would be, should be—but none of it worked! Why the hell did you do it, Lewis?" Harry walked away throwing his arms up in the air.

Lewis stood up. His face went from fearful to pissed off in less than two seconds. In a clear, low voice, Lewis quietly answered, "Because of you, Harry. I wanted, for once, to be better. To be right. To show you I could outdo you."

"Well, look at yourself, Lewis. Happy? Mother's life will never be the same. Over five million dollars of Dad's hard-earned money is gone because of Lewis, the joke. Not only have you hurt Mother, you've stolen from her and lied to both of us. You've dragged the family name down in the mud with you. I hardly know what to say. I'll defend you, Lewis, but only because you're my blood, and I wouldn't dare disgrace my own family the way you would. After that you're on your own. I don't even want to know you anymore."

Lewis stood still, emotionally beaten to a pulp. He was unsteady on his feet as he moved across the room toward the front door.

"No, thanks," he said. "I'm on my own as of now." And with that, he slammed the front door and walked out on Harry.

They hadn't spoken since that fiasco nearly six years ago. Lewis and his cronies hired some high-powered Birmingham lawyers who got them off with some stiff fines and six months' prison time at some posh, white-collar camp outside Atlanta. Charged and convicted of investment fraud and some FCC violations, Lewis eventually returned to Tuscaloosa stronger and even more determined to make loads of money.

With that all behind him, Lewis went on to become one of the most recognized voices in sports radio. That's the funny thing about being in the media—sometimes a prison stint makes you even more interesting!

Over the last few years, Lewis made his and his mother's money back with book deals and appearances.

Bit by bit he worked himself out of the red, and without any help from Harry. I don't think Lewis ever forgave Harry for treating him the way he did. Truthfully, I'm not sure it ever really mattered to Harry.

When their mother, Julia, died two years ago, Harry had stayed around after the service to watch Julia's casket descend into the muddy Southern earth. I left him down near the gravesite alone to say goodbye to his beloved mother. He was always her favorite and he knew it. But Julia's constant doting on her favorite eldest son put responsibilities on Harry that otherwise wouldn't have been there. Harry felt the weight of the world on his shoulders. The Heart legacy, the Heart name, was his and his alone to propel into eternity, for the world to know and respect.

Much of the family, Julia included, had already written Lewis off as an unredeemable philanderer. Booze, gambling and women all seemed to gravitate in Lewis's direction. It was Harry that everyone depended upon, counted upon. And as in every aspect of his life, Harry would have to be perfect. He expected it of himself more than anyone else did. Eventually the perfection he insisted upon became unbearable for, well, both of us. I'd come to realize that there were only two things Harry really cared about: his career and his mother. His drive for perfection didn't seem to exist when it came to romance and marriage. Lately, it seemed as though these things were only an afterthought for Harry, if he had ever really considered them at all.

The day they buried Julia, I could see that Harry felt guilty. Guilty that he hadn't done more, guilty that he hadn't been able to save her like he always had, guilty that she never understood the whole story of why Lewis left the family. Harry had protected her from the God-awful truth. Now that she was gone, I think he was also partly ashamed for never forgiving Lewis.

When Harry was saying his last words to her, just before they began to crank the casket down, he looked up to remove his glasses, dabbing his eyes, and he caught Lewis in his peripheral vision. A starched white shirt, dark crimson tie and khakis—Lewis's work uniform. He had obviously just left the pre-season show on campus. That Bama crimson is what caught Harry's eye. He hadn't laid eyes on Lewis in person for over four years, and the sight of him clearly took his breath away. He was caught. I could see the emotions warring within him as I watched him try to decide how to react. The Heart Book of Emotional Rules clearly states, "Hold a grudge with a white-knuckle grip—especially if it is against a family member."

Yet the sensible, responsible Harry decided to make an amendment to the rule. *Unless the person begrudged needs to say goodbye to his dead mother.* Harry himself would not break the rules. No, he was too "Heart" for that. As Lewis approached from across the rain-soaked cemetery, Harry kissed his first two fingers and gently touched the coffin, and then turned away. He did not speak to Lewis or even motion a wave or an acknowledgment. He just turned and walked away. He had allowed Lewis to approach, and that amendment to the "Rules" was enough. While I'm sure he'd never admit it, I could tell that part of him wanted to scream at Lewis for not being a better son, a better brother, a better anything. But another part of him, I knew, wanted to grab him and hold him. He was, after all, the only family Harry had left now. But he did neither. Instead, he made his way up the hill to me.

That's the same Harry I saw in the police station as we looked at the muddy clothes strewn out upon the desk. A Harry needing to speak, but unable to utter a sound.

"Well, Miss Vivi," Sonny pushed.

Vivi sucked in a deep breath, and I slipped my hand in hers as she began to nod.

"Yes, Sonny, that's probably what Lewis was wearing. I believe those are his clothes."

"Thank you, Miss McFadden. That's all we need for now."

Sonny was matter-of-fact. He glanced over at me and then at Harry. "We'll be in touch." He handed the soggy bag back to Officer Dooley and gave him a nod, cop-speak for, "You know what to do."

Officer Dooley trotted off into the darkness of the long hallway as the three of us turned to head back into the midmorning mist.

"Blake." Sonny caught me. He cleared his throat. "Can I see you a minute?"

I saw Harry glance back at us, but he only said, "Go ahead. We'll head to the car."

I turned to Sonny. He looked concerned. "Blake, we need to talk."

I sat back down under the slow-moving fans and got comfortable. I knew Sonny well enough to know that nothing with him only takes a minute. Nothing. Sonny was slow and steady, much like Harry in that way. I guess that's always been my kind of man. A rock of a guy with a strong shoulder to lean on. It balances my overly emotional side.

Sonny looked at me without blinking. His dark brown eyes were speaking silent messages to me but I couldn't quite make out the code.

"What is it?" I finally said.

"I was just thinking," Sonny began. "Blake, as you know, we're still waiting to hear whether those body parts belonged to Lewis. Without that, it's still a missing person case."

"I know."

"Well, I am a little concerned about a couple things," he continued in his thick-as-molasses Southern lilt. "I'm worried 'bout Harry, Blake. I saw him look at that bag of clothes."

"Yes. So?" I said.

"C'mon, Blake, the guy missing is Harry's brother. How's he gonna deal with that? You know? Separate the emotions from the job? I mean, hey, I know you lawyer types can do all sorts of gymnastics in the courtroom, but this might be one cartwheel too many."

"What are you saying, Sonny?" I leaned forward and put my arm on his desk. Sonny leaned in toward me, just inches from my face. I could feel my face growing hotter by the second, though I knew this wasn't the time or place to be getting riled up. It's just that I hadn't been this close to him in ages. I could smell his trademark peppermint gum, and his Stetson cologne hanging in the air.

"What I'm saying, Blake," he continued, "is that Vivi Ann deserves a lawyer with a completely clear head. We've got a press conference in less than two hours and someone has to speak to the press. Frankly, we both know Vivi is a loose cannon, and I don't think Harry's up to it."

That was Sonny. Just telling it like it is.

"Blake." Sonny leaned even closer as if telling me a secret. "I care about you. Your heart is showing on this one. Stop a minute and think about what I'm sayin'. You need to make sure you get off on the right foot. No missteppin', you know? With Lewis being the star that he is, it's a real muddy case already. I know you know that. Someone will need to be the family spokesperson for Lewis. Please don't take offense. I'm just callin' it like I see it."

Sonny had that protective, nurturing quality about him. That's the part I'd always loved. Well, that and just the pure physical chemistry that had always been part of our story. I felt this passion whenever I was around him…always simmering just under the surface. For both of us.

"Just who do you think should handle the press?" I asked.

"Well, honey, there's only one Deep South debate champion and University of Alabama speech and debate scholarship winner in this group. Seems to me she'd be the perfect spin doctor for a prickly case such as this. Sweetie," he continued, "I'm looking at her."

Something exciting bubbled up within me at his words. He'd remembered my awards—something I was sure Harry had long forgotten. That easily won Sonny a trillion points. He had me in the palm of his hand. I looked into his eyes like I used to do when I wanted something. I knew how to handle him, too.

"How do we take care of this? I'm not sure Harry's going to like this news. I mean, we both know he isn't one to miss an opportunity to speak to the public. And a case this big? That's some serious exposure. Even if it's about Lewis, I've got a feeling Harry's gonna be focused on what this could mean for his career," I explained.

"I know, honey, it puts you in a strange situation with Harry."

Does he want me in a strange situation with Harry? I wondered.

"Even so, we must have a lead counsel, and I don't think it should be him. I say you talk to him now and volunteer for the job. Tell him you're worried he may reach a point where he becomes less objective."

"Sonny!" I said. "Harry would never compromise his legal duties." *Not even for family.*

"Okay," he said, backing off a bit. "Just think about what I've said." With that he reached over and slowly but deliberately laid his huge, protective hand on top of mine and squeezed.

"I care about you, Blake. You know that never really went away." He slid his hand back. "Take care, now. I'll see y'all in a couple hours at the press conference. It's at Denny Chimes. Remember, this isn't going to be your average press conference. Lewis's fame will draw quite the crowd. We've been getting calls at the station from the media all day. With Lewis missing, every reporter from all of college football is gonna be swarming Tuscaloosa like flies on manure. They want to know what happened to their star announcer and who will be taking Lewis's spot in the broadcast booth this season if he isn't coming back. We're gonna leave that one to the Bama spokesperson. I'll be speaking, too, but we're gonna try and keep this short and sweet. I need you to prepare a statement from Vivi, but don't let her anywhere near that microphone. We don't need a repeat of her storytelling from the Tutwiler. This is not the time or place for her to deal with this kind of pressure—and with all the attention and live cameras, I'm afraid her nerves will make her say something that could hurt her case."

I must have looked apprehensive because Sonny paused and said, "You can do this, Blake. All of it. Now put that debate champion hat on and get out there for those two people you love. I'll be right there next to you."

My heart was speeding and my palms were damp and I was ashamed and excited all at the same time. He had this effect on me. I only had to be in the vicinity of him and my heart would try to leap out of my chest. I took a breath and turned toward the door.

Though I had been married for years, Sonny comforted me in a way that was uniquely his own. And he made me feel so protected and secure, yet strong and confident. He never cast his own shadow over me. I had an ally in this whole mess in him. He still understood me and wanted to protect me. I was filled with invincibility. And a little heated excitement.

As I stood, Sonny touched my shoulder and winked.

"How's Laura these days?" I asked, needing to remind myself that we were both off-limits.

"Fine, I guess," he said. "I hear she's fine."

"What?" I asked. "Aren't you still…?"

"Divorced," he interrupted. "About a year now."

"Oh, I am so sorry," I said. *Was I?*

He began to walk me out. His hand was still on my shoulder. "Blake, no poor woman can ever live up to you." There was sarcasm in his voice, but something in his eyes hinted at the truth.

As I made my way to the door, I turned to him. He

looked at me and winked again, leaned down and kissed my cheek. I stepped out onto the sidewalk and noticed slivers of sun beginning to peek out from behind the clouds. I felt guilty for feeling excited. I was still married. But it was very clear to me now what was missing from my relationship with Harry. Attention, passion, heat, emotion. Apparently the list was pretty long. I was shocked at the clarity a simple touch from Sonny could bring. As I made my way to the car, I realized I had a choice. I could act on the heat I felt between us, or I could be my usual good-girl self and try to put the fire out. Somehow I knew my halo didn't quite fit anymore.

8

I left the station and arrived at the car, Vivi already strapped in. She had been crying and she looked shaken, knowing the clothes she had just seen belonged to the love of her life. Things did not look good.

Harry was on his cell. By the tone of his voice I could tell he was talking to Dan Donohough, an old fraternity brother who was now Harry's campaign manager.

"Uh-huh. I know. I know. I won't. Really, it's not an issue. Got it," he said into the phone. I knew he was talking about Vivi and the possible threat this case must be to Harry's image. Image was, after all, the very most important thing. Harry's Senate run was approaching fast and nothing would be allowed to tarnish the shimmery Heart image they had worked so hard to create. Not Vivi, not even a possibly dead brother. Dan was Harry's handler. And it was his job to make sure Harry didn't…well, step in it, so to speak. Unfortunately for Dan, it seemed that Harry was pretty much surrounded by a barnyard of *it,* nearly all the time. Harry always meant well, and though we were having our problems, even I had to admit that he was still one of the good guys deep down. Only lately, the good was buried a little deeper than usual. The run for Senate was changing him.

Dan was great at his job. He was one of those political hounds—supersmart on the inside but on the outside, well, let's just say he'd give James Carville a run for his money. Bald and loud and skinny, he'd tell it like it is, even if you didn't want to hear it. Harry needed him, depended on him. They made a good team and I knew, our relationship aside, that Harry would make a great senator. I felt confident he would always get my vote, whether or not we stayed married forever. But *forever* suddenly sounded like a really long time.

"You okay?" I asked Vivi as I got into the car.

"I'm so confused, Blake," Vivi answered, her voice shaking. "I have so many questions. In my heart, I just cannot believe Lewis is dead. I mean I left him layin' there. I swear I thought he was dead, but then where could he have gone? Did somebody come in and take him? Dump him in the river? I just don't know if I can stand this. The truth is, I always act like he and I just loved screwin', you know? But, Blake, I loved him— *love* him."

"I know, Vivi, I always knew that. And, honey, truth be told I know he loved you, too, even if he was born with an overdose of testosterone. You are the girl he has always loved. I know it."

Vivi lost it right there, sobbing uncontrollably. After a few minutes she stopped, inhaled deeply, wiped her nose and cheeks with the cuff of her white cotton sleeve. A good and proper Southern girl would at least use a tissue. Vivi was always good, but hardly ever proper. The big breath was followed by silence. Vivi looked at me. Eyes bugged out, brows up high, she announced, "Sonny thinks I did this, that I hurt Lewis, and threw him in the river. Why? Why, for God's sake?" It was all hitting her like Dorothy's house hit the Wicked Witch's sister—all at once, laying her out flat with only her shoes sticking out.

"Vivi, get hold of yourself!" I said. "That's what we're here for. We're gonna take care of you, and Sonny is just doing his job. I know him. He knows you didn't do this."

I reached for her shoulder and brushed her tears from her cheek. "Vivi," I said, "you are good. A bit from the fruit and nuts department of the store but still good, and everyone knows it. This whole town knows it and some of them know you inside and out. It will be okay. There's nothing the two of us have ever faced that we didn't conquer. We climb mountains together. We have since the fourth grade."

Vivi broke my serious monologue with a huge burst of laughter. "Oh, my God! Sister Pauline! I'd almost forgot about that." Now her sad tears mixed with laughing tears and she couldn't decide whether to start laughing or keep crying. But it was a release, which she definitely needed, so I just let her do both. It was a tremendous release for both of us.

I pulled right in behind Harry as we arrived at Denny Chimes, the beautiful old bell tower right front and center of the University of Alabama's campus quad. When the bells ring, the harmony gives the campus a sound all its own. The bells chime every fifteen minutes, so

I knew this would need to be a quick conference in between the musical melodies. The car rolled to a quiet stop. I looked over at Vivi. She had pulled herself together. I, however, didn't feel quite so settled. My heart was thumping so hard and quick you could see my chest jumping under my blouse. I couldn't decide which was scarier, the thought of being live on TV talking about my missing brother-in-law, or facing Harry and telling him I'd be the one doing the talking.

"Honey, you can let go of the wheel now, we're here," Vivi said with her eyebrows up.

"Oh, I didn't realize." I glanced down at my white knuckles glued to the wheel and tried to let go, but I needed to hold something, squeeze something, and the wheel was what was in front of me.

Harry got out of his car looking nervous but confident as he made his way over to me. I knew that walk. It was part of his game face. I kept thinking, *I have to tell him.* As he walked toward me I ran through the words in my head.

"Harry," I practiced, *"I think I should be the one speaking to the press."* No, that wasn't forceful enough. He'd run me over like a bulldozer. *"Harry, I'm going to do all the talking."* But then he'd say, "What else is new?" and laugh it off. I just couldn't find the right words. For once I was speechless. That had to be a first.

"Blake," Harry interrupted my private drama. "Didn't you hear me, honey?"

"No, sorry. Just thinking," I said.

"Well, we're here. Let go of the wheel."

"I was just thinking," I continued, "you know, about Vivi and this conference. I, uh…"

"Yes," Harry interrupted again. "Let's talk about this for a minute."

He helped me out of the car. Even in my heels, he was nearly a foot taller. At five-four in my best daytime pumps, Harry always towered over me. I knew he would be a much more commanding presence on camera than I would. I began doubting Sonny's idea. Camera time is so important to a man with his aspirations and obviously it would be very appealing to him. A good lawyer and future politician lived for that kind of thing, so I knew Harry would really want this moment. Plus, the missing guy was his brother! Who better to talk to the press than a direct family member? *Yes, Blake,* I said to myself, *the missing guy is his brother and that's exactly why he can't do it! Because he's not just the victim's brother—he's Vivi's lawyer. That would be sending mixed signals, not taking a clear stand. For a politician, that is not a good career move! You can't be seen as the wavering type, Harry. How would that look to the people? Yes! That's it!* That's what I would tell him.

"Blake." Harry grabbed my shoulders. "What's the matter with you today? Listen, I really need you to get it together. I think you should be the one to talk to the media."

Hang on. What did he just say? You'll have to wait on my response, Harry. I'm busy swallowing my tongue.

"Oh, honey, are you sure?" I said, batting my eyelashes and looking all concerned. I needed an Oscar. I couldn't believe how easily this had played out. I didn't even need to say a word.

"You're a great speaker, Blake. I'm not feeling quite up to it at the moment. I'll be glad to take over if you need it, but I have a feeling you won't need it today."

"Are you sure?" I pressed, thanking God and all His angels.

"Yeah, you take care of it."

I reached back through the open window of the car and gave Vivi's hand a squeeze. I felt in that single second the world was mine. I knew I could make it so that by the time I was through, Vivi and Lewis would look like the Pope and Mother Teresa. Well, maybe that was taking it too far. At least I could try to help them not look like two horny idiots screwing each other to death....

Okay, I thought, *time to get the pumps on the concrete. Put the "I mean business" red lipstick on, get behind the mic and take care of Vivi.* I winked at her and we walked toward the Chimes. Looking over at Harry, I realized that Dan must've had something to do with this. Harry wasn't just being nice to me. And he wasn't stepping down because of his feelings about Lewis, either. No, this was all motivated by his perfect little campaign. There was always his image to consider, above all else. Harry was distancing himself from the media today all because of Vivi. I was sure Dan convinced him to stay away from the microphone. None of this would be good for the campaign. Harry speaking for Vivi as attorney or even friend would not help the business of the fall election—she was a loud-mouthed, frizzy-haired, wild one who may or may not be involved in a crime. He couldn't avoid being seen with her on camera, but Dan would definitely have advised against him speaking for her. I was a little disappointed when I realized Harry backing away from the mic was really for himself and not because he really believed in me.

But it was no surprise that Dan was involved. Dan and Harry go way back. In college, Harry was always running for something—fraternity president, student senate, student body president. His ambition and perfection were major attractions for me. I just loved those power suits and the yummy man inside them. I loved his desire and determination, his goals and his drive. Plus, he was deliciously gorgeous.

When Harry was running for student body president during our senior year, Dan was his campaign manager. The opponent was a sleaze and stupid on top of that but another gorgeous frat boy just the same. As part of his campaign, Billy Cane handed out rocks. Yes, I said rocks. He sent some fool pledge down to the river to gather hundreds of rocks, about the size of your hand, and painted on them, Vote for Billy Cane, solid as a rock. He handed them out all over campus. Not to be outdone, Dan came up with a campaign strategy for Harry, too. They found as many of those Billy Cane rocks as possible, then, working alongside the pledges, sorority sisters and fraternity brothers alike, we had reworded the slogan to read, Vote for Billy Cane, DUMB as a rock. It wasn't very nice, but it sure was effective. Billy was a laughingstock, and Harry was voted president. Even today, Dan was at Harry's side for all his campaign needs—and I had a feeling his "approach" hadn't changed a bit.

Harry and I stood at the back of the press area for a minute and hashed out our strategy. We were always good partners when it came to our work. I could predict his behavior, even better than he could predict mine.

"Blake, listen," Harry began. "I know you can handle this all by yourself today."

"Harry," I interrupted, "stop. I'm fine. I know what to say. The gist of things is that we support Vivi, we know she is innocent of any questionable events. She is a very good friend to Lewis and nothing more. And we are doing everything in our power to find Lewis and get him home safely."

"You do know how to spin it, Blake. Thanks." Harry looked relieved and I caught him looking over his shoulder at Dan and giving him a wink.

"Harry," I continued. "The sports media is here and I know we will need to take questions from them about the upcoming season. What do you think should be the spin there?" I wanted him to be in the moment, here with me, and not on the campaign trail...just for a second.

"Uh, hmm, well, say that we believe Lewis will be there right in the broadcast booth where he belongs," he said.

The quad was covered with media. The satellite trucks were set up along University Boulevard for a mile. The president's mansion across the street even allowed parking in the driveway to help with the traffic flow. Camera equipment and cables and boom mics were everywhere. Reporters were setting up with microphones being attached to the podium, now right in front of the chimes.

The quad at the University of Alabama is a huge field of green grass covered in winding lighted paths and a forest of trees. It's like a park, breezy and serene, though it is covered in students most of the year. The atmosphere felt a little different today with all the press buzzing around. Directly behind Denny Chimes is the famous old Amelia Gayle Gorgas Library, a Greek Revival building with a huge sweeping front porch and eight sturdy columns across the top of the front steps. The reporters were swarming clear across the quad from the chimes to the library steps. Loudspeakers were set up along the base of the chimes so our voices could be heard by the multitude of journalists. The anxiety was palpable as Harry and I approached Sonny and Vivi, who were already on the steps of the chimes.

"You ready?" Sonny asked, knowing I was but looking down at me with that curled-up smile that let me know he knew I was fine and in control. He had no anxiety at all on his face and that relaxed me. Just what I needed as we began. I looked at Vivi and smiled a confident smile and nodded my head to her as Sonny stepped up to the crowd of reporters.

The press pushed their mics forward. Sonny began. The cameras rolled. Harry and I stood stoic, aware that we must at all times project confidence in our client. But when your client is the redheaded town wild woman, well, Harry and I were going to need Academy Awards for this performance. Vivi stood between us wearing those giant Jackie O. sunglasses and a fashionable spring duster in lime and turquoise billowing in the gardenia-scented air.

This was a big story that would become huge before it ever ended, and Lewis was the reason. His bad-boy lifestyle was followed with intrigue and excitement by fans far and wide. He was Tuscaloosa's own slice of celebrity and definitely a publicity hound—a handshakin', back-slappin', good ol' boy, but of the upper class. His voice had become synonymous with Alabama football. His face often appeared on the society pages as well as the sports page, usually with an expensive stogie in one hand and a two-olive martini in the other and he was almost always standing next to a cleavage-baring socialite.

He had big, blue-gray eyes with eyelashes so long and dark it should be illegal for them to belong to a man. He had an incandescent thousand-watt smile, framed by big, deep-set dimples and a head of shiny, thick, jet-black hair. Women loved him. Men wanted to be him. But he had a softer side he showed only to Vivi. Turns out that despite all the bravado, he was really a hopeless romantic who sent her flowers and wrote the most beautiful, spicy letters. They had a free and open relationship, but lately Lewis had been seeing Vivi almost exclusively. Vivi hadn't seen anyone but Lewis in at least a year.

What I needed now was for the media to forget his playboy reputation and instead garner as much sympathy as possible—that's what it was gonna take to have everyone on our side and free Vivi of any suspicions. God bless me and all my debate trophies.

As Sonny spoke, my gaze darted around the sea of reporters, scanning the outstretched arms clenching microphones. And then my eyes locked on one person in particular. A blonde (bottle of course—no, more like a keg) standing to my left. In her thigh-baring miniskirt, with over-glossed lips and skin like milk-and-honey cream pie, she was beautiful in that flashy sort of way and I knew she was about to eat this story up, especially since I was involved.

Dallas Dubois had been in and out of my life since I was sixteen. She was only fourteen when my mother married her father and we were twenty-six and twenty-four when they finally divorced. We had been many things to each other over the years: friends (for one day), loathing enemies, backstabbing competitors and step-sisters. She wanted to go to law school, too, but didn't get in. It wasn't a big surprise—she'd spent all her time partying and messing around with a variety of guys instead of actually studying. But she concocted some completely fake story about how she blew her LSATs on purpose and that Mother and Daddy were pushing her too hard to be just like me. Dallas was the original drama queen.

Since then, she had been married three times and divorced three times, all in a matter of seven years, but after the third one she kept the name. I remember she once said to me that Dallas Dubois sounded like a movie star. I thought it did have a nice ring to it—but it sounded more like a porn star name to me. The movie star thing was always top of her mind, though, mainly to get back at her mother, who had left her when she was only four years old to run off to Hollywood. Eventually, Dallas had become a big-time television reporter and that was sorta like being a movie star…at least to her.

Sonny continued talking to the crowd, but my eyes had become lasers burning a hole through the mass of people to Dallas. With her here, it was impossible to concentrate. She was always out to get me, so this just seemed like a perfect opportunity. My mind began to buzz with all the awful things she could ask, with the way she could take anything I said out of context. If I was a spin doctor, Dallas was a spin queen. My confidence wavered and the nerves kicked up a notch.

"Blake!" Harry whispered loudly and gave me a body shove. "You're on!" My laser eyes retracted. *Oh, my God, what had Sonny said just now?*

"And now I'll turn the mic over to the appointed spokesperson, Blake O'Hara Heart. Y'all can direct your questions to Ms. Heart at this time."

You have got to be freaking kidding me. I panicked. Debate champion? Hell, I was doing all I could to keep from uttering a bunch of mumbo-jumbo at this point. Dallas's eyes caught mine as I approached the podium. It would sure as hell have helped if I had heard a syllable of Sonny's account of the situation.

As the reporters shoved their mics under my nose and the cameras panned over to me, the questions began to fly.

"Ms. Heart, can we have a statement from Ms. McFadden?"

Harry grabbed hold of Vivi's hand so she wouldn't speak. He would have thrown his hand over her mouth but that might have been too obvious with the cameras and all. I glanced over at Sonny. He winked and nodded as if to say, *Go on, baby, you can do this.*

Of course I could. Talking is one of the things I do best. But if I'd had a judge before me right then, I'd have pleaded temporary incompetence and extenuating circumstances. I mean, just consider everything working against me: Vivi is my dearest friend of all time, so I had the added pressure of representing her perfectly. Besides, I'm a perfectionist anyway. Next, the missing person was my brother-in-law. The police chief and lead investigator was my former lover, and I would have to work with him side by side. My partner in representing Vivi was my husband, and our marriage wasn't exactly what you'd call rock-solid anymore. The gossip queen, investigative and often sensationalist reporter was my former stepsister and number one teenaged rival. And to top it all off, her microphone, as well as her breasts, were shoved in my face along with about a hundred other mics, cameras and pushy reporters. I was feeling like a turkey in November.

"Ms. Heart, where did Ms. McFadden last see Mr. Heart?" Dallas asked, knowing damn well the answer.

"My client and Mr. Heart were in a meeting." Well, technically they were. Plus, we had it on record in a statement made by Vivi for Sonny at the Tutwiler. They were in a "conference."

"Isn't it true, Ms. Heart, that in fact, your client and Mr. Heart were last seen at the Fountain Mist?"

Sonny stepped in and saved me. "As I indicated earlier, only one question per person."

"What is the relationship between Ms. McFadden and Mr. Heart?" asked a sports reporter from ESPN.

"Well, they are very close, and she is as eager as we all are to find Mr. Heart," I replied.

"Is she jealous of Mr. Heart's many romantic escapades?" Dallas piped up again. "Maybe she just got tired of all his flirtin' and finally decided to do something—"

"Only one question per person!" Sonny interrupted, cutting Dallas off midaccusation.

I jumped in quickly. "I'd like to read a statement on behalf of Ms. McFadden now."

Cameras flashed and the crowd hushed as I began to read Vivi's words. "I am very upset and confused regarding the disappearance of my good friend of many years, Mr. Lewis Heart. I will do anything in my power to be of assistance to the authorities in their efforts to discover what happened to Mr. Heart. Thank you."

The questions kept coming, like missiles, and I dodged and defended as best I could. A reporter from

Sports Illustrated yelled, "Any word on who might be the replacement in the booth if Mr. Heart doesn't make it back for kickoff?" I was beginning to fidget at the podium. Sonny stepped closer to me and I could feel his body like armor around me.

"We believe Mr. heart will be found and back in the booth for the season. We have no reason to believe otherwise at this time," I managed to say. *Uh, yeah, except a few body parts and his clothes from the river. Yep, no reason to worry.*

"Ms. Heart, with you being Mr. Heart's brother-in-law, doesn't that put you in an awkward situation? I mean who are you speaking for here, Mr. Heart or Ms. McFadden?" Dallas asked, just trying to get me upset. Nothing would make her happier than to see me lose my cool and get that on camera for the six o'clock news. I was ready to fire missiles back myself. I pressed my lips together, took in a deep breath and glared at her. "It is true that I am Mr. Heart's sister-in-law and Ms. McFadden's co-counsel. That puts me in the perfect position to speak on both of their behalves. We believe Ms. McFadden will be important in helping us locate Mr. Heart." I cut her off before she could go any further. "Next question, please." I was feeling my power, but Dallas just couldn't seem to get enough attention.

"I have decided to establish a *Find Lewis Heart* campaign," Dallas announced, partly to me but mostly to the other cameras and reporters. "As a citizen of Tuscaloosa, I feel it is my duty to join in the efforts to bring Lewis home. I'm sure y'all are working really hard with this case, and I want to volunteer my assistance."

I couldn't believe what I was hearing. On one hand, it seemed like a generous and caring offer. But I knew

Dallas, and that meant she had some kind of ulterior motive for taking on this cause.

"I'd like to set up a hotline for anyone who may have any information whatsoever regarding the whereabouts of Lewis Heart, our dear Voice of the Crimson Tide. If you've seen Lewis or spoken to him lately, if you know anything at all about where he could be, please be in touch with me through email, text or phone." All the cameras had swung around to her, exactly like she must have planned. Her glossy lips and whitened teeth sparkled in the light of the camera flashes.

Sonny stepped up to the mic in an attempt to control the damage.

"All information *must* come into the police department. We have an investigative unit set up with a hotline. I encourage anyone with any details to call the hotline at the police headquarters. It will be answered twenty-four hours a day, seven days a week. While I appreciate your help, Ms. Dubois, this matter cannot be taken lightly."

"Officer Bartholomew, we are just trying to help. Of course we will send you all of our info as it comes in," Dallas said while her cameraman was rolling on her. It was so typical that she would make herself the center of attention. It was her specialty.

Harry stood shaking his head. I saw Dan the man talking on his cell. It would be very hard to distance Harry from this new segment for the TV station. And I knew Dan had a whole new heap of *it* to keep Harry from stepping in. I began to wonder if there would be a shovel big enough for Dan to use, 'cause he was sure gonna be shoveling *it* now.

The reporters kept the questions coming, all shouting

over each other with their mics outstretched. I could not make sense of any one question in particular, until one reporter from the Birmingham news hollered over the noisy crush, "Ms. Heart, is it true that clothes washed up on the shore of the Warrior River this morning that belong to Mr. Heart?"

The cameras all swiveled back to face me. I nearly threw up. Everyone was suddenly quiet, waiting on the answer. I hate those damn police scanners. I looked at Sonny immediately. He leaned over and was about to speak. I knew he wanted to protect me, but I wanted to make sure I handled this myself. "It is true that what looked to be clothes did wash up on the banks of the river," I responded calmly, "but no test results are back at this time. The items recovered could belong to anyone."

Sonny stepped forward, pressing against me, and took the mic. "That will be all for now. Thank you to everyone for coming." At least that last question had gotten the attention back on the press conference for Lewis and off the Dallas Dubois show.

Turning off the mic, Sonny leaned in and whispered to me, "Good job."

"Thanks," I said. "Glad it's over. Can you believe that Dallas?"

"Unfortunately, I can. Nothing she does ever surprises me," Sonny said. "But this time, she better step softly. I don't want any interference on this investigation and search. That hotline's gonna be real busy for the next week or so till all the excitement and shock dies down. That's when we'll get our best leads."

"Thanks for everything," I said. "I don't know what I'd, uhm, I mean, we'd, do without you." He smiled at me, realizing what I had said. With Vivi in the eye of the storm, and Harry caught up in his world of politics, I suddenly felt it was Sonny and me, alone in the search for Lewis. I squeezed his arm and turned to Vivi. "You did great. And now, I'm gonna go pop that skank's balloon. She will not make this investigation all about her. I'll see to that."

"Well, good luck, Wonder Woman. It's gonna take more than a caped crusader to stop that egomaniac. She better not mess up this hunt for my Lewis." Vivi looked stronger. Angry. I liked seeing her this way. Vivi wasn't about to take Dallas's limelight-lovin' hot air lying down. She'd fight for her Lewis. And that was the Vivi I loved.

"Don't you worry, I've got on my cape *and* my lasso of truth and I will tie her up one side and down the other with it if I have to," I promised. "I will see you in a few. I've got a media queen to talk to." I smiled at Vivi and she smiled back as she removed her oversize sunglasses and winked at me.

Before I made my way to Dallas, I walked over to Harry. He had left the steps of the chimes and was standing in the wet grass with Dan.

"Hey, there, Blake, you were awesome up there, a regular pro. You're gonna be great this fall on the campaign trail," Dan greeted me as I approached them. His comment made me feel like I had been dropped from a roller coaster. I had forgotten what would be expected of me as the hopeful senator's wife. Mostly standing next to my man, nodding away and smiling and waving. I had to shove that thought aside for the moment and deal with the crisis at hand: Dallas and this campaign of hers.

"Hey, Dan," I said, reaching out for a hug. "This guy keepin' ya busy these days?" I chided as I reached over and patted Harry's chest.

"Yeah, but we got it all under control, Blake." Dan was from New Orleans and had the thickest Southern accent. He was a good guy and great at handling Harry. And Harry needed a lot of handling.

"You know this guy's a winner if I can keep him outta the frying pan, so to speak. No problem at all." Dan was always so sure of himself. And Harry. He had become the brother Harry no longer had in Lewis since the family breakup years ago.

"Okay, well, y'all make your plans. I am going to visit our local attention hog," I said, gesturing to Dallas who, get this—was now holding her own impromptu press conference talking all about the *Find Lewis Heart* campaign.

"Looks like you might be the one needing Dan this afternoon," Harry said with his eyebrows up.

"No," Dan said with a smile. "She just handled the entire sports and investigative media from all over the country, I think she can handle a local reporter. She's just fine." Dan gave me his vote of confidence. I turned and saw that even though Sonny had ended the press conference, the journalists continued to shout questions and shove their mics at all of us wherever we walked. The unpleasant accusations seemed to hurtle through the air at us like softballs at a carnival dunking booth. Eventually, one would hit and throw us all, with Lewis's clothes, into the muddy Warrior River.

Campus security inched back the reporters, who eventually began putting away their equipment and trotting through the wet grass back to their station cars.

Everyone except Dallas. She just kept right on slinging her long golden locks as she spun around to first one then another of the male reporters. I don't think they were exactly listening to her as much as they were just watching her move that *Penthouse* centerfold body of hers. She hung around just beyond the security line, buzzing around like a wasp that had spotted her prey, biding her time for just the right moment to sting. She saw me coming toward her, as I made a beeline toward my wasp.

She acted like she didn't see me, hovering around the last security guard, batting her fake eyelashes and talking over her shoulder. My pumps were spiking into the wet ground as I walked, but I was full of determination to get this awkwardness behind me. I had nearly lost my focus once, and if I didn't go speak to Dallas now, I'd be stuck in this mud-wrestling match with her, and there was no time for that.

"Well, well…if it isn't Miss Law School Queen, in the flesh. Hey, honey." Dallas leaned over and gave me a meaningful air kiss. "My, my, sugar, you sure do look like life is treating you nice."

I swallowed a catty response. Dallas was always so genuine.

"How are you, honey?" I said, returning all of her sincerity. "You look great yourself. I like the blonder hair. I'm sure it really works for you." *Or helps you work,* I thought to myself.

"So," Dallas said, "aren't you in quite the little situation?"

"Whatever do you mean?" I asked.

"Well, sweetie, everyone knows Vivi has always been, shall we say, a convenience for Lewis? And vice versa? I mean, Blake, for God's sake, her life has always been an open book."

"Your point?" I gritted out between clenched teeth.

"Blake, honey, I know I don't have to draw you a picture. I mean if it walks like a duck…"

"What are you saying, Dallas?" I cut in. "That Vivi is somehow at fault for Lewis's disappearance because she had sex with him? Well, sweetie, I guess that makes you guilty, too, now doesn't it?"

Mission accomplished: I had stung her first. I knew Dallas had been a "convenience" for Lewis, too, years ago.

Silence followed. The wasp had retreated. I'd put her in her place.

"Anything else I can help you with, Dallas?" I said with a smirk.

"Yes, honey. I had just one more question. How can you defend Vivi when Lewis is your brother-in-law? Just because he and Harry have been on the outs doesn't mean he's not still family. I mean, you must be colder than I even thought. I used to tell your boyfriends to watch out, if they kissed you real quick, they'd get an ice cream headache." She bent over sexily to pick up a microphone, laughing at her own joke.

"Dallas, we both know Vivi. She's no threat to anyone. I can defend her even though Lewis is my brother-in-law because I know she's completely innocent. And besides, she's always been like the sister I never had." Ooh. Sting number two.

"Yes, well, we never really were very good sisters, were we? But, Blake, honey, you never needed anything but achievement to keep you happy. As long as you had all your trophies in bed with you at night, there was never any room for anyone else. I hope you at least pulled a couple to the side to make room for Harry—or do y'all sleep in separate rooms?"

"Dallas, you are still so transparent," I said, "looking to be famous just like always. Wow, some people never change." Dallas had entered every single beauty pageant from here to North Carolina and never got that coveted crown. Eventually she decided to become a TV reporter and then at least she could sign autographs every now and then. While Vivi and I grew up and went on with our lives, somehow Dallas got stuck in her own little selfish desires. Her drive every day came from one question deep in her soul: *What can I do to be famous?* She was the very definition of narcissist. That's why I knew this little Find Lewis campaign would be huge. And believe me, it wouldn't be all about finding Lewis, it would be all about promoting Dallas.

"Oh, Blake," Dallas said, "you know this will help the police. If I get involved and my fans help out, we may just dig him right up before kickoff. Sure can't hurt, since no one *you* know seems to have a clue where he might be. If I get a good lead, I'll be just as happy as can be to call Sonny. And you know, I'll make sure we get lots of publicity about our search. I have already called the news director and he loves the idea. Says he's gonna make it a whole new special report segment on the news every single night till we find Lewis. Now what could be better than that?"

I could think of a multitude of things, even cleaning toilets after burrito night, but I tried to be polite. She wished she'd had just one trophy. She didn't even have a crown. Dallas was still looking for recognition. That was confirmed when she looked up at me after grabbing her (fake) Prada bag and said, "I don't know, Blake. I think I smell Emmy Award all over this one."

"Oh, Dallas," I said, shaking my head. "I want you to know there is no story here. Nothing has been identified. Vivi believes she was the last one to see him, but we don't know for sure. This is still all very new. So you have no story—and you certainly don't have one that could hurt Vivi. And this little news segment of yours will just fall flat when people see you are just being as shallow as usual."

"Blake, you always think you have the upper hand don't you? Well, maybe not this time." She smiled.

"Are you saying you have some kind of information?" I pressed.

"What if I do?" she responded smugly.

"Well, honey, I can subpoena you, for a start."

"I received a phone call this morning," she began, clearly trying to tease me and get me interested.

"And?" I said.

"I am a reporter, Blake. It's confidential." She had her eyebrows up and was smirking.

"Dallas, do you know something?"

"I may have received an interesting tip already," she finally gave in, "and I cannot tell you anything more."

"Well, like I said, I can subpoena you."

"You can't."

"What? Of course I can. You know *that* much, I'm sure."

"I received a phone call this morning," she repeated. And I knew it would be about all I would get. But I kept pushing."

"And?" I said.

"Don't you always win the argument, Blake?" She was clearly enjoying this banter.

"Dallas," I pushed, "what do you know?"

"I have a source," she finally admitted. "I don't know who it is. I can't even make out what sex the person is. But this person called me and said they thought they spotted Lewis near a bank in Birmingham, after he had already been reported missing. That's where I came up with the brilliant idea of hosting a search. Maybe lots of people have spotted him." Dallas pulled her suit jacket back on and straightened her skirt.

"What else?" I asked. I had to admit she had me interested.

"I couldn't get that out of them. This person said that they thought this might make a good story with spring training going on and Lewis may be about to do something big. Then next thing you know he disappears. And I know he has owed Harry money before. Sounds like he's in another mess to me."

"Look, Dallas, we have this under control," I told her, "but it sounds like you're determined to be involved come hell or high water. Just make sure you get Sonny every single detail that comes in. He's in charge, along with the rest of the police department. Not you and certainly not the rest of the TV stations." I smirked and turned toward Vivi and Sonny back at the chimes. They were still talking with Harry and Dan. I knew that from this moment forward we'd be seeing a lot of Dallas Dubois. Like it or not.

9

Late that night I stood in front of the bathroom mirror, thinking about Dallas. She had the opportunity of a lifetime in her hand—she could drag Alabama's star announcer's name through the mud, and gain prestige and power while she did it. It didn't matter to her who she'd leave in her self-absorbed wake. Vivi, Lewis, me, Harry—we'd all be awash on the wrecked shoreline of Hurricane Dallas. All of us collateral damage. This is why we'd been enemies for as long as I could remember. She was the same way in high school, doing whatever she had to do to win. Especially when she was competing with me.

I remember when Mother announced to me when I was sixteen that she was marrying businessman Sweeney Sugarman and my first thought was, *Oh, dear God, why?* I'd known that family my whole life. LuAnne, Dallas's mother, was a joke till she left and was still one when she got back after Hollywood had eaten her up and spit her back out. After she returned she had nothing to do with Dallas anymore. She soon left Tuscaloosa and wound up in Birmingham and sang in a bar for a while.

After our parents' wedding, Dallas and I were friends for a very brief time. We were around the same age and seemed interested in similar things, so Vivi and I decided we should try to welcome her into the fold. But it wasn't long before Dallas blew into my house and began stealing my clothes, along with my boyfriends. When she got caught doing something stupid by our parents, she'd try to pin the blame on me. And even at school she wouldn't let things be—starting ugly rumors about Vivi and me to anyone who would listen to her.

I continued to watch my clothes drape Dallas's ass and listen to her talk about me to her trashy girlfriends at school, until eventually I just couldn't stand another minute. I said to Vivi, "I think we need to make her understand her place in my house and in my life." Now, remember, we were all of seventeen, but right then and there we concocted a plan. Of course.

Vivi and I were family. We had pledged a sisterhood years before, in junior high. Vivi and I and our friend Rhonda Cartwright established an exclusive club. We called ourselves the Sassy Belles and created a constitution of sorts, stating now and forever we would have each other's backs. "No matter what, even in cases of jail or worse," we vowed. We were Southern Belles with attitude and a splash of fun. Nobody could break the circle. Though Rhonda moved away in tenth grade, Vivi and I have always remained the Sassy Belles. We take care of each other, we stand our ground and we do it with high heels, big hair and lots of lipstick.

Now, Dallas was certainly not a member of this exclusive club, despite our initial efforts to include her.

She was the type of female who would never be a girl-friend. She preferred the company of men and would never be able to put her female friends first. Dallas was competitive with women and a flirt with men. She could never be a Sassy Belle. Regardless, we were forced to inhabit the same space day after day. Eventually, it was bound to come to blows.

Vivi and I set to work on our plan like it was a new religion. The Miss Warrior River beauty pageant was one for the record books, though looking back on it now, it was not one of my finer moments. The day of the pageant, our lake house was a swirl of activity. It was a sunny, fragrant Saturday in May, and hot rollers and taffeta, crinoline and mascara were everywhere. It was a day of spa pedicures and crystal beaded gowns. It was my favorite kind of day—primping all day long—but if everything went according to plan, Dallas would remember this day in quite a different light.

Vivi arrived in an old model Saab convertible, her red frizz set in hot rollers. I ran out to the circle drive to greet her.

She hugged me and asked in a conspiratorial whisper, "Got the goods?"

"You better believe it," I said. We sounded more like mobsters in New Jersey than pageant girls in the South—although some would say they are interchangeable.

We walked inside feeling smug, until I saw Dallas had my rollers in her hair.

"Why in hell didn't you use your own rollers?" I asked her.

"'Cause mine weren't hot yet and yours were ready."

"Yeah, they were ready! For me!"

Any second thoughts I'd been having about our plan evaporated. She was gonna get it. Vivi winked at me as she left the room and went down the hall to Dallas's room. Her white organza and silver-sequined dress was spread out across the bed. Vivi took out the big guns— the itching powder, scissors, needle and thread that were all hidden in her pocket. The powder wouldn't be noticed until the dress was worn, so long as Vivi put the powder inside the dress where it would be right against Dallas's skin.

Vivi spread the powder all under the straps and at the base of the breast cups. Then she cut the straps and sewed them back with only one tiny thread holding them. With a figure as voluptuous as Dallas's, there was only one way this event could possibly play out. Oh, dear, there might be itching and scratching. And all that movement when the straps were hanging by only a thread—who knows what might pop out? Whatever would we do?

Vivi came back to the bathroom and smiled as Dallas was taking up all the space and all the energy. I finally got her out of my rollers and out of my bathroom. She went downstairs to find the double-sided tape to keep her ginormous boobs from falling out of the sides of her dress and to tape her jiggly butt into her swimsuit. I smiled at that one—little did she know she'd never even get to the swimsuit competition.

"You ready for the big show?" Vivi said to Dallas, her voice just dripping with sugar as we were about to leave the house.

"Yes, Vivi, I do believe I am," Dallas answered with a heapin' helpin' of confidence. Vivi winked at me. Hell, Dallas *was* the show. She just didn't know it. We all zipped our gowns into our dress bags and loaded the car with the makeup kits and the shoe bags for our sparkly, strappy heels and left for the Bama Theatre, where the area-wide pageant was being held.

The Bama Theatre is part of the fabric of downtown. It was built in the 1930s through FDR's New Deal and was one of the most stunning buildings I had ever been in. I always stood mesmerized in the actual theatre, under the indigo-blue ceiling dotted with twinkling stars. It was one of the last of the grand movie palaces built in the South, with sweeping staircases up to the balcony and tapestry carpets running throughout. The entire auditorium is actually a copy of the courtyard of Davanzati Place in Florence, Italy, complete with the twinkling stars and the clouds of a night sky. Flower-filled iron balconies hang halfway up the walls and face toward the grand stage.

My mother, Kitty, had actually worked there selling popcorn when she was in high school. She met my daddy there. He never came there to see the movie. He was always there to watch his own movie of Kitty selling popcorn. They got married right out of high school. To this day it is a special place to me.

When we arrived at the parking lot out back, Dallas got out first and pulled her things out, rearranging the back of the car and throwing mine and Vivi's things to the side. My dress bag hit the gravel.

"Well, excuse me for also being in this pageant, but you just threw my dress on the ground," I said, yanking it up as quick as I could.

"Oh, honey," she oozed, "I am so sorry, I had no idea that was your dress bag. It looked like where they keep the spare tire." Typical Dallas. She prissed off, swinging her hips from side to side.

"Ugh!" I looked at Vivi in total exasperation, but she just smiled back, reminding me that Dallas would pay.

We went into the back doors of the theatre and found ourselves a spot to spread out. We hung up our dresses on hooks in the dressing rooms and the theatre began to fill with anxious families and, of course, a few stage mothers putting lipstick on their precious daughters and going over the dos and don'ts of the proper pageant poses.

The nervous girls spread Vaseline on their teeth to help with the constant smiling and to make your teeth look pretty. The rips of double-sided tape sounded like a bunch of angry dogs as the flurry of activity heated the room. The humid air caused Vivi's hair to frizz up even though she had rolled it on hot rollers twice already. I dug through my caboodles and gave her two crystal hair clips to hold some of it down.

Vivi had a gorgeous emerald-green dress that made her eyes sparkle. She looked beautiful. My dress was pale, icy blue and it made my eyes just pop. I loved it. It was antebellum styled with a huge skirt. I wore a large crinoline hoop skirt underneath to make it even bigger, and it rustled when I walked. It was strapless and had a scalloped bust and lace draped in scallops around the bottom swept up with tiny satin blue-and-white bows.

I loved looking like a Southern Belle. I *was* a Southern Belle. For sure. My strand of pearls was right in place. And ready to choke someone, if need be.

Dallas looked like a lounge singer in her dress. I knew she wouldn't be in it for long, though, seeing as how it was full of itching powder and was redesigned to fall off with the first scratch. Vivi and I were thrilled when they gave the numbers out for us to pin on our gowns and Dallas got the number one. Perfect! All of us waited until the last minute to put our dresses on so we wouldn't get any makeup on them.

"Ladies, please get dressed. We will begin in twenty minutes."

We dressed and got in line. Vivi and I were number three and four. We lined up at the wings of the stage, waiting to begin. The nerves and anxiety had us all in their grip, but Vivi and I were more focused on holding in our hysterics. Just about then, the lights were lowered, the spotlight came on and the music began. Then Dallas started to itch—right on cue. She pulled at her breasts, complaining, "Oh, my God, my boobs are so itchy." She kept pulling till the double-sided tape was rubbed completely off, and her boobs began to drip out of the sides of her gown.

"What the heck is happening?" Vivi acted concerned.

"Oh, my goodness, honey, what's wrong?" I said.

The curtain raised and the announcer said, "Number one, Dallas Sugarman." As Dallas walked out, everyone began to mumble in appreciation. But as Dallas kept itching and fidgeting, her walk made her look like a chicken in a barnyard. She moved and danced and tugged at her breasts and her straps till her right strap broke and her breast almost did its own dance for the audience, but she caught it just in time. Nothing could stop her now, though—she was itching, picking and poking at herself as she moved. Vivi and I were dying with laughter backstage. I could hear the audience laughing and talking. Dallas deserved this, I kept telling myself. I laughed till my own mascara was running and Vivi had nearly lost her own strap as she doubled over.

After another minute, Dallas gave up and ran backstage and ripped her dress off. Screaming and unzipping her gown, she hopped around, shouting, "I'm having an attack of something!" Her breasts were red and her thighs were itching and then she caught her reflection in one of the lighted makeup mirrors. She looked straight at me and Vivi as my name was being called. Vivi winked at her.

I went down the runway, never missing a step, smiling my Vaseline smile and returning to the wings to watch and cheer for Vivi. She walked like she would rather be at a disco. But her red hair and bright green eyes looked stunning. I could see her soul. And she was especially beautiful that night, her face flushed with laughter. We were sisters. Sisters of the Sassy Belle Order. Dallas would never be my sister. And she'd most certainly *never* be a Sassy Belle.

The top ten were called and Vivi and I went out to walk the stage again. Then the top five, and only I went back out to answer the social "We love the whole world and world peace" questions, then the winner was announced—Blake O'Hara.

All the while, Dallas sat backstage, a cool towel draped across on her breasts. She had washed all the makeup off her face, and she was sitting in an overstuffed chair in her white swimsuit. She didn't get to model it for the swimsuit competition, because her midsection was too itchy.

I went out to accept my crown and trophy. It was my year to reign as Miss Warrior River. I could see Kitty standing in the front row, her bangle bracelets clanking as she clapped like a super fan and blew me kisses.

I came backstage to see Dallas in this awful state with the towels across her itchy body, and that's when it all suddenly hit me. I instantly felt terrible. I looked at Vivi and she looked at me and I could tell she felt bad, too. What had we done? We were angry, hormonal teenagers who'd been repeatedly taunted and abused by this girl, but looking at her then, it didn't feel like a good enough excuse for stooping so low. The very worst part was seeing how alone she was. At that moment, I realized something that hadn't sunk in till that very second. Dallas had no mother. She'd had no one to teach her any better growing up. No one to shower her with the affection Kitty lavished on me all the time. No one was there to tend to her. I suddenly didn't feel like wearing my tiara anymore.

I've always regretted that prank—though Vivi tried to remind me of the list of hideous things Dallas had done to deserve it. Still, I tried to apologize. I shared my clothes without complaint, even though she took without asking. I covered for her to our parents when she messed up, and I did my best to reach out and include her in things I did with Vivi. But Dallas remained her mean, backstabbing, shallow self, despite my efforts. And today at the press conference, she'd just proven herself once again. She was using Lewis's disappearance to her own advantage rather than genuinely trying to help. At some point, I knew, she'd have to be held responsible for her own actions. And I'd have to forgive myself for the little incident with the itching powder.

It was near midnight as I lay in bed reflecting on the events since we'd first heard about Lewis. A heavy thunderstorm had crept up like a ghost. Quietly, then with a sudden startle, the thunder crashed and the lightning ripped open the night sky. I made my way to the bathroom and filled the old crystal drinking glass with water from the tap and swallowed a sip. *I'm just tired,* I thought. *I can handle this.* It was good to have Sonny around again, too. He brought a comfort to me like no one else. Harry had been like that, in the beginning. But lately it just felt like we were roommates rather than friends or partners. I missed just being held. I missed going on a date and laughing. We still went out, but all talk was centered around our cases and the future of Harry's inevitable political run. I was so sick of work talk. I wanted to feel like a woman again, desirable and feminine. Some flirting would be nice. But Harry was so wrapped up in his own goals that I wasn't sure he even remembered how to flirt.

Sonny, on the other hand, made me feel so feminine it was making my head spin. For the millionth time I reminded myself that I shouldn't be having these thoughts about Sonny. Problems with Harry aside, we were all in the middle of such a mess, just worry and anxious nerves every minute, and getting caught up in these emotions wouldn't help anyone. Still, Sonny was on my mind.

I opened the bathroom door and turned off the light. The rips of lightning stretched across the white sheets illuminating a snoring Harry. I crawled into bed and drifted in and out of sleep, my mind wandering to Dallas and what she'd said about her source. What was she hiding? Or, rather, *who* was she hiding? Between the heavy thunder and heavy snoring, not to mention the inescapable thoughts of Sonny and the case with

Lewis, there was no real rest for me that night. I'd decided, in the morning, Dallas and WTAL-TV would get a visitor. Me.

"Blake, I've already told you what I can."

The TV monitors flickered and fax machines beeped in the newsroom of WTAL channel 30. They already had a banner hanging in the newsroom that read, *Find Lewis Heart.* The thing had taken on a life of its own, just like I knew it would. Dallas sat with her legs crossed in a bright turquoise suit with a very short skirt. She wore high-heeled sandals revealing hot-pink toenails. Her jacket was draped over the back of her chair, her sleeveless, low-cut white blouse just a smidge too tight.

"I have a meeting with my news director at nine-thirty, so I'm running out of time. And I've been running low on patience since you arrived twenty-three minutes ago unannounced."

But I wasn't giving up, especially not to her. "Dallas, you and I both know that you know more than you are saying. So just spill it. I don't have time for your games."

"Oh, my, look at you, Blake. Are you begging me for something? Wow, what a difference a few years can make."

Dallas fingered her large gold chains and shifted her weight in her chair, eventually dropping the necklaces down her cavernous cleavage. I could see I was getting nowhere and her satisfaction at that was no longer worth it. I had to cut her off.

"Okay, fine. If you want, I will have the subpoena drawn up and served. Enjoy your meeting." I grabbed my cream Chanel bag and began to walk away.

"Blake. Wait." Dallas got up from her chair. Her

height in those four-inch heels was overwhelming. Her legs went on forever.

"Reconsidering?" I asked, with my eyebrows up.

"Listen, you know that even if I wanted to, I can't divulge my sources. Honestly, I really don't know who it is. You can subpoena me and I will still have nothing. That's how anonymous tips work."

Part of me believed her, but I couldn't help feeling there might be more. I couldn't let her see my confusion.

"We'll see, Dallas. Call me if you get any new information." I turned and swung my long dark hair at her and clicked my Jimmy Choos out of the newsroom. She wasn't the only one with hot-pink polish today.

10

"Hey, Vivi! Hey, Arthur! How's everybody this morning?" I tried to sound upbeat as I pulled into the gravel drive at Vivi's, talking to them out of my rolled-down window.

"Well, hey there, yourself, Miss Blake," Arthur yelled back. "How you doin'?"

"I'm good, Arthur, and yourself?"

"Not too shabby," he answered.

I walked toward them, the scent of fresh-cut roses surrounding us. Vivi had been working these gardens with Arthur since she was a child. With her mother so sickly and her father running wild, Vivi and Arthur had spent the years making these gardens their own. The flowers, and Arthur, were her friends. Arthur looked good. His aging face full of lines—every one of them probably put there by Vivi. He was about eighteen years older than me and Vivi, but only about twelve years older than Bonita, his new love interest. He was gentle as a summer breeze and smart as could be—and funny.

Always laughing. His hair was short, a salt-and-pepper gray. His smile was beautiful and infectious. When he smiled, you smiled. You just couldn't help it. He had a dimple on only one side. And when he was really laughing, which he did often, it would always deepen. His eyes were his most stunning feature. A light amber-brown, they glowed like dim flickering candlelight. His rough hands were dry from yard work, and he waved at me from a distance as Vivi approached.

"Do we know anything?" Vivi said under her breath when she reached me, out of earshot of Arthur.

"I was just with Dallas at the TV station," I said.

"Oh, my, my. Do tell." Vivi took a carrot stick from the pocket of her apron and crunched into it as if she had a snack ready for the afternoon matinee.

"She knows something."

The crunch stopped midchew. "What?" Vivi nearly choked. "Please, Blake, tell me. Anything."

"Well, I don't think she knows much, and I certainly couldn't get her to come clean to me. She doesn't know where Lewis is or anything like that. But she said she got a strange phone call the morning after his disappearance."

"What kind of phone call?" Vivi put the carrot stick back in her apron pocket. "Let's go inside," she said.

We sat down at the big oak table that took up most of the kitchen. Vivi shifted anxiously in her seat. I felt so bad for her in that moment, with her weary eyes begging me for anything…any shred of anything. Her desperation melted me.

"Oh, sweetie." I reached over and grabbed her hand. "We'll find him. I know we will."

"Yes," Vivi said, her eyes welling up, "but in how many pieces?"

"Listen, Dallas got a call after Lewis went missing. Apparently, someone thinks they saw him at a bank in Birmingham."

"Oh, my God, really?" She smiled and her tears fell down her cheeks. "Oh, Blake, is it for real? I mean could he be alive? Maybe he has amnesia." Vivi was so hopeful. I hated to tell her that at least ten calls of sightings of Lewis had come in since Dallas launched her campaign. It was exactly what I feared would happen. Everybody and their cousin coming out of the woodwork calling the TV station trying to get their fifteen minutes of fame. Vivi wiped tears from her cheeks with her bare hands. Dirt from the garden under her fingernails left streaks of mud across her face. I tried to calm her down. "Don't get excited. Since Dallas went on the air this morning announcing the new *Find Lewis Heart* campaign, the phone has been ringing off the hook. I have already called Sonny and he is checking things out. We don't think any of the tips are credible yet."

Vivi got up and walked over to the sink, turned on the spigot and shoved an old Anchor Hocking glass under the running water. "I don't get it," she said. She turned off the water, took a sip and used the rest to rinse her face, grabbing a dish towel and dabbing her cheeks.

"Look," I said. "First of all, it was Dallas who said this happened. So that means maybe it did, maybe it didn't. You just can't trust that big bag of hot air. I went to get more information about the source, but Dallas was, well, being Dallas. She just loved the fact that I needed something from her."

"So she wouldn't talk?" Vivi asked, exasperated.

"To be honest, I'm not sure she had anything else to say. She just enjoys watching me need something from her. I left telling her I'd subpoena her, but really, I think she's pretty clueless at the moment."

"More than usual?" Vivi added with some sad sarcasm. Vivi had been pacing around the kitchen. She had pulled down some pink glasses from the white cabinets and poured us both a glass of sweet iced tea, the house wine of the South, while she paced. Vivi made her way to the cupboard and took out a fresh jar of Dreamland BBQ sauce and grabbed a loaf of plain white bread. Time for a snack. We sat dipping the bread into the sauce and sipping our tea. Who needs ribs when you've got the sauce? She looked so exhausted, and I knew she needed answers.

"Are you scared for yourself?" I asked. "You know there is no body right now, and I truly believe there won't be. He's out there somewhere. At this moment, Lewis Heart is simply a missing person."

Vivi dropped her head down on the old table and began to sob.

"Blake," she started, but couldn't get the words out. "I...I..."

"What is it, sweetie?" I became worried that Vivi needed to say something.

"I'm not worried about myself. I just...well, I'm just..."

"I know, honey. I've seen it in your eyes. What is it? I know. It's that you love him, right?" I asked.

"What?" she said.

"Lewis...you love him...that's it, right?"

Silence.

"No, Blake." Vivi finally got it together. "No, Blake,

that's not it. I mean, I do. Of course I do. But I thought that was obvious." She paused. Then she looked deeply into my eyes. "I'm pregnant."

I dropped my glass to the floor and it broke to smithereens.

"I know I did not hear that right," I said. To Vivi, I am sure it looked like my brain had just fallen out of my head. I said nothing. I moved nothing. The iced tea was all over the floor.

"Blake." She leaned over and locked her eyes with mine. "Say something. Anything."

"I know I heard something, but I know you did not say what I thought I heard. Did you?"

Arthur appeared at the door, the sound of the glass crashing having alerted him. He rushed over and began to pick up the pieces when Vivi jumped up and told him she'd get it.

"I am so sorry," I said, still shaking. "Let me."

We all began to nervously clean up the tea like it was an oil spill—in a panic and in a hurry. It was awkward. Both of us needing Arthur to return to the rose gardens and leave us to continue the newsflash. She looked up at me with such desperation.

"Blake," she began.

I stopped her. "You don't have to say it again," I said, gesturing to Arthur's presence. I couldn't speak anymore. I looked at her. I had a million questions. I got down on my knees next to Arthur to be eye to eye with her. I couldn't think of anything appropriate to say, so I held her. And there we were, in her kitchen, on the floor, on our knees hugging. It reminded me of my wedding proposal. Why, during all the monumental moments in my life, am I on my knees? No one would ever understand this moment with Vivi. I did. She loved Lewis pure and simple.

She sniffled on my shoulder and whispered to me, "Blake, I really want to do this."

"Like there is even a question here." I smiled at her. I had to lighten it up or both of us would startle poor Arthur. Nobody else needed to know just yet.

"That sure must be some real expensive tea for y'all to be laid out all over it like this." He was so warm and funny and instantly lightened the mood. We both let out a giggle so he would know we heard him and hurry it up out of the kitchen.

"Of course," I said, smiling at Vivi as we all cleaned up the mess. She knew it would be okay. I could see it in her red, teary eyes. We stood up and I rested both my hands on her shoulders. Arthur smiled and headed out the back door with a paper towel full of glass shards and wet with sweet tea without asking any questions. Surely he thought we were just crazy as usual and saw nothing out of the ordinary.

"We're going to spoil her rotten," I said with a wink. "And we will get to the bottom of this whole case, and if your Lewis is out there, I will find him and bring him back to you and this baby." I was full of determination. Full of promise. The stakes had now been raised—the famous Bama Broadcaster was not only missing…he was also gonna be a daddy!

11

My cell phone began ringing. The caller ID indicated Harry was on the line. As I left the kitchen, Vivi grabbed my arm and gave it a yank. I looked back at her. She put her finger to her lips and shook her head.

I nodded. "No one but us," I whispered.

"Hey," I answered, moving into the other room. "Anything going on?"

"I'm with Sonny at Lewis's condo on campus. He said it was time to do a search."

"Find anything?" I asked.

"Not yet, but I think we need to talk to Vivi. She spent the most intimate time with him recently. She'll know things no one else will know."

"So true," I answered. *More than you could ever guess,* I was thinking.

"Anything going on with you?" he asked.

Just a pregnancy. You know, typical stuff like that. I kept up the acting job. "Nothing. I'm with Vivi now and I've got a meeting with the Myrnas today."

"Well, I want to be there when Sonny questions Vivi again. We're wrapping it up here, so how 'bout three o'clock at the station? Will you be done with your meeting by then?"

"Three is fine, but the station makes her too nervous. Let's go to Mother's. She'll relax there," I said. "I'll call Meridee and let her know. She's leaving for her sister's today, so we won't have an audience this time. That will be perfect."

"Okay, sounds good. I'll let Sonny know." He hung up.

I closed my phone, holding it to my face as if holding on to something familiar, then I turned to Vivi to let her know the plan. I left her standing in her kitchen with a hug.

"Okay, listen," I said matter-of-factly. I wanted her to feel strong, to pull it together. "I've got a meeting in half an hour at the office. This Myrna case is reaching fever pitch, so I'm sure I'll be tied up for a while. But, Harry and Sonny need to see us at three at Mother's. I'll be by here to pick you up, okay?"

"Did they find out something?"

"No, just some strategy ideas. Now, get cleaned up and I'll see you in a few." I walked out to my car and waved bye to Arthur and drove to my office, where I knew the Myrnas would be waiting.

For three months I had been tied up in a legal battle over a magnificent old house in the center of town. The Brooks Mansion was not your typical old Southern plantation. Stories from all over the South had been told and retold about this famous old place. It was even featured in a book on Alabama ghosts. Of all the supposed haunted houses in Tuscaloosa, and believe me there's more than you might think, the Brooks Mansion had become the Holy Grail if you were looking for apparitions—it is unquestionably known as Tuscaloosa's most haunted house and is such an important part of Tuscaloosa's history. It was constructed in a unique mix of Greek Revival and Italianate architecture and was built in 1837 by the then-owner, Dr. Robert Brooks. Many stories say Dr. Brooks himself still walks the halls and that his wife, who also died there, starts fires in the bell tower. The hauntings are the reason the house does not sell and is not kept up. But it is certainly a place that attracts the ghostbusters.

The Brooks Mansion was owned by a church, and for the past few years it had been listed as one of Alabama's Places in Peril by the Alabama Historical Society. Being born and raised in Tuscaloosa gives you a sense of pride in the town's history, and I've always felt that it's important to preserve what we can of our past, so I had been fighting alongside the Tuscaloosa Historical Society to save the mansion. I even became a member of the Preservation Society myself.

The Myrnas are one of the wealthiest families in town, but they have little respect for history or preservation. They wanted to buy the land this grand old home sits on and tear it down for a shopping center. For the Myrnas money trumps antiquity any day. I had been trying to get the place listed on the National Registry of Historic places so the Myrnas couldn't touch it.

I was meeting with them that afternoon because they thought we could come to some sort of agreement. I knew they believed that any problem could be solved with the right amount of money, but I was not about to let Tuscaloosa's rich history be bought—not for any price. They were about to see the challenge they had in front of them. Me. A passionate soul that fights tooth and nail for the things she loves. I just wished it were as simple as buying the whole place myself and caring for it. If I could, I would have made it into something special again. Something the town really needed, that everyone could enjoy. Unfortunately I wasn't quite as well-off as the Myrna family. But no matter what, I knew I would never give in to their little proposition.

I parked on the street just outside my office and went in the front entrance instead of my usual spot in back. Wanda Jo was sitting at her desk. I was a few minutes early.

"Hey Wanda Jo," I said as I grabbed my mail off the side credenza. "Everything on schedule?"

"Yep, they've already called to confirm. Those people scare me," she said, "always sho'in' up in such formal suits and every one of 'em have shady smiles. Where I come from, you just know folks like that are up to no good." She unwrapped a Hershey's Kiss from the candy jar near her computer and popped it in her mouth.

"I know it and I agree with you," I said. "But believe me, there's no way on God's green earth that Brooks Mansion will ever be torn down. Not as long as I am breathing." I was already sounding impressive.

"You know I knew your grandfather, Blake, and he would have been so proud of you," she said. "You are so much like both of your grandparents. That's what makes you such a damn good lawyer. You always fight for the underdog, just like your grandmother, Meridee. You have enough passion for the things you believe in to go 'round the moon and back. If I could sell tickets to this showdown here today, I would. And my money's on you, sugar."

"Thanks, Wanda Jo. I feel pretty good, too. I mean, Tuscaloosa supports their own and their history. Even if they try to tear that beautiful old place down, there would be a sit-in a mile wide on the grounds." We smiled at each other. "Okay," I said as I turned. "I'll be in my office. Let me know when everyone gets here and I'll meet them in the conference room." I headed down the hall and closed my door.

I wished Harry had been working on this one with me, but I remember when the case came in, he was just putting his campaign staff together and was too preoccupied to get involved. It's just one of many cases we now handled independent of each other. I missed working with a partner. That's what I thought we were doing when we started our practice together. I sat there thinking about that and the disappointment fluttered into my head for a moment. I shook it off. I knew I had to focus to deal with the important case at hand.

I got out my file on the Myrnas and made some notes. Wanda Jo buzzed me over the intercom and announced that Ms. Crabtree, the Historical Society president, had arrived. I had wanted to meet with her ahead of time to hash out the strategy.

"Send her on back," I said. Ms. Crabtree was about sixty-five years old but looked older than her years. She wore her brownish-gray hair on top of her head in a small bun and carried her purse on her forearm. She was a proper woman. Always in a skirt and jacket. She had retired from the university where she had spent nearly thirty years as a history professor. I respected her and we had a great working relationship.

I heard Wanda Jo walking down the hall and she opened my door to let Ms. Crabtree in.

"Have a seat, Ms. Crabtree," I said as she entered. "So nice to see you again."

"Thanks, Ms. Heart, good to see you, too." She took a seat in the leather chair in front of my desk.

"What can I get y'all to drink?" Wanda Jo said. "I know what you want, Blake, another Diet Coke, but what about you, Ms. Crabtree? Coke, tea, whisky?"

"Wanda Jo!" I said it like I was surprised at her, but I wasn't.

"Oh, I'm just kiddin'. But those Myrnas sure make me need a swig."

"I'll have iced tea, please," Ms. Crabree said. Wanda Jo went to the office kitchen and returned with the drinks and shut the door.

"Well, I believe we are ready," I told Ms. Crabtree. "Do you have any questions?"

"I just want to make sure this is gonna work. So many people are counting on us to save this building and restore it."

"It will be fine. I was assured that as long as the National Registry is working on this, it is not a possibility for the Myrnas to go ahead with their plans to tear it down. Just follow my lead and we can hold them off for a little while longer."

"Oh, I hope so. We need this building for future generations. We need to pass down our history!"

Wanda Jo interrupted us. The Myrnas were early. I smiled at Ms. Crabtree and we joined the group already waiting in the conference room.

"Good afternoon," I said as we all sat down at the large oval table. Wanda Jo had put a pitcher of sweet tea and some glasses at the center of the table. The Myrna men were old rednecks that had come into a fortune buying and selling property—mostly commercial, but they owned a few rental houses, too. Nobody around town trusted them too much. Both the older Mr. Myrna and his son were at the meeting that day.

"Ms. Heart, Ms. Crabtree, we don't want to waste any of your time with chatter so let's just cut to the chase here," old Mr. Myrna began. "We understand that you believe it is of the utmost importance to keep that old haunted shack intact for the future generations of Tuscaloosans, but we feel just the opposite. We feel that building a shopping center and parking deck will help bring back a lot of jobs, and Ms. Heart, we all know how bad the economy has been all over the country. Our plan brings in money and your plan costs money."

"I don't believe you have the right at this time to have any say-so whatsoever on the future of the famous Brooks Mansion," I shot back. "It's not anywhere close to being yours. So, while I am extremely impressed by your concern over Tuscaloosa's future generations, we're not quite ready to hear your thoughts on the matter. Now, let's proceed with today's business." I needed to establish that we were in control and would not be bullied.

"Suit yourself," the younger Myrna said. "But, we'll see about that."

"Here is a copy of our petition to have this home put on the National Registry of Historic Places. And here's a copy of our petition to have it continue to be listed on Alabama's Places in Peril. As long as those petitions are under review, you can't budge with your bulldozers.

There is no deal on the table." I passed out the copies of the petitions and glanced confidently at Ms. Crabtree.

"And we would like to present a little paperwork of our own." Mr. Myrna Jr. opened his briefcase and passed out a copy of the real estate offer on the home and the date the offer was made had been highlighted for all of us to see. It was dated one week *before* our petitions. My stomach dropped like it did when Harry told me Lewis was dead and Vivi might be involved. But I didn't let a beat go by.

"I will need some time to investigate this. When we filed our petitions we were told that no real estate deal was in play." I was in shock but hoping those great acting skills would take over any second now. I played it as cool as I could although my nerves were about shot. "Ms. Crabtree, you also checked on the real estate deals and offers on the place, as well, and did you find anything at all like this?"

"No, I certainly did not." She held it together.

"Well, Mr. Mryna, until the deal goes through, the Brooks Mansion is not yours. So you still cannot proceed with any plans. "And—" I looked at Ms. Crabtree "—I heard things can stay tied up in commercial real estate for what seems like an eternity. Didn't you hear that, too, Ms. Crabtree?"

"Yes, I most certainly did," she said. She was quite the team player.

"I think that will be all for today until I can find out some more details regarding this offer. I'll get back to you and set up the next meeting. Thank you for coming." I stood and shook hands and walked them to the front of the office. Ms. Crabtree hung behind.

"Blake," she said, "thank you. You were wonderful and we do appreciate it."

"Ms. Crabtree, I will get to the bottom of this. Don't worry. We made a good team in there," I told her. "I'll be in touch."

She hugged me and walked out the front door. As soon as it closed, I collapsed into one of the chairs in the lobby. I felt like I had been shot out of a cannon, hurtling through the air and having no idea where I was about to crash.

"You okay?" Wanda Jo asked. "You don't look so good. Want me to run and get your Diet Coke?"

"No," I answered, "but how 'bout a shot of that whisky?"

"Comin' right up." She smiled and jumped up, trotting off to the kitchen, pitching me a Hershey's Kiss through the air as she went. What in the world would I have done without Wanda Jo? I should have been driving a fire truck that day 'cause all I seemed to be doing was putting out fires.

Vivi and I were already waiting in Meridee's kitchen when Harry and Sonny pulled up in their separate cars at exactly 3:05 p.m. I had called Meridee to let her know we were coming for a chat, so even though she was on her way out, she had put the coffee on and set the creamers out on the yellow table. The table sat in the center of the kitchen and it held a jar of spoons and an old sugar container in the center. It was perfect for a little private heart-to-heart.

Meridee was leaving today to go with her younger, party animal, seventy-five-year-old sister from north Alabama on a trip to celebrate Meridee's upcoming birthday, which was in a couple of weeks. My great-aunt had come down to pick her up because Meridee's car was in the shop. Meridee insisted on driving my grandfather's old car and the parts were hard to find when something broke down. The car had been sitting in the shop for a couple of weeks waiting on parts that had to be shipped in, but that wasn't about to slow down Meridee's plans. Now the two of them were headed on a gambling adventure in Mississippi. Even at nearly eighty, Meridee was full of life—and sometimes full of the devil. Her constant sarcasm and dirty mind were the source of many side-splitting evenings of laughter in her house. She was a tiny woman, all of about five feet tall and maybe one hundred and ten pounds…soaking wet. But her laughter was large and full and her heart was even larger.

She had left us a note with the creamers on the kitchen table: *Y'all have fun, I know I will. Love you, Nanny.* I pressed the note to my chest, wishing for the simpler times when this tiny woman was at the center of my universe and our reason for visiting her house was just so we could spend a little time with her. Just then Harry and Sonny stepped in through the back porch.

"Hey," I said as I hugged Harry with one arm. I reached behind him and grabbed Sonny's hand and he squeezed it. Harry let go and moved across to Vivi. Sonny leaned down and kissed my cheek. Harry didn't even notice. Sonny always seemed to feel my emotions. He just knew the stress I felt. He could see it in my eyes. He was tuned in, definitely more than Harry. But the kiss? It did make me feel better and it stirred something in me that I couldn't quite understand.

Vivi sat nervously sipping her over-sugared coffee,

looking like she had something to hide. Okay, she did. A *baby!* But it was not the look we were going for. I looked at her and shook my head.

"Let's all have a seat," Sonny said. The kitchen windows were open and a steady summer rain began. "Vivi, look, we gotta get a few things outta the way. We've been at Lewis's condo all morning. We've turned up a few cigarette butts and some bank statements, an extra set of keys identical to the ones found at the Fountain Mist. Except this set from the condo have a few extra," he said, eyebrows up.

"Do you know what they might be for?" I asked.

"They look like they might fit a safety deposit box," Harry answered. "Do you know about a box, Vivi?"

"No," she said. "My relationship with Lewis was never about such private things as what could be in a safety deposit box. Only…other private things."

Oh, here we go, I thought. It was obvious that she was just going to be playful. It was her cover. She'd be a broken, nervous wreck on the inside, and outside, she'd be sexy and silly. She'd been using this tactic since the ninth grade.

"As you know, Vivi, anything you tell us can be used to help us find Lewis and make sense of all of this." Sonny really had no patience for her this afternoon.

"Well, if I don't know, then I just don't know, Sonny! The only thing I *do* know is that Lewis is out there somewhere—I can feel it. Maybe he's got amnesia. Maybe he's been kidnapped. But we had a connection. I feel him now. I…I…just know. That's all." She subconsciously placed her hand on her tummy. Maybe she did know.

Vivi started to tremble, but she took a gulp of her

coffee and continued. "Sonny, something you said does confuse me, though. You mentioned cigarette butts. Didn't Lewis quit smoking about ten years ago? I know he did."

"Yeah," Harry answered. "It was a bet, right? With one of his radio buddies. It was for a thousand dollars. He bet Vince Landry over the LSU game. Bama lost that one, so Lewis had to quit cold turkey and pay Vince a thousand dollars."

"He did it like he was puttin' down a glass of water," Vivi interrupted. "Lewis was like that."

"Yeah, not much could shake him," I said.

"Or defeat him," Vivi added.

"Well," Sonny said, "the cigarettes weren't his, unless he was into more than we could imagine."

"Like what?" Vivi and I said together.

"Like cross dressing," Sonny said in his sober baritone.

"Oh, what in hell are you talkin' about?" Vivi seemed almost personally insulted.

"The cigarettes were stained with lipstick," Sonny said. "Bonita was with us and she was the one who spotted a few butts stained in pink. She took them to the lab."

Dead silence fell over the room. Vivi put down her cup. The look on her face was one of shock and surprise. I could tell this news was like a jab to her soul.

"We're having the butts tested now. It would help if we all submit to a DNA test," Harry said. "I know that seems odd, but for one thing, Vivi, we'll need it to prove those cigarettes *didn't* belong to you."

"I don't even smoke!" Vivi exclaimed as she brushed a tear from her eye.

"I'm sure there is a good explanation," I said to Vivi.

"If he had a woman in his condo the night before he saw me, she could know something. Oh, God! We've got to find her." Vivi was thinking out loud. And amazingly she was thinking of only Lewis's safety, not the fact that someone with a pair of hot-pink lips had been visiting with her Lewis.

And at that moment I knew she really loved him. She loved him unconditionally and without hesitation.

I left the group sitting at the table and headed down the hall to the bathroom. I felt a range of emotions hit me—concern for Lewis, sadness about Harry and excitement over the prospect of the baby, for starters. I passed the living room and the screened front porch beckoned. I never made it to the bathroom. I sat down on the old glider and took a few minutes to let my swirling thoughts form some sort of sense in my head.

This is where I used to come to talk to my great-grandmother after she died. I know. I said *after* she died. Mother's house seemed filled with ghosts. And crazy people. I leaned a little to the crazy side so it was understood that I talked to all the ghosts. It smelled musty out there with the afternoon rain stirring the dust, and I listened to the rain splatter on the broken sidewalk. The sound of the rain helped me clear my head. My thoughts kept returning to Vivi's news. *A baby.* Under normal circumstances this would be such a happy time, but with Lewis missing, the news had a bittersweet quality to it. I felt the tears begin and quickly shut them off. *Change the topic,* I told myself. But the rain kept falling and so did the tears.

My mind turned back to the information we had all

just learned, and as I thought about the lipstick-stained cigarettes, a jolt of realization hit me.

Dallas smokes! To maintain her ultra-trim figure, of course. She smells like an ashtray, but to cover that, she sprays fragrance all over and it wafts through the air every time she makes a move. And, like Dallas herself, there was nothing subtle about it.

I thought back to the conversation we'd had after the press conference. Dallas had gotten that phone call from an anonymous source once the news had spread about Lewis's disappearance. Dallas said her source talked about Lewis being at a bank. Could Dallas have met with Lewis the night before he disappeared? If so, then why?

I wasn't getting any answers just sitting there, so I reluctantly left the familiar comfort of the screened front porch and returned to the kitchen to find Vivi pacing the green vinyl floor.

"Blake, who could have been there with Lewis? Who?" Vivi said, talking to me as if I had never left, although I had been gone for at least ten minutes.

"I have no idea right now, but we'll figure it out," I said, just sort of blowing it off. I didn't want to let on about suspecting Dallas just yet. I needed a little more to go on before getting Vivi all worked up.

I looked hard at Sonny to try to read his face. He looked at me as if he wanted to believe me, but he and I both knew this case was growing deeper and dirtier by the day. His eyes spoke all I needed to know. After all, this was Lewis Heart we were talking about. The Voice of the Crimson Tide.

"Let's go ahead and get these DNA tests ordered,"

Harry said as he poured himself another coffee. "I want Vivi cleared of any suspicion ASAP." We all did.

Who did that lipstick belong to, hot-pink and imprinted on those cigarettes? One thing was for sure. Lewis had visited with another woman hours before he was on his back, naked, with a cowgirl named Vivi.

12

Late afternoon came and dusk settled over my college town like a curtain falling on a summer theatre production. The early evening brought with it a much-needed deep breath. The songs of late spring strummed along outside with a comforting rhythm, like a symphony. Wanda Jo had called to let me know that the most recent package for the Myrna case had arrived.

"Perfect," I told her. "I'll prove those Myrnas wrong once and for all, then the Preservation Society can get to work saving that priceless old place. Did you sign for the package or do I need to come in?"

"Of course I signed for it. I know what I'm doin' here, now, don't I?" she said. "I'm goin' home early tonight, okay? The championship rounds of *Jeopardy!* are on and my damn tape player is on the fritz. I'll turn the answerin' machine on before I leave."

"Okay, Wanda Jo, thanks for everything," I said. She wasn't asking me if she could go early, she was merely letting me know of her plans. It was actually a comfort to have someone there at all times keeping our little ship afloat.

Before I let her go I said, "I'll swing by the office on my way home and pick up the package. I'll give you a call tomorrow once I know what we need to do to get another meeting scheduled with the Myrnas."

"Sounds fine to me, Blake, but now, if you don't mind, I've got to go. My show is on in fifteen minutes."

The sun set and the rain returned, this time falling in a sideways downpour. I drove over to the office to pick up the package before I headed home. I parked out front along the sidewalk and ran inside the front door to my office. It was dark and closed for the day. Wanda Jo had left the lamp light on at my desk and the Myrna real estate package was in my chair. The large envelope contained the original real estate offers on the old Brooks Mansion and all the paperwork from the Historical Society and the Preservation Society and even the National Registry of Historic Places. I knew there was a hole in this thing somewhere and I intended to find it. There was no way we could have filed anything with the National Registry if there was a real estate bid on the mansion at the time. I knew the Mrynas were trying to pull something and I was going to call their bluff.

I put the large envelope in my red Gucci satchel and headed back to the front office and out to my car. The rain was coming down in torrents now and I was out in it getting soaked. Hurrying around to my car door, my eye caught Sonny standing in the door of the police station. He motioned for me to come over. I reached in the backseat of the Navigator and grabbed my umbrella, but it was no use, I was already drenched. I ran across the street and ducked inside the station, my wet white blouse now clinging to my skin and hiding nothing.

"Hey, Blake, I'm sorry to make you run through the rain. I thought you'd just do a U-turn and drive up to the curb out there." I caught his eyes drop to my chest and a shy smile curled his lips as he spoke. "What are you doing at work this late and in this flood?"

"I had to pick up a package on that real estate case I'm working on—you know, with the old Brooks Mansion?"

"Oh, yeah," he said, going over to a small closet in the hall and grabbing out some hand towels. "I heard about that case. Maybe it was Harry who mentioned it. He's helping you on this one, right?" he asked, rubbing the towels over my shoulders and down my back.

"No, he's so busy with the campaign and, well, I can handle this myself." I was getting lost in his touch and his height over me and his cologne and…

"Oh, I have no doubt about that," he said, smiling. "I'm positive there's nothing you can't handle by yourself." He kept talking and as I took the towels and dabbed my wet face, the rainwater dripping off my hair and running down my neck.

"I called you over to tell you how much I appreciate your dedication on this case with Lewis. You are my strongest ally on this. Your passion is in the right place and I think we make a good team for Vivi. I wanted to make sure I told you that, I just had no idea you were gonna go for a sprint in the monsoon."

"No big deal, it's just water. I'll dry." I was rubbing the towels through my hair. "And thanks. Sonny, I feel the same way about you on this. We do make a good team."

I looked up at him and smiled. His eyes were so tender and his face was soft and sweet, still boyish with all those freckles. Sonny was the chief investigator for the force. He was a suit and tie guy, not in a uniform. But he carried his gun in his holster on his hip. He was so tall with broad shoulders and big hands. He wasn't like Harry, always slick in a Hugo Boss monochromatic suit. No, Sonny was more like a khakis-and-tweed-sportcoat kinda guy. Usually in a dark-hued classy tie and a light-colored button-down shirt. He was a man's man. Rugged and tough, but tender and emotional when the time was right. Was the time right, right now?

I stepped away from him, realizing my shirt was now see-through as it clung to my body, and my pink sheer bra was very visible. I knew I wasn't hiding much as Sonny kept glancing down. We were alone in a nasty thunderstorm and just a dim light on at his desk. He took the towels back and reached down and gently grasped my hand and began dabbing my fingers, then moving up to my neck just under my cheeks, he rubbed my skin softly. He was dabbing and sliding the little white cloth down my neck, then he began to glide the towel to the front, inching toward my chest into the collar of my wet blouse, which was open down to the third button.

Looking down into my eyes, he said, "I guess you better take it from here." I wanted him to keep moving, but I instinctively held his wrist as he let go. His skin was warm and his touch was sweet and tender. I knew I had to step back. My heart felt stuck in my throat. The chemistry we had always had was still there, more than ever now that we were adults. I was scared at what I thought could happen between us, and I was ashamed at myself for what I wanted to happen.

"Let me get you something else to put on," Sonny suddenly said, realizing the room was getting hot in so many ways. I could see him looking at me with intensity. The tension between us was building and I felt my pulse race. I was sure he could see my heart pounding under my wet blouse. I wanted something to happen but I knew it was very wrong. I just couldn't help being excited and I could see Sonny's face flush red as he turned to head up the hall.

"I keep an extra set of clothes back here in my office closet. Never know when I might need to change after looking for bodies and criminals." He walked down the hall to his office and I followed him without even thinking. Sonny was always the caretaker. That's why I always felt so safe with him. Not that I needed caretaking, but I sure liked it. He opened his office closet and took a white button-down dress shirt off the hanger and handed it to me.

"Here's my shirt and you'll find some little white plastic bags under the sink in the bathroom for your wet things."

"Thanks Sonny, you're so sweet. I could have made it home and changed. But this will be much more comfortable," I said.

"Well, it's the least I could do, seeing as how I made you get all wet." He smiled with his cocked eyebrow up. I smiled and shook my head at his little innuendo and took the shirt. He had been that way since I had known him and his comments always made me smile. I felt desirable around him. So feminine. I headed into the bathroom and changed out of my soaked blouse and bra and returned to Sonny's office with the white plastic bag full of wet clothes. Sonny's shirt came down past my hips to the top of my thighs, and smelled like his Stetson cologne. It began to make my head spin as I was now enveloped in "Sonny." My head told me I needed to leave but my body kept telling me to stay.

"I better go, I've got a lot to do tonight. What are you doing here so late anyway?" I asked, trying to ignore my body.

"Oh, I'm here waitin' on DNA results on that pink lipstick from those cigarettes. I think that's gonna tell us a lot. I wanna be here when it comes in."

So dedicated, I thought.

"Do you need me to wait with you? I mean, do I need to be here, too?" My body was still speaking instead of my head. Wait there all night with Sonny, in his big dress shirt and wearing no bra? *Smart, Blake, really smart.* Not a good idea, especially when I had so much work to do, being in the middle of both of these incredibly stressful cases. I squirmed and tried to shut my body up.

"As much as I would love for you to be here, I'm okay and it sounds like you have a full plate for tonight." The heaviness of the moment lightened as I turned to leave. "Besides, Harry called and I told him the results were coming in late tonight. He said he'd be swingin' by in a few." I took a deep breath, realizing Harry did not need to see me in Sonny's shirt. I sped things up.

"Oh, okay. Well, I better get going so y'all can work and I can get going on my file." I swallowed hard, not wanting to leave the security of Sonny but knowing I needed to. I reached up and hugged him around his neck and he held me around my back, pressing me to him tightly.

"Thanks again for the shirt. Y'all call me when you get the results, okay?" I said, releasing him.

"Will do. Don't work too hard," he said with a smile. It was a tender, awkward moment. We both felt something was happening but the timing was off. I smiled and headed back to the front of the station. As I reached for the door, I turned back and looked at Sonny leaning in his office doorway, hands in his pockets and smiling at me. Something stirred in me that I hadn't felt in a long time. It was prickly and uncomfortable and soothing and intoxicating all at the same time. I breathed in a deep breath.

Outside, the rain had stopped and the street was dark as I made my way back across the lot to my car. On the short drive home, Sonny's cologne kept drifting under my nose, wafting around my face. It made me feel good. I caught myself smiling.

At home I changed into my loose cotton shorts and kept Sonny's shirt on. The lights were dim, the ceiling fans turning slowly as I made my way to the bed with my file. Opening the envelope, I spread all the papers and my notes out all over my bed and made myself comfortable. I tried to concentrate but the smell of Sonny was all over me, and I didn't want to lose it. I began sifting through the evidence, the real estate files and my own petitions. None of it was making sense. Everything looked legitimate but their dates weren't coordinating with the petitions and I knew I must be missing something. I was going over everything with a fine-toothed comb, but I knew I would need more information and that would have to wait until I could call for additional files in the morning. I was pretty confident I could string it all together with just a tad more info. Besides, I was fidgeting and restless, wrestling with the essence of a certain favorite cop.

It was later that evening and when I decided I needed to stretch and take a breather. I walked into the bathroom and put my hair up in a ponytail. Home was dark and cold that night. The house was so quiet.

I'm usually pretty independent. I'm the one people turn to in a crisis. But tonight's damp air, along with all the thoughts swirling in my head, not to mention Sonny's cologne drifting over me, had left me a little lonely, and I felt drawn to go back to Meridee's. I was a little emotional and seeking some comfort and Meridee's is my port in a storm. If I was going to spend the evening alone, I wanted to do it somewhere safe, and Meridee's was just the ticket. I knew it would relax me and that's just what I needed. I changed into a pair of sweatpants and a warm sweater, then hopped in my car for the short drive to Mother's.

Her house was dark and a little damp. Someone had left the kitchen window open from earlier today and the feel and smell of the rain had crept inside. With Harry and Sonny working and Vivi safely tucked in for the night, we were all separated for the first time since Lewis had gone missing. I think we all needed a break.

I walked down the hall and switched on the lamp that sat on the old phone table and opened the linen closet. Never very organized, Meridee's towels and sheets were all thrown mish-mash around the closet, crammed in here and there. I knew she kept a box of pictures and old love letters from her beloved Frank on the back of one of the shelves, and I felt like reading them. With my marriage to Harry feeling very tenuous, I thought it would feel good to read those letters and remind myself of the real love that Frank and Meridee had for one another. I knew it would remind me that that kind of love really did exist.

I shoved my hand between the jammed linens until I felt the hard side of the box. I pulled it out and sat on the old tapestry carpet right there in the hallway. I didn't even know what I was looking for. Evidence that passionate love was a real thing? Maybe I was just needing the comfort of Meridee in the middle of all this. I was suddenly swimming in a memory from one of my favorite summers—one that I like to call "the summer of the voices."

That summer was so extraordinary we had to title it. One hot August day, my friends and I were playing in the cool, damp basement at Mother's. It was after my grandpa Frank had died and the Ouiji board was in its heyday. Right in the middle of our game, we heard the ceiling creak and crack, but we thought we were alone. We ran upstairs to explore the house. Finding no one, we returned to the basement and our game when…it spoke.

"Blake."

Something said my name.

"Did you hear that?" my friend Kathleen asked.

"Uh…yeah," I replied nervously.

And then again, *"Blake."*

The voice was breathy and low and a little gravelly. It was Frank. I heard him and I just knew it. He had been dead several months, but I guess he just wasn't ready to go. I understand that now, but back then, at eleven years old, the Ouiji board had come to life.

Me, Kathleen and Vivi jumped up, scared out of our wits, and went screaming and running out of the basement at full speed. We ran out of the house, jumped the hedges and kept going three houses down all the way to the playground.

Later, Vivi and I would laugh about that day, but underneath, we knew what we had heard. I laughed out loud as I sat there in the hall, and I heard my own laughter echo through the empty house. I sat still, listening for ghosts that night.

But the house was silent. Chillingly silent. I kept sifting through the box. Beneath the pictures, I pulled out a pack of tattered envelopes held together by a rubber band. I had read these so many times growing up. Meridee used to show these to me proudly with such a sweetness in her eyes and voice. They were her love letters from Frank. Some of them dated back to the thirties, and they were always signed, *Your Lover, Frank.*

They were so romantic and sexy and gave me such an insight into Meridee as a young woman. She was alive and passionate and so in love. I loved reading these old letters, especially with Meridee. I loved hearing her voice, now shaky with age, repeat the words of her former self and her "Lover" from decades ago. For myself as a young child, it was like hearing about people I'd never met, even though I understood that this was the story of my grandparents. It was a soul-hugging treat. And it made me love her even more, just watching her face flush with passion and her eyes spill over with tears as she read.

After skimming over a few, I put the letters back, shoving them into their place underneath the pictures, when my hand brushed another rubber band. *Another bundle of letters?* I pulled it out and realized I had never seen them before. The handwriting was certainly different. I searched the envelopes for a return address, but none of them had one. I looked at the dates and postmarks. They were much more recent than the thirties. They were all stacked in order…starting about six years ago. That was the year that Lewis and Harry split the Heart family in half. Broken and bloodied forever, it had never healed and probably never would. I kept studying the bundle. All had the same handwriting. All had no return address. The author of these letters had purposely left it off. *But why?* I wondered. I felt that sick feeling in the pit of my stomach.

I sat there unsure of my next move. Did I intrude into my grandmother's privacy? She had never shown me these letters before. Maybe that had been on purpose—maybe she didn't want me to know. My natural curiosity—or nosiness—was wrenching at me, squeezing my breath away. Maybe there was a reason she didn't want me to know. Maybe this information would hurt me or change my life. My heart raced, my mouth felt dry and sticky.

I sifted through the letters and looked at the postmarks again. They were from out of town. Birmingham, Atlanta, even South America. My stomach clenched tighter and a lump formed in my throat. I thumbed the envelopes like a deck of cards. I felt flushed and hot. I fanned myself with the stack. Then, the rubber band broke.

I sat still, staring at the scattered letters on the floor around me. No one would know if I peeked. No one but me….

13

November 30, 2006
Dear Meridee,
Thank you for the other night—the warm bed, the hot black coffee and the offer you made me. The Heart stories of you are true. You are the saint and savior of us. That's what Grandad always said.

I know you said you owed us after Granddad helped Frank years ago, but you really went over the top with your generous offer to help me. That amount should be enough for now. If I need the additional, I will let you know.

Meridee, your faith in me is overwhelming. You are the only one who has faith in me at this point. I won't let you down.

In your debt,
Lewis

I felt as though I had the wind knocked out of me, as though I had fallen ten stories into a pool of dark water.

My mind worked in a fury. *What the hell had I found? Meridee helped Lewis all those years ago? Why would she? Why would he even go to her?* I thought about it for a minute and I knew why. Meridee never turned anyone away. She took in anyone who needed her. That's why her house became the headquarters to everyone and anyone. It was our Mission Control. Meridee could fix anything. Her kitchen always held comfort food and hot coffee…with a shot of good booze if needed. There were lots of empty beds, too, since everyone had grown up and moved away. And Meridee had a way of consoling even the most damaged broken soul. Just her presence meant all would be okay.

But why did he go to her after the big blowup with Harry? She was my grandmother, after all, not Lewis's or Harry's. I knew I shouldn't read another word. I'd promised myself I'd only read one letter. *But this is evidence now,* I reasoned. *This could lead us to Lewis.* I checked my watch. 8:10 p.m. Sonny had mentioned it would be at least 10:00 p.m. before they knew anything. I shuffled through to the next letter.

December 5, 2006
Hey Meridee,
I know you said on the phone last night that you had arranged to have all the money wired through. I really appreciate that. But I met with my attorney this morning in Birmingham. I need to get them a retainer. It looks like my new address might be a 6x12—you know, prison—at least for a little while. It's okay—I won't be in with the murderers and gangsters. I'll probably get sent to a white-collar place in Atlanta for the FCC violations and

fraud with the advertising. Some stuff I don't totally get but the lawyers here are the best. Anyway, I've gotta get them some money pretty soon.

Harry and Blake still haven't spoken to me since all this came down. Maybe you could talk to Blake? Maybe you could get her to talk to Harry?

Meridee, I've asked you for so much. I know you've said this is a long overdue gift, but I swear, one day, I'll be here for you just when you need me. Let me know about the bank transfers. I left you all my info the other night.

You are an angel!

Lewis

December 26, 2006

Saint Meridee,

The transfers all made it and to all the different accounts. That was a brilliant idea to split them up so nobody gets too crazy. It looks like I may need that extra we talked about before it's over. I have to help get Mother resituated.

Harry is trying to do it on his own with his share of the inheritance but Mother has become completely immobile. The crippling arthritis has hit her legs and the whole house has to be redone for her. Harry can't do it without the share that I blew, and the Birmingham lawyers took a huge retainer. So if there's any way, that extra money would really sew it all up.

Either way, you are definitely a saint, just like Granddad always said.

Hey, Merry Christmas! I still plan on making

all this up to you some day. Thanks for still believing me.

Love,

Lewis

January 22, 2007

Dear Meridee,

I'm glad we decided to communicate this way and not get anyone else involved. As you said, it's no damn body's business anyway. You are the most courageous woman I have ever met. All the final transfers arrived safe and secure. Thanks so much for the additional. The expense of this whole case is killer.

My arraignment for the FCC violations is next week. My lawyers are telling me to plead guilty. It will be the quickest, least expensive way. I will get some fines and maybe a little slammer time. They say it won't hurt my career. Hey, who knows? Didn't that dude in Birmingham go to jail for a while? He did okay after that, I think.

Maybe I'll do the Grand Return…after a leave of absence. Anyway, Meridee, you have been my lifeline. Hell, I'm not even drinking anymore. You tend to bring out the best in people just by believing the best is there in them, even when we can't see it ourselves. Harry could benefit from having that kind of attitude. He is just the opposite, especially when it comes to me. You make me believe I'm not all that bad.

I have transferred some of the money to Mother. Now she's getting what she needs and I have repaid the money I lost of hers and paid the lawyers. If I have to go to jail, I will. I'll come out ready to make it all right.

Meridee, I never told anybody else, but you know I've been seeing Vivi on and off for years. I think…I think I love her. This is a strange feeling for me, but in case anything happens, just let her know for me, okay?

I'll keep you posted.

Love,

Lewis

I felt breathless. Like the feeling you get at a white-knuckle, edge-of-your-seat movie or on a massive roller-coaster ride at an amusement park. I felt sad and full of love and filled with so much guilt for both Meridee and Lewis. I felt guilty for the ways I had thought about Lewis. I had taken Harry's view of him as my own, always ready to shake my head in disappointment or disgust when anyone mentioned his name. When I'd heard about him and Vivi getting involved, I'd been full of snobbery and disapproval and always thought Vivi could do better. Truth was, I'd never developed my own opinions—I just followed in Harry's footsteps.

I was ashamed. I spent my days clicking my Jimmy Choos as if I was all that, but I hadn't even bothered to think for myself. *How could I be a successful attorney,* I wondered now, *if I let Harry do all my thinking?*

I stopped reading and sat still, wondering what in the world I had become. I don't think I was ever more ashamed of myself as I was in that moment sitting there in the dark, damp hallway of Meridee's house. How long had it been, I wondered, since I had thought for myself? Since I had made my own decisions? I had spent the past ten years trying to become what Harry needed. What Harry wanted me to be. I wasn't myself anymore.

I felt awful for poor Lewis. He'd never had a chance with me because Harry had decided he was unredeemable. And, worst of all, what kind of friend had I been to Vivi, loathing and detesting the man she loved without ever looking at him through her eyes? But she'd never ever said anything to me, even knowing I had behaved like a royal jerk. A pompous ass, as full of myself as Dallas has accused me of being for so many years.

I started to cry in the silence of the hall. I knew I could be better. I was sad for what I did to Lewis all those years ago. Not speaking to him and not giving him a chance, while there was Meridee, my own dear grandmother, helping him and believing in him. He was asking, nearly begging for her to get through to me. He'd lost his family and had been trying to prove himself to everyone, but no one gave him even the benefit of the doubt.

I was not only sad for Lewis, I was sad that I had blocked myself from *myself,* from my own thoughts and feelings and decisions. I had let my soul go on autopilot and had become lazy. The Crimson Tide wasn't the only thing that had lost its voice lately. It seemed I had voluntarily lost my own voice over the years. No wonder everyone came to Meridee in a crisis. She was the one who was *all that.* She never seemed to judge anyone, and it wasn't because she was a softie, it was because she was Hercules in an apron.

I pulled myself together. Sitting there in my sweats in Meridee's hallway, I vowed to never let anyone do my thinking again. I would never be afraid to go against anyone if I felt my judgment was right. I stopped crying and knew I had to be stronger. Be better. For Lewis and for Vivi. And for myself.

I was totally confused. A traffic jam of emotions swirled inside me, and I still had a lot of questions. At the top of the list was whether any of the information I'd learned from Lewis's letters to Meridee had anything to do with his disappearance. Those letters about the money were from so long ago that I wasn't sure how they could connect to what was happening now. I checked my watch. 8:50 p.m. I had to finish the letters before ten. Harry would be calling.

February 12, 2009
Hey Meridee,
I'm sure you've seen the papers. I've enclosed the one I have with the headline, "The Voice of the Tide goes to Jail." The news is everywhere.

Six months in the slammer and pretty much what was left of the "gifts" from you are all gone. But after the last few years with all the depositions and crap, this time away might seem like a vacation! It has taken my lawyers the past three years to catch a break, but I'll only be in six months, which is a big improvement. I think I can make it—I owe that much at least.

I am glad we are able to stay in touch by phone for a while. It's always good to hear you. For now, we will have to go back to the letters. I'm sure Blake and Harry know I'm in jail, but I never hear from them. I guess we've done all we can do on that front.

The project we spoke of should be in the works now. Nothing like being down and at rock bottom to fire you up to say, *Never again!* I will make you proud of me, Meridee! Do not worry. I will be fine. Out by the end of summer, just in time for kickoff.

Love,

Lewis

April 10, 2009

Hi Meridee,

Thanks for all the kind words and prayers. If only Granddad or Dad was alive today, I know they wouldn't be surprised by your generosity. You are helping me help Mother. They all still don't know where I got the money to help pay for her care, but at least the work goes on at Belle Garden to accommodate her. She's in a wheelchair now, I hear.

Harry still hasn't spoken to me. Can you believe that? Not even a "Go to hell" since that Thanksgiving! What a guy! He always looked down on me. I'm not a lawyer, but it was never in me. Seemed the Hearts had that one covered. Maybe you get me 'cause Frank was a play-by-play announcer for the Tide, too. I know it was only part-time for him, but I have a feeling it might have been his passion. Anyway, he was a special guy. Thanks for telling me about the details of Granddad helping him years ago. I never knew, but now I understand. Granddad saved Frank's reputation as well as their practice. But you sure don't owe *me* for that. You do not need to go to any more stocks. You have been my angel. Three more months to go. Thanks for

believing in this with me. It will all come back
to you. Promise.
Yours,
Lewis

What the hell? It seemed that not only did she bail
him out but she also invested in something else with
him. What had Meridee done with our family fortune?
I knew that all the answers might not be here in these
letters, but I would have to look into this. I would have
to tell Meridee that I read these letters and hopefully she
would fill in the blanks for me. I knew she could refuse
to divulge the secrets she held for Lewis. She would
also know that I'd broken into her private things. But
it was too late now to have regrets about reading those
letters. I couldn't stop thinking about what I had just
learned. With that, I opened the last letter in the stack.

September 28, 2009
Cartagena, South America
Meridee!
I am a free man! I know you heard. It's all over
the media. I did my big comeback interview on
the steps of Denny Chimes. All the publicity has
been great for the radio station. "He's back!" the
papers have been shouting. All the media has been
so positive for me. Did you pull something with
your friends at the papers? What a turnaround. I
am motivated beyond my own craziness.

Now I'm taking a little trip out of the country
to lay the foundation on that deal we talked about.
It's a sure thing. The money is coming from down
here. These investors are great just like you said.

These people are in it for us and I am so glad they share our vision! I know you believe in it, too. I'll tell you all about it when I see you. I will be able to pay back everything soon. I am doing everything right this time.

I'll see you next week after my trip.

Lewis

P.S.

If you see my wild little redhead, tell her I miss her, okay?

The back door slammed. I checked my watch. 9:45 p.m. I wondered if Harry had gotten the DNA results and had decided to come tell me in person.

"Blake!"

That was Sonny's voice. But he was supposed to be with Harry. I quickly gathered all the letters and shoved them into the pile of towels. I wiped my face with the soft sleeves of my sweatshirt, pushed my bangs from my forehead and stood up. My damn foot was asleep from sitting on the floor for so long. I shook and shook it but the pins and needles would not stop. I limped up the hall to the back door.

"Sonny?" I entered the dimly lit kitchen.

"Hey," Sonny said. "I thought I'd find you here." With the emotional roller coaster I had been on all night, the sight of him was like a deep breath, freshly exhaled.

"Are you looking for me?" I asked, rather puzzled and still shaking my foot. "Where's Harry?"

"Well, the results are a little delayed. Harry called to say he'd got caught up in a meeting with Dan. He'll be heading over to the station in a while. I wanted to stop by and check on how you were doing since I had time to kill. I drove by your house, but when I saw your car wasn't there, I knew you'd be here." The tingling in my foot was finally stopping, but I began to tingle elsewhere. Sonny was big. Overpowering. But there was something boyish about him, too—a twinkle in his dark brown eyes that always made me feel good, even after I married Harry. His size alone made me feel protected from the heavy world I sometimes created. Okay, I can be a drama queen, it has been said.

I knew I couldn't tell him about the letters I had just read. They were too serious to share before I knew what they really meant, so I needed to talk to Meridee first.

"Well, you were right. I've been here for a couple of hours." My intense reaction to him was unsettling, and I kept telling myself it was the damp evening causing it, but I knew it wasn't.

"We know that the results should be in before midnight. We've ordered a late dinner. Some Chinese food, it should be there in about half an hour. Whataya say? Hungry?"

Ten years, I reminded myself as my mind started planning all the ways I could keep Sonny here alone with me instead of returning to meet Harry at the station. I twirled my wedding ring round and round. *Hungry,* I thought. *That doesn't begin to describe how I'm feeling.* Maybe that's why I wanted him—I just needed strong arms to hold me. He was safe. Maybe it wasn't about sex, but a place to hide out from this crazy situation and the stress and confusion that came with it.

I put one arm around his back in a halfhearted hug and said, "Yeah, I'm a little hungry. I've just been sitting here kinda thinking and listening to the rain, readin' old love letters."

"Oh, yeah? From who?" Sonny stepped closer and put his arm around my back, my hip now pressed up against his toned thigh.

"Not from you," I said, glancing up at him only for a second.

"Who, then?" he playfully retorted. "Harry?"

"No, not even Harry," I said. "They're private." And I let that dangle in the air for a minute.

And then, unexpectedly, Sonny turned to me and, with a hand on each shoulder, leaned down and kissed my forehead. Oh, dear God, his lips were so warm and soft. I felt my other arm slip around him and I looked up at him like a lost girl. That's truly what I felt like at that moment. We were standing in the darkness of someone else's kitchen, with only the lamp of the distant hall table light to provide any illumination. Our closeness was so powerful, so intense, but also so wrong— which only made it all the more tempting.

Why am I doing this? But that was only a fleeting thought, cut off as suddenly as it appeared when he kissed me again, but this time not on my forehead. His lips on mine were so tender, but he pulled away quickly, astonished at himself. But I moved into him, telling him it was okay. More than okay. He began to speak. I knew he wanted to apologize, but I put my finger to his lips. My eyes let him know it was all right. He leaned toward me again and I met him halfway. He kissed me like he meant it this time. And so did I. It was long and tender, damp and warm, and I tingled all over from my lips to my thighs. A shudder pulsed through me with each tilt of his head. Before I was ready, he pulled away, my head still hanging sideways, my mouth still open and hungry.

"I'm so sorry, Blake," he said, speaking quick and

breathless and shaking his head. "I don't even know what I was thinking," he mumbled under his broken breath.

"It's okay." I held his hand and spoke with tears stuck in my throat. "Sonny, we're both exhausted. It's okay. We haven't slept in days." He held me against him. This is what I loved and wanted. To be held by him. Sonny could make the world go away with his big ol' hugs. He always could. From my memories of us back in the high school halls, his hands around mine, his arms around the small of my back pressing me against him—it felt just the same now. The same, and also completely different from being close to Harry. Especially the Harry of the past few years. I never felt that sense of safety with Harry. Harry's emotions were buried deep. To be honest, I wasn't so sure he had any feelings about me anymore. Sonny's emotions were close to the surface. At least when it came to me. That was obvious that night.

I began to sob. Time seemed to have crawled by from Lewis vanishing, to Vivi's pregnancy, to Harry's relationship with Lewis, to Meridee and all of those letters—and all along, my feelings for Sonny were simmering just under the surface. The release valve had been tapped with one kiss, and I was flooded with emotion. It was an overload.

Sonny pulled me closer. Now aside from all of the other concerns, there was this added complication. This kissing and feeling and *him*. Sonny caressed my hair, still in a ponytail. I felt him loosen the band and slide it off my hair. My long waves fell loosely down my back and around my face. He rubbed his hand down my hair and held it in his grasp. I looked up at him and he kissed my tear-covered cheek, then wiped my wet face with his fingertips. Too soft for a cop, I thought. His fingers felt sweet to my skin and even sweeter to my soul. Sonny gazed down at me and smiled slightly. He slipped one side of my hair behind my ear.

"You'll always be part of me," he said.

"It's been a long day. I'm—"

He stopped me. "No regrets, remember?"

It was our high school motto. We were on-again, off-again so much during that time that we began saying "No regrets" when we were off again.

"Right. Never."

Sonny backed away. "Chinese, thirty minutes?"

"I'll get Vivi and be right behind you. Just let me lock up."

"You okay?" he asked.

"I grew up here, remember? I'm home."

Once Sonny had left, I went back to the closet to put the letters away properly. I needed answers, but did not know how to get them without hurting Meridee. Questions swirled around in my mind: Did Lewis ever pay her back? Did the "project" ever fly? What did any of that have to do with Lewis's disappearance? I just couldn't make the information click.

And it was no wonder—since I could barely even walk straight after that kiss with Sonny. Reading the letters had only made me want Sonny more. They had reminded me of how much Harry had changed me, how much of myself I had lost. And Sonny was a living, breathing reminder of all the parts of me I had forgotten.

I didn't want Chinese food anymore, and I definitely didn't want to see Harry. I was so angry at him for being such a bastard to Lewis all his life and for dragging me into it. I could see Harry now as clearly as I could see myself. And I knew I certainly couldn't lay eyes on Sonny after tonight. I was mad at myself for my weakness with him.

The women in my family were a lot of things, but weak was not one of them. So, as I began to close up the house, I decided I was not acting weak with Sonny. I *wanted* to kiss him. I was mad at Harry and I wanted a kiss and I wasn't going to Harry for it! So I took it from Sonny. I was mad at Harry for not being altogether fair to Lewis and for being a bit of a control freak with me. So I rationalized that all of this was Harry's fault. It was good to get that all settled.

All of this insanity made me think of Kitty. She always said, "Never explain anything. Your friends don't need it and your enemies won't believe it!" She got away with quite a bit of bad behavior using that line. But people came to expect it from her. They'd shake their heads and say, "Oh, that's just Kitty."

Of course, she didn't think her actions were at all questionable. She'd drag home the hunky bartender from the corner dive once in a while. The bartender might be thirty years her junior but nobody said a word. They'd just shake their heads and say, "That's Kitty." That young bartender might be there all night—no, he *would* be there all night. Nobody ever raised an eyebrow. It was Kitty, carefree and crazy. With all this stress piling up, I decided a big dose of Mother Kitty was just what I needed. Like all good Southern girls, when something awful has happened, we burst into tears and call our mothers, and I guess I'm no different from the rest of them.

14

It was just after ten when I heard the back door slam for the second time that night. I had high hopes that this second visitation might result in a little less guilt than the first.

"Mother, I'm in here," I called. I could hear her heels pad across the tapestry carpet in the living room and turn to head into the kitchen where I was waiting.

"Mama's here, baby. What the heck is going on? You sounded awful on the phone. What in the world is this hissy fit all about?"

Let me make something very clear. In the Deep South, sometimes women cry and get very upset. These moments are known around here as hissy fits and sometimes they're called conniption fits. Now, don't get these confused. The hissy is short and loud and abrasive, often ending as quickly as it came on. The conniption fit, on the other hand, is an unfortunate day-long event. It's chronic. There is clearly a difference and we don't *have* them, we *pitch* them. That night I was having what we can consider a major hissy fit. Kitty grabbed me as I stood up and she held me tight against her ample bosom. Her rotund rear end looked bigger than ever in her lime-green suit. I was so glad to see her—which was actually quite a surprise. I needed to take that in for a minute. The sight of Kitty making me happy was not an everyday occurrence.

Kitty and I had always been close, but had not always gotten along. She was…hmm, how do I put it? *Different*.

Kitty had been married a few times, and after she divorced Dallas's father several years ago she went back to telling everyone she was "between husbands." She was still in the real estate business and selling houses and she was great at it, too. She had a very driven spirit and an outgoing personality—maybe just a little too outgoing. Growing up, I hated the endless parade of husbands. I knew my mother had a big heart and a lot of love to go around, and I learned to accept that she had never found the right man to settle down with. But she had a tendency to keep her relationships secret until she was ready for her big announcement. It always began like this.

"Oh, Blakey, guess what?" And I knew, *Here comes another fool*. She would sweep out her left hand from behind her back to reveal the sparkling diamond on her ring finger. I think it was her way of trying to protect me—an attempt to keep the bad apples away from me completely. But even the ones she finally conceded to marry would never replace my daddy. To Kitty's credit, she never tried to push any of those men on me. They were *her* husbands, not *my* fathers, and she never tried to force me to accept them as if they were.

My dad had been a self-made man, a local politician,

even though he had been raised on the poor folk side of the tracks. He represented those people well; he was the head of the local service clubs and had a personal line to the governor's office. He'd accomplished so much—all before he died in a boating accident down on the Gulf Coast when I was six. I always thought Kitty kept marrying because she was busy looking for him. Nobody would ever replace my daddy. No one. I knew that, but Kitty kept right on trying.

Dr. Sandoval was husband number two. I liked him, but Kitty was so loud and her real estate business drove him nuts. That marriage lasted about six years. She would answer her phone seven days a week and never said no to a client. Her career came first. I was as frustrated as he was with her lack of attention, but when he finally had his nurse take his temperature one too many times, Kitty had enough and sent him packing.

Kitty and I were so different. I wanted predictability and she thrived on adventure. She was loud and ruthless and I was emotional and…well, okay, I was loud, too. But at least I try to think before I speak! Not Kitty. She was such an unpredictable mother, but she loved to love me and show me off.

She carried a massive purse at all times and was quite round herself, so she took up a lot of personal space. That purse. My God. It was like Mary Poppins's bag. I will never forget, as long as I live, the one day I was late to school and I was eating buttery toast in the front seat of the car as we drove. I was in seventh grade and it was an early morning and the skies were overcast.

I said, "I'm getting crumbs all over me! I wish I had a plate." And my mother actually pulled a plate right out of her purse and said, "Here you go, baby," and just kept right on driving as if it were an everyday occurrence to have a plate in your purse. I sat there with my toast and my mouth dropped open. But that was just Kitty.

Though Kitty and I will never be the same, and she drove me nuts most of the time with her sheer presence, this was one time I was thrilled to feel the heavy weight of her purse on my back as she squeezed me tight. She was quite obviously reveling in the fact that I needed her, something I'd never admitted. As she held me tightly, I became limp in her arms and began to cry.

"Baby, what is it? What did he do?" I loved her for that. For just knowing what it was before I even said a word. And she immediately blamed Harry—she was always on my side. "I know," she soothed as I continued to cry. "I always thought that stuffed shirt would eventually push you away." Before she could say another word, I pulled away.

"No, Mother, it's not Harry. It's me."

"Well, baby, let's go sit a minute and get this outta you, okay? No time like the present to vent. I'm a big believer in venting." We walked back up the hall to the kitchen table and sat down.

"Spill it, sweetie. Mama's listenin'."

I told her everything. Not that I meant to, but the venting thing was working. It felt so good to get it all out. I told her about Lewis, the body parts, the DNA tests, the hot-pink-stained cigarettes in his condo. I told her about seeing Dallas, and how she got a phone call after Lewis disappeared. I was still tearing as I spilled. My soul kept shouting, "Watch yourself, you're with Kitty!" But, God, if I couldn't trust my own mother then things really were bad. She'd always been there for me before, and I had no doubt she would be here for me now.

Kitty was a fixer, not a commiserator, though. She was another Sassy Belle for sure; a strong Southern woman you can count on in a crisis, smart as a whip and full of attitude. I had to remember that. Maybe deep down I knew that. Once I spilled the dirty details, I wasn't going to get, "Oh, poor Blake. Mama's here for you." Instead, I'd get, "Oh, quit your whining, honey, it's not that bad. Don't be a pain in your own ass. Let's fix this." And she'd get to work fixing whatever it was at the moment. In other words, she was good medicine for both a hissy fit *and* a conniption fit.

I hesitated for about two seconds before I decided to tell her about the letters. And then about Sonny.

"Oh, my word! I knew that cop still loved you. You know, I ran into him about a year or so ago at Ruby Tuesdays? He had his significant other with him, that milk-toast cardboard wifey, if you ask me. He asked about you, and when he spoke of you, those big brown eyes of his just twinkled like the night sky. He's always gonna love you, Blake."

"Mother, I'm married." I chose not to tell her he had since gotten a divorce. That would have opened up a huge can of Kitty worms!

"Well, for goodness' sake, it was only a kiss. Any tongue?"

"Mother!" I winced.

"Well, no tongue, no sex, no harm…and no fun." She burst out laughing at herself. "I really don't see the problem here. What else you got?"

I shook my head and tears fell onto the table. "Please," I said. "I'm guilty."

"Do you love him?"

"I did. I do. I just…I don't know."

"Well, maybe it was just the rain and the darkness and all of this emotion. It's understandable. Let's just pretend it didn't mean anything and enjoy it for what it was. It did feel good, didn't it?"

"Yes," I said. "Too good."

"Maybe you are more like me than you wanna be. One's just not enough." She smiled, only half joking. "Now, about those letters."

I looked at my cell phone. Three missed calls. "I'd better call Harry first. They were expecting me an hour ago for Chinese takeout at the station."

On the first ring, Harry picked up. "Blake! Thank God! Where the hell…"

Before he could finish I told him Kitty had stopped by and I had lost track of time. "No, everything's fine," I said. "Just catching up. Any results yet?"

"Yes," Harry replied. "That's one of the reasons I've been calling. The body parts do not belong to Lewis. The rest is inconclusive."

"Well, that's good news! At least we don't have a murder," I said. "Go home and get some sleep and I'll be home in about an hour."

"I assume you ate something with her, then?"

"No, honey."

"Lost your appetite when Kitty arrived?"

"Yeah," I said, knowing full well I lost it the minute Sonny laid his lips on me and started making out with me in my grandmother's moonlit kitchen. "I'll be home soon."

As I was putting the cell phone in the pocket of my

sweatpants, I looked up to see the lime-green suit rummaging through the linen closet in the hall.

"Mother!" I shouted.

"Blake, where are the letters? I've got to see them." She kept dragging things out and towels and sheets were falling to the floor in a heap.

"Mother! Have you been in the sauce tonight or what?"

"Blake. This is family money we're talking about. Oh, here they are!" she announced. And she began walking back to the kitchen table with the stack of letters from Lewis.

She got through all of them in about twenty minutes, then put them all down on the table. She offered nothing but a "humph" as she chewed on the stem of her bedazzled reading glasses.

"Well, it looks like the old woman gave away the farm. The question is did she get it back?"

She began processing everything out loud about Lewis, Vivi, even Dallas and the phone call. Finally, "There's got to be more. More to this that we don't know. The only way to get the answers we need is to go straight to the source."

"Mother, Lewis is missing, possibly dead," I reminded her. "Are you planning a séance or something? You know I'm not a fan of those Ouija boards."

"Not Lewis, honey. We need to talk to Meridee."

She stood up and put her glasses in her purse. "Now go home, Blakey, and kiss your husband, and see how he makes you feel. If you really feel guilty, you're an ass, and that means you still care about being with Harry. But if you feel the least bit justified or satisfied with

Sonny, you better find out why." Well, that was Kitty—always ready with a game plan.

Kitty scooted her chair back under the kitchen table, pulled and straightened her skirt, leaned over and kissed my forehead. "Mama loves you, Blake. I'll handle Meridee. Don't you worry, she'll never know you found those letters. I'll tell her I was looking for pictures to make a gift for her and I stumbled upon them. Okay?"

"Mother, please be careful, and for once, use some tact. I can get you a definition of that if you need it."

Kitty giggled. "Good thing you've got my little sense of humor. Your mama will be fine, don't you worry your pretty little head. Go home now and rest it on the pillow next to your man and leave the rest for me." She turned back to me just before she stepped out the door. "I know y'all weren't really plannin' my birthday party the other day since all this mess was goin' on. But, there's still a month before the big day, so baby, y'all have plenty of time."

She winked, grabbing her keys and her giant bag, and with a jingle of her bangles, she was off.

15

The morning sun streamed across my face as I turned over in bed. Harry was standing to my left, in front of the large mahogany antique armoire. He was putting his cuff links into his starched, white European cotton oxford, staring into the mirror as usual. God, he did know how to dress. He looked absolutely perfect—straight out of a magazine. He strived for that and expected it from me, too. I knew that as he got closer to that Senate run later this year, he would need even more "perfect" out of me. But I wasn't sure I could play the part of Senate wife. All the nodding and smiling and keeping quiet. I couldn't begin to imagine how un-opinionated I would have to be. I started squirming in my own bed at the thought. I didn't even remember crawling into bed with him the night before. I must have been exhausted after all of my encounters at Meridee's. I stretched and moved in bed, getting his attention.

"Mornin'," he said without taking his eyes off the

mirror. He kept fussing with his cuffs. "What time did you get home last night?"

"I don't remember. You know Kitty. Talk your ear off all night long if you let her."

"Well, I'm glad you had a chance to see her. I know how much you've missed her," he said with more than a hint of sarcasm.

I kept watching him and trying to gauge my feelings toward him. *Am I feeling guilty, or do I want more with Sonny? What am I doing?* I turned completely over and buried my head in my down pillow.

"That bad?" Harry asked.

"Oh, yeah," I assured him sheepishly. "You know Kitty. She just wears you out."

"I know," he said. "You know, last night Sonny smelled just like rose petals and it reminded me of that French milled soap you use all the time. I told him he smelled a little prissy and he just laughed."

Harry was tying his tie and just kept talking. I was dropping off a building with the shock of that statement ringing in my morning-groggy head. I was so ashamed. I turned over and faced the window so he couldn't see my face. "Well, I guess some people can be full of surprises." I was not used to being a bad girl. Did Harry know something? I wondered. I worried.

He turned and went into the bathroom to finish his hair in the larger lighted mirror.

"Are you seeing Vivi today?" He changed the subject, thank God.

"Yes," I said.

"Okay, well, you need to let her know about the DNA results."

"Wanna see her later?" I asked.

"Not necessarily," he answered. "You can bring her up to speed. Call you later. I'll be at the office. Wanda Jo called last night and she needs me to drop by and sign some papers this morning. She has a delivery to make to the courthouse on the Spiller case later today. Then I've got lunch with Sonny. Join us?"

"Uhh…" How would I face Sonny? Sitting there between these two men, it would be written all over my face. "I'll see if my schedule works out. Hopefully, I can catch y'all."

But by then he was already halfway out the bedroom door, answering his phone as he left. I sat up in bed as I heard the door slam, reaching for the phone and pushing speed dial 1. I needed Vivi this second.

"Hey, Blake, any word?" She answered on the first ring. She was clearly anxious for any news.

"Yes, actually. There was no match on the body parts, which means you were right! That was definitely not Lewis! Tests came back inconclusive on everything else—the clothes and the lipstick. But, Vivi, you need to get over here now!" I was talking at the speed of light. "Honey, so much has happened since I last saw you that I cannot even talk about it on the phone."

"Okay, I'm on my way."

We were on our third cup of coffee by the time I told the whole sordid tale of my moments with Sonny, both at Meridee's and the one just hours previous at the police station during the storm. I also spilled the dirt on Meridee's letters, Kitty's jet-fueled arrival and departure, and my unimaginable guilt.

"Good God," Vivi kept saying, shaking her head, sipping from her cup, her eyes wider and rounder with each new revelation. There was silence between us after I finished, and she stared into her coffee mug deep in thought. I waited, not exactly sure what would come next.

"Do you love Harry?"

My mouth opened wide for a quick answer, but no words came. I was shocked, but not at the question. I couldn't believe my lack of an answer and how confused the question had made me feel. I wanted to say, *Of course I do,* but all I managed was a weak nod of my head. Another "Good God," from Vivi, and I knew I was all too transparent.

"What? I mean, yeah…yes. Of course I do!" I said. "I do!" But I was a little too defensive. "Oh, Vivi, I don't know what happened with Sonny. I just… It felt… familiar…safe, you know?"

"Why the hell do you need safe, honey? Somethin' else goin' on?"

"Well, don't we have enough going on here?" I shot back sarcastically.

"But you're the legal diva here. Aren't you used to a lot going on?"

I peeked over the steam rising from my cup and met her eyes.

"It's just that…Sonny made me feel like it all wasn't real. This, all of this—from Lewis, to the baby, to all those letters, even Dallas and her stirring the pot. It was all just too much and I went for something that was safe, predictable…an escape."

"Honey, I'm real experienced in this area. And the choice to kiss Sonny Bartholomew was not what I'd call safe," Vivi reprimanded me. She took another sip and then without looking up from her cup, she spoke four words that stopped my heart.

"Do you want more?"

Once my heart stopped, it rose in my throat and choked me. I decided not to answer. I had no answer. I didn't know the answer. So I sat. I could hear my own breath. A deafening silence fell over my kitchen. Seconds swept slowly by on the French country wall clock. My eyes fixed on it while I felt Vivi's eyes burning a hole through my face.

"Well?" Vivi was both asking and accusing simultaneously. A true talent and one only my best friend could get away with.

"Oh, Blake. I knew you had never really gotten him out of your system. What are you gonna do?"

I felt a tear, but it never spilled. "I love Harry. You know that, right?"

"Are you trying to convince me or you?"

The tear fell. "Sonny and I have a history, Vivi. It's something else. I don't know. It's unfinished."

"Is he still married?"

Silence.

"If he is or if he isn't, it makes no difference," she continued. "He's always loved you. Always wanted to devour you. I've seen the way he looks at you. He's never stopped looking at you like that. He can't even stand near you without getting a serious woody!"

I stopped the tears and laughed. It was ridiculous of Vivi to bring it up, but it was true and it made me smile. He was always ready to take me the second he saw me. It was one of the things I loved about him. He made me feel so desirable. So beautiful and feminine.

That chemistry had been there since we first laid eyes on each other back in the ninth grade.

I decided that Vivi should know the whole story, so I told her about my plans to talk to Harry about a separation on our anniversary.

"Oh, my God, I had no idea you were so unhappy. Why didn't you tell me?" she asked.

"I don't know, I guess I feel more comfortable in the role of the strong shoulder, you know? I'm never good at sharing my own problems."

"It makes me feel good to help you, too, sometimes," she said. "Listen, it's obvious that this kiss with Sonny is not the cause of your problems with Harry—it's a result of them. So don't feel guilty. I think if there's trouble with Harry, Harry surely knows it, too. This is something the two of you are gonna have to face sooner or later, because you can be damn sure Sonny isn't going anywhere."

Vivi stood up and grabbed her brown Coach bag. "Don't think too much about it. Let it go for today. I'm off to the baby doc. Can you imagine?" She kissed me on the cheek. "I just know Lewis would be happy." She paused and smiled to herself. "He loves me, you know?" She took a deep breath. "Find my man, Blake. I know he's not dead. He'd never want to miss all this." She arched her auburn eyebrows and winked, patting her slowly changing belly.

I watched her head to the porch and I heard the back door slam and her car leave my driveway. As the sounds of her car became more and more distant, I felt my namesake creep in.

"I'll just think about this tomorrow." It was the Scarlett O'Hara way. *"Tomorrow is another day,"* and today was about finding Lewis.

16

By noon I was dressed with full makeup and ready for anything. Tight black pencil skirt and crisp white blouse, cherry-red lips and, of course, my pearls. I got to the office for a quick half hour meeting with the Myrnas. This whole mess was intensifying every day. They were pushing for us to get out of their way and let the bulldozers roll. No way was that going to happen. They had called first thing that morning and demanded a face-to-face meeting with me, wanting to know what I had found out about the real estate deal. I told them I had asked for the final bid to be sent to me and that put the whole thing on hold for now. I told them I should have the information very soon and we would call them to set up the next meeting. But they insisted they had to come by the office to hear that message in person. I spent the next thirty minutes with old man Myrna and his son going over the same damn details we'd discussed at our last meeting. I have to admit that Southern men have a knack for wearing you down with plain old perseverance. But it was not going to work this time. They were not going to wear me down. The historical society was counting on me and I would not let them down.

"Those folks drive me nuts, Blake," Wanda Jo said after the Myrnas had finally shut the front door. "I swear, I really don't know how you put up with them. You are so patient."

"Not really, I just needed them to leave," I said as I straightened my skirt. "I don't have the new property bid yet. My lord, we just requested it this morning and they come barging in here. I swear, bulldozing is their middle name."

"Me, I got no patience anymore. Everyone gets on my nerves equally," said Wanda Jo. We both laughed at her genuine honesty.

"Okay, Wanda Jo, I'm outta here for now. I'm meeting Sonny and Harry at the University Club for lunch," I said, grabbing my black patent Chanel bag and keys.

"Well, that oughta be entertaining," she said, full of scarcasm. "You know that boy still has the hots for you, Blake. Everybody knows it."

"Can I bring you anything?" I offered, smiling and hoping that she couldn't see right through me.

"Are you asking me to give up my plans for some KFC and *The Price is Right?* My lunch breaks are serious *me* time, honey. You go on to your fancy club and think of me sittin' here with my chicken. Only the best for the help." She laughed as she talked, walking to the back of the office where the TV was.

I stepped out into the warm sun and got into my car. I kept thinking about where Kitty was on this whole Meridee thing, so I decided to give her a call.

"Hey, darlin'," she answered.

"Hey," I said, "have you talked to Meridee yet?"

"Nope. She's still on that damn gambling boat off Biloxi. We'll have our answers soon, so don't you give it another thought."

"Mother, I want to say thanks."

"For what, baby?"

"Well…just for being there last night."

"You know that mamas just do what mamas gotta do. Love you." I sat there holding the phone under my chin. "Love you, too, Mama," I said in the silence. And I did. I was just beginning to realize how much.

I was feeling a little more courageous after talking to my girls…Vivi and Kitty. Today, they were two of the three strongest women I knew. Meridee, of course, was the third. I'd have to face Sonny and Harry sooner or later, since we were all working on a case together. I had to get my head on straight. It wasn't ninth grade anymore. I called Harry as I was driving.

"Hey, honey, where are my boys?" I froze, stunned. *I cannot believe I just said that!* They were already waiting for me at the University Club, Harry said, so I told him I'd be there soon and then hung up as quickly as possible.

The club was truly one of the most beautiful spots in town. I had my bridesmaids' luncheon there. It was one of those old columned homes with the wide porches all the way around, shaded by 200-year-old giant magnolias. Men and women in black serving attire and white gloves waited the tables and kept the sweet tea flowing. The club's specialty? The very best Southern cooking anywhere: fried chicken, of course, along with mashed potatoes and black-eyed peas, corn bread, turnip greens with a chunk of fat back, fried okra and corn on the cob. It made my mouth water just to think of it. Then there was the dessert tray filled with the most delectable, scrumptious Southern confections. Peach cobbler, lemon meringue pie, chess squares and, my personal favorite, red velvet cake. I drove up to the circular drive, parked and handed the keys to the valet, then ran up the front porch steps. A salt-and-pepper-haired gentleman greeted me with a smile.

"Welcome, miss. Do you have a reservation?"

"I'm meeting Mr. Bartholomew and Mr. Heart for lunch. I'm not sure which name the reservation is under."

"Right this way, miss." He gestured toward the beautifully appointed dining room.

The University Club was originally an old plantation house. A sweeping staircase commanded the front hall along with a cloakroom, a powder room and two parlors. Toward the back, behind the stairs, was a grand dining room full of original fireplaces trimmed with gorgeous moldings.

I heard the sounds of crystal glasses clinking and silver tapping against bone china as I made my way down the spectacular grand hallway.

I followed my host behind the grand staircase to the dining room and spotted Harry and Sonny at a table by a window. Both stood as I approached. Harry touched me first. Arm extended, he reached around my waist, pulling me into him for a quick squeeze and a kiss on my cheek. I was staring straight at Sonny. My face felt hot. Sonny stretched his hand out, so I leaned over and he pecked my other cheek. *Uh-oh,* I thought. *Some-*

body's gonna see that look on my face. Oh, dear God. Come down from holy heaven and punish me now. I am a bad girl. I am having bad thoughts.

I needed to pull it together. "Hey, you two. What have I missed?"

"Unfortunately, not much." Harry replaced his napkin in his lap as he sat back down. He spoke in his usual professional tone, not making eye contact with anyone.

"Yeah," Sonny agreed. "Without more information, we're gonna be back to square one here before long."

"What do you mean?" I asked, adjusting myself in my chair. "Yes, iced tea would be great, please," I said to the waitress who'd appeared by the table. "Un-sweet, extra lemon."

"The test results on those body parts showed they belong to a man by the name of Walter Aaron. Bonita is on the case. There was a barge accident about a week ago up the Warrior, north of here, and he fell off. I think he suffered a little slicin' and dicin' under the boat because of the propellers, which is why he turned up in the state he did. They'd been lookin' for his body ever since the accident. Bonita is investigating it because allegations are that he was *helped* off. What we know for sure is that it isn't Lewis." The conversation and the iced tea flowed, as though nothing—but everything—was somehow different.

Sonny looked at me, then glanced at Harry as he finished his last bite of corn bread. "Hell, Blake. We gotta keep digging."

"I'm working on a few leads," I announced. "I'll let you know when I figure anything out."

"What? You got something new?" Harry said,

looking at me as if he should know this. As though he couldn't believe I'd made progress without him.

I ignored him. "Can't we run the DNA on the cigarette butts with another lab? Maybe in Birmingham? There's got to be the chance that we just missed something," I suggested.

"I thought of that, too," Harry said, quick to insert himself into the plans. "Might as well. We have nothing else at the moment."

"How's that Find Lewis campaign going?" I asked Sonny. "I hope Dallas is sending everything she hears to you. Are there any leads coming with any credibility?" I asked.

"We did get a bunch of crazy calls sighting Lewis from here to Texas, but one call this morning caught my attention," he answered. "I asked Bonita to follow up and get back to me. She's working on it right now."

"Really?" asked Harry as he straightened his cuffs to hit the cuff links. "What is it? Where was it?" He never looked at us. His eyes were darting around the room to see if anyone noticed *him.*

"That first call that came in the morning after the disappearance, the one that said they saw him at the Birmingham bank…that same bit of info has come in over and over. Seems like several people saw him at that same bank. I thought we should check it out," Sonny explained.

I had an idea. "Dallas said the call came in after Lewis went missing. What time was that call made exactly?" I asked. "It takes an hour or so to get to Birmingham. We could begin to figure out if these calls are credible simply by knowing the time they claim to have seen him. It needed to be at least an hour after the Lewis and Vivi 'meeting,'" I said to Sonny.

"Exactly what Bonita is working on right this minute."

Harry saw a judge he knew across the restaurant who was fixin' to give him a big endorsement. He excused himself and headed over to her table, making his way around the dining room the long way so as to shake as many hands as possible. He was smiling and back-slapping; you'd never know we just came up with the first plausible lead in his brother's disappearance. When Harry was out of earshot, Sonny spoke.

"You okay?" he said.

"Yes, actually," I said, "doing great. You?"

"I had a hard time sleepin' last night, but uh, other than that…" He smiled at me. "Blake, seriously, I was thinking… You know, things look pretty good for Harry and this run for office. Have you thought about what it will really be like if he wins?"

That was a stunning question. I felt a wave of shock and breathlessness bolt through me. Yes, I had been thinking about it, but when Sonny said it, out in the open, and it was hanging in the air between us, it choked me.

"Well, yes," I said, my voice trembling as I spoke. "I have…" I stopped midsentence and swallowed hard. "I guess I haven't really thought about it in such a way as I…" I trailed off again. I couldn't get the words out. I knew what he was asking. Did I realize that if Harry wins, I would be moving to Washington, D.C.? I would be leaving Tuscaloosa, my family, my practice. I couldn't even imagine. Then, I suddenly realized, I would also be leaving Vivi…and Sonny. I felt tears coming and swallowed hard. I cleared my throat and took a sip of tea.

"I didn't mean to upset you, Blake. I'm sorry. I was just thinkin', ya know? I mean after last night and…" Sonny was so sincere. He was leaning across the table wanting to grab my hands. He touched my wrist lightly, then retreated. We were trying to be discreet. This was one time I was glad Harry was soaking up all the energy in the room.

"No, Sonny. You're right. It's all coming up soon and it *is* something I need to think about. I know it's out there but I never really imagined it like it was real." I smiled a fake smile and looked away at Harry laughing and talking. At that second, I couldn't imagine moving to D.C. with Harry. I knew my life was in Tuscaloosa and I had some major decisions to make. *Good thing I have nothing else going on in my life right now, so I can give this my full attention,* I thought.

"Maybe he won't win." That broke the tension. We both laughed. Harry returned from his little impromptu campaign stump and sat back down.

"Judge Shamblin will be publicly endorsing me at our next fundraiser. That is a big one. Her backing is superimportant to the strategy." Judge Jane Shamblin was one of the Shamblin judges, a long line of judges for several generations. They were filthy rich and had a ton of political power. She and Harry had a mutually respectful relationship. Both of them sat on the zoning board for the city and I knew he needed her backing. A person with that much power and influence could mean the election. Harry took a sip of tea, proud of himself for all the lunchtime stumping. His cell phone rang and he put one finger in the air as if to stop us from speaking and slid right back out of his chair. It was Dan the man. "Yes, I got it, just now, uh-huh, she says by the next fundraiser…" He was talking as he stepped out on the side door to the sunroom. I looked at Sonny. He smiled a dry smile. He knew I didn't want to leave Tuscaloosa, but he was gentleman enough to let me make my own decisions.

"Blake, if you do wind up moving, just know there's a cop here that's really missin' ya."

Sonny melted me. His curled-up smile and glistening brown eyes had me. I smiled as the waitress appeared again and filled my glass.

Lunch ended with cobblers for the boys and red velvet cake for me. Then the three of us left the University Club, the valet going for our cars and me standing there stuck between Harry and Sonny. My past on one side, my present on the other and my future…well, maybe that was me, alone in the middle.

17

Somehow during lunch I had managed to hide a mountain of secrets. Sonny and me. All those Lewis letters. And the news about Vivi's baby. The letters would start an absolute wildfire with Harry, and poor Meridee would be at the center of it. She had no idea. I could just see her on that boat, throwing dice and laughing hard with a salty margarita in her hand. She always threw her head back when she laughed. She loved the gambling boats on the Mississippi Gulf Coast. She never bet much. Didn't win much. Didn't lose much. At least that I know of. Since reading those letters, I wasn't really sure what I knew about her. That tiny woman had kept her secrets. And who knew if there was more to it than just those letters?

I saw I had a missed call from the office so I called Wanda Jo.

"Hey, Wanda Jo, what's up?" I asked as she answered.

"That package from the state real estate office came

in. You know, that one you ordered on the Brooks Mansion?"

"Great," I said. "I'll be right there." I hung up and headed to the office. I knew that new file would have a lot of answers for me. It had all of the information about the dates of the real estate offer filed by the Myrnas and their partners. That old place held special memories for me. It's where Sonny first kissed me when we were only fifteen years old. Our ninth-grade prom had been held there. It was a Tuscaloosa mainstay, and one I intended to save. I hurried over to the office from the University Club. I knew Wanda Jo had to drop some papers off at the courthouse for Harry, so she would be gone or on her way out by the time I arrived.

I settled into my desk chair, opened the large envelope and pored through the materials. I studied the dates of the offers but even more importantly the dates of the acceptances, as offers on the Brooks Mansion had come in by the handfuls over the years. All of them were lowballs because of the ghost stories and all the ghost hunter groups that showed up on a regular basis. But it was such a stately place, sitting in the geographical center of town. Most of the surrounding grounds of the old plantation house itself had been sold. Over the years, the town grew up around it. So the mansion sat alone, surrounded by a frenzy of modern-day activity and newer structures, sort of like a spirit hovering over Tuscaloosa. It had a definite feel and personality, standing tall for over one hundred and seventy years. I couldn't imagine a Tuscaloosa without its centerpiece, and I knew I had the power to save it.

Just then, I saw it. The dates of the acceptance of the offer from the Myrnas and their partners. It was one day *after* our halt petition was filed in order to present our petition from Alabama Places in Peril. That was it; the petition that stopped all activity until a review is performed. I knew it! I had to prepare a brief on it now, and let Wanda Jo know to set up the next meeting. Besides, the old place wasn't zoned for commercial property anyway, so that would be another hurdle they would have to jump before an actual shopping center could be built. They could still mow the mansion down if they got their hands on it. But I was determined they would never own it.

Just as I was getting ready to leave, Harry walked in through the back door.

"Hey, what are you doing here?" he asked, like he was surprised to see me.

"I work here," I replied straight-faced.

"Ha-ha, very funny, Blake." He was rushing around looking for something.

"I'm actually here working on that Myrna file. Over my dead body will that old Brooks Mansion be torn down," I said as I stood and gathered up my things.

"I never understood your love affair with that old place," he said.

"I've told you a hundred times. I had my first prom there, my first kiss there. It's just a part of me. Plus it's a major part of Tuscaloosa and so many people feel just the same way. I'll stop those Myrnas, believe me."

"I thought your first kiss was with Sonny in junior high or something?" He found whatever he was looking for and actually stopped and looked at me while he put a file in his briefcase.

"It was," I said. "And it was there, in the Brooks Mansion during our ninth grade prom."

"Well, good luck," he said, but I could tell he still didn't get it. "I'll be late tonight. Got a campaign thing." And he turned to the door without waiting on me to answer. The back door shut and I was standing alone in my office. Why did I feel like a storm just blew through?

I left a note for Wanda Jo on my findings and instructions to set up the next battle—ahem, meeting. I locked up and left to head over to Vivi's.

I drove along the river and before I knew it I was on the long gravel driveway to the McFadden plantation. I rolled my window down to smell the jasmine and the honeysuckle. I heard the gravel crunch under my tires as I pulled around to the front porch near the fountain.

"Hey, Arthur," I called over to him as I parked and climbed out of my car.

He looked up from the tomatoes planted on the side yard, wiped his hands on his apron and started over to me.

"What brings you by, Miss Blake?"

"A girl's gotta have a reason to come see her favorite people?" I chided.

"'Course not." He was grinning as he reached out to hug me. "So good to see ya." And I knew he meant it.

"You look nice today, Arthur."

"Well, Miss Bonita'll be around directly. She's gonna be helping me sample some new recipes at my BBQ place. That woman has good taste."

"Uh-huh, and she sure loves your cooking, too," I said with a wink.

"Miss Vivi's inside making iced tea. Why don't you go on in and have some," he said, trying to hide his bashfulness.

"Arthur, if I drink any more tea today, I'll be floatin' down the river myself," I laughed. "But I'll go on in and have a visit."

"Okay. Tell her I'm almost through here, then I'm headin' out to my restaurant to wait on Bonita."

The Moonwinx was out back and to the right side of the plantation itself, with its own little gravel drive to the front of the stand. It was the type of place where you walked up to the screened counter and ordered. It wasn't really meant to be a restaurant, just a few picnic tables and the smokehouse kitchen—small, mostly for pickup and takeout. Arthur kept himself busy getting ready for the fall grand opening. Of course he wanted to be ready for football season and all the tailgatin' parties. And now with Bonita by his side, he'd have a partner.

"Okay," I said over my shoulder as I headed up the stairs. The screened front door slammed behind me and I immediately smelled homemade buttermilk biscuits and heard the teapot singing. I had been coming in this house for as long as I could remember. The beautiful round solid mahogany table sat in the front foyer with an oversize milky-white vase of fresh blue hydrangeas. They grew in massive bushes on either side of the wide front porch. A curved staircase invited you upstairs to the left and parlors bathed in sunlight framed the back of the entryway just behind the staircase.

I walked through the right parlor and headed back to the kitchen.

"Hey, Vivi," I shouted. I waited for the usual, "Hey, honey," but all I got was silence. I walked into the kitchen to see a big rear end bent over and a head shoved into the back of the fridge.

Vivi was in a yellow sundress with an old apron

tied around her waist. Her rear end was bouncing to the radio, causing the sundress to swing wildly back and forth.

"What the hell are you doin'?" I said, laughing. She bumped her head bringing something out of the fridge.

"Oh, hey, honey, come on in. I'm lookin' for some lemons. I got me some tea made and Arthur has cut me some mint. But, oh, well, no lemon."

I walked over and hugged her.

"Okay, spill," she said. "I know that hug. What's going on?"

We sat for an hour and hashed everything out again.

"You know, Blake, we're all just needin' each other in a time like this. You gotta let those walls crumble, honey. Let all the ones you love in. It'll help. It's not a bad thing to be needy every now and then. I know. I even enjoy it sometimes."

"What am I doing in the middle of all this? I'm making out with Sonny. I'm married. I am a fool. I have jumped in with sharks. Everyone has so many secrets and I'm in on all of them. How can I help anyone without betraying someone else?" I didn't want to bring up the question Sonny asked me at lunch about me moving to D.C. I knew it would just upset her.

"Sweetie, you have secrets of your own brewing and I am here for you like you are here for me. You don't always have to be the strong one. Sometimes I can be that for you, too, you know? So let's come up with some answers here, okay?" She got up from the table to get a pen and paper. She was serious. I got a hold of myself and grabbed napkins from the center of the table and dried my eyes.

"Okay, then, first things first. Number one: you gotta make sure I'm not giving birth in jail."

We both burst out laughing. Yes, Vivi had a point. That did seem to be the most important thing, that she not go to jail—not now, not ever.

"This baby, after all, will be your niece or nephew and it deserves a better start than to draw her first breath in a 6x12 cement block."

"Vivi," I said, "you are not going to jail. There is no way that is ever going to happen. No one has yet been able to even say whether Lewis is actually dead. And nobody anywhere believes you are a murderer! Plus, you've got his baby growing inside you. It will never happen. Got it? On Mother Teresa's grave."

"Okay, number two: you gotta tell someone about those letters. I mean, besides Kitty and me. You gotta tell someone who can actually do something with them. I think they have a lot of clues and they might help us."

"Well, Kitty said she'll go to Meridee when she comes home tomorrow and see what she can find out."

"Okay, we'll give her a couple of days. But then you gotta go to Harry or Sonny. Deal?"

"Deal," I agreed.

"Next," she continued, "we gotta find out about that hot-pink-colored cigarette. Honey, the thought of that has made me sick. I can hardly sleep over it. And that pink…well, it makes me think of Dallas, which gives me the willies. I just cannot believe Lewis would be with someone else twelve hours before he was playin' cowboy with me—and especially if it was Dallas. That's not like him. Not since we, he and me, well, since *us*. You know. Well, that's really number one on my list. Next to finding him. I guess that would be my number one."

"Okay, that's a given," I said, laughing.

"Next, Sonny." She raised an eyebrow. "After I don't go to jail and my Lewis is found…" She hesitated, and I knew she was thinking that there was still a chance he could be found…not alive. She cleared her throat. "When he is found alive, and you get to the bottom of those letters and the damned cigarette, and all of this is untangled, you better figure out those feelings for Sonny and how deep they run. Are they real, or were they just symptomatic of everything else going on? If they are symptomatic, it's totally understandable considering the pressure you're under. But if they are real, Blake, you may have your own set of long-term problems."

"Thanks. I think."

"Now, that's the entire list," she said with finality in her voice, hitting the pen to the pad with a flourish as she wrote the last question mark. She shoved the paper across the table to me.

1. No giving birth in jail for Vivi.
2. Find Lewis—alive.
3. Figure out those letters.
4. Pink cigarette. What the hell? (Dallas?)
5. Sonny. Real or symptom?

That was our to-do list. Vivi had a way of simplifying things and making them black-and-white. From a missing body, a possible murder and a pregnant suspect, we now had a list of five simple things to do and we'd all live happily ever after. At that moment I wished I was more like Vivi.

I looked out the back window over the sink and saw Bonita and Arthur finishing up some ribs at one of the picnic tables. She cleared things away and then made her way up to the house.

"Hey, girls, how's it goin' today?" she asked as she came through the back door.

"We are doin' just fine and how 'bout yourself? Can I get you somethin' cold to drink?" Vivi offered.

Bonita shook her head and rested her hand on her ample belly. "Honey, I could not fit one more sip of anything after that lunch. Mm-mmm, that man can cook."

"Any word from the other lab on those cigarettes?" I said.

"Nothing yet, but we are expecting the results pretty soon. We had hoped we'd get them sooner but we had to send them all the way to Birmingham." She changed back to her favorite subject. "Ain't that Arthur just something?" she said, going over to the sink to wash the rib sauce off her hands. "He is just the sweetest thing. He's taking me to the movies tonight." She didn't realize how big her grin was growing as she spoke. She was wearing a pink-and-black Chanel suit and black patent heels. Her silver charm bracelets caught the afternoon sun and sparkled as she dried her hands on a nearby dish towel. She was a lucky woman to have Arthur and I knew she was good to him. They weren't quite a thing yet and he was nearly twelve years older but she liked the gentleman in him and he loved her sassy ways and bubbly personality. And of course, she loved to eat and he loved to cook. It was a really good match. When two people have that much fun together, the rest just seems to fall into place.

"Have y'all seen those billboards of Dallas all over town?" I asked, changing the subject to see if Bonita had anything new on the calls coming in.

"Yes, that girl will get that Emmy she's after, that's for sure," Bonita said.

"I even saw a TV commercial yesterday," Vivi joined in.

"What in the world does she think she can really do?" I wondered. "You just know she's hoping she can be the one to find Lewis. Can you imagine? Her popularity will go through the roof."

"I know it, and it seems that's already happening. I saw it in the paper this mornin'," Bonita said. "The ratings are going sky-high over there since they launched the Dallas Dubois segment on the six o'clock news the other day. The article said they are breaking ratings records every day now."

"But, the problem with this little campaign is that it attracts all the crazies," Vivi said. "You know those idiots who just wanna be on TV. To me it's an interference with the real search. Just a flashy distraction."

Vivi got up and poured herself another glass of tea, bringing the pitcher back to the table with her. Bonita turned to us.

"Well, that is the very definition of Dallas herself, is it not?" I said. "A flashy distraction." We nodded to each other, smiling as if I had hit the nail on the head.

"Y'all won't believe this but I saw her story last night and she was actually reporting live from a house near the edge of town—hon, that woman she was interviewing swore up and down she had seen the face of Lewis in her toast that mornin'! In her toast! I said to myself, good Lord, he ain't even Jesus and people are seeing his face carved in their food. I mean I know people claim to see the Lord in their sandwich sometimes, but *Lewis?* What is the world comin' to?"

Vivi and I burst out laughing and Bonita was laughing, too, and shaking her head. I wanted to tell Vivi about the sightings of Lewis at that Birmingham bank, but I knew she would just lose it and I didn't want to give her any false hope. Still, I thought she should know, so I led the conversation in that direction to see if Bonita would tell us the latest. I knew Sonny said at lunch that she was checking on those leads.

"Bonita, have y'all gotten any significant calls or info from any of this?"

"As a matter of fact, we did get something we thought was worth checking out," Bonita said.

"Oh, my, what did you hear?" Vivi asked, sitting up straight and looking big-eyed at Bonita.

"We have had a pretty significant number of calls stating the same sighting so we thought it was worth looking into."

"Oh, I hope it's not a body to go look at."

"No, Miss Vivi, it's not. At least ten people have called saying that they think they saw Lewis at a Birmingham bank after you reported him missing."

"After?"

"Yes, after. All have described him in the same clothes, at least all in a similar color of clothing, so we have asked the bank to provide records and videotape and we will have a look for ourselves."

"That's fantastic! At least he was walking around and breathing if he was at a bank. That's all I need to know. Oh, I feel so much better." Vivi was wringing her hands and a hopeful glimmer was in her pretty green eyes, not wet with tears this time, just shimmering with joy.

"I will let you know when we get the file from the bank."

"This just might be the lead we've been waiting for," Vivi said.

"Listen here, Vivi," Bonita said, turning to us at the table. "I have a strong gut feeling we are about to break this case wide-open. I believe Lewis may be out there somewhere and somebody that smokes and wears pink lipstick knows something. I intend to find her and shake her till she talks. Trust me. I'll get to the bottom of this."

Vivi and I looked at each other and held in our giggles. We knew we were looking at the newest member of the Sassy Belles.

The next day proved to be another busy one. Harry called around four to say he'd be late with another campaign event. I still had a big workload in front of me and would also be working late, so we agreed to meet at home at eight and order in something quick and easy. But it was only six when my stomach started rumbling, so I made my way into the back room to grab a snack and catch the news. I could not believe they had moved Dallas's Search for Lewis segment up to the very beginning of the six o'clock newscast. The main anchor tossed the story to Dallas who was reporting live from Walmart.

"Lewis Heart seems to be everywhere and nowhere these days. Billy Wayne Carmichael says he spotted him today in the drugstore section of Walmart on Skyland Boulevard, standing in the ointment aisle. Mr. Carmichael, please tell us what you saw."

"Oh, I know it was him for sure. He was standin' near the Preparation H, fidgeting from side to side. I could tell he had himself a problem. I had gone in with my wife today 'cause she had a problem, too, and so we was headed right down the same aisle when he looked up at us. He knew he was spotted 'cause he took off without his salve."

"Thank you, Mr. Carmichael. I do appreciate your… candor." Dallas turned back to the camera for her sign-off. "This is one of many such sightings of missing play-by-play announcer Lewis Heart. We will continue in our dedicated campaign to find the missing voice of our Alabama Crimson Tide. Reporting live from Walmart, I'm Dallas Dubois, WTAL."

I nearly threw up. She was so transparent. There was now a billboard on every corner; Dallas and her enormous cleavage, with her perfect megawatt smile and her microphone. I was sick of seeing her. In fact, it put me off accomplishing anything else that evening. I finished what I was working on, then closed up and headed home. It was nearly six-thirty by then and I decided to call Kitty as soon as I arrived at my driveway. This would have to be the day Kitty talked to Meridee, or I promised I would do it myself.

I grabbed my cell phone from my leather Hermès as I pulled into my driveway and hit speed dial for Kitty. Ringing… Answering machine…

"Hey, Mother, it's Blake. Look, today is the day. You have to talk to Meridee. It's been way too long and she could be a vital piece of the puzzle here. I need this done today, do you understand? If you don't talk to her by tonight, I will."

I hung up and sat in my car in front of the house when I realized Harry's car was there. I wasn't expecting him home for at least another hour or more, but I wouldn't have been surprised if he'd stopped by to get some things he'd forgotten for the campaign event tonight. Seeing his car made me nervous. I had gotten up my courage earlier and planned to try to talk to Harry about the separation over dinner. It would be the perfect time. We had been so busy since Lewis went missing, and the Myrna case had started to escalate, and Harry's campaign was growing. I just hadn't had time to have the talk with him. I thought that since I finished earlier than expected, I'd try to get home and actually fix supper for a change. It would relax me and help me prepare for what I was about to tell him. But now, seeing him home early, another thought struck me—maybe he was really trying this time. Maybe *he'd* gotten home early to put together a special dinner for us. We had kinda missed our anniversary. Despite the fact that Sonny and I had been getting closer, and that Harry and I had been slipping apart, there was a big part of me that still loved him and thought we deserved a fighting chance. After all, ten years of marriage should not be given up on lightly.

I hurried up the steps of our porch, thinking of candlelight and my crystal vases full of flowers, my heart filling with hope. As I put my purse on the front hall table, I could smell the coffee on and something sweet in the air drifting around from the kitchen. I was smiling ear to ear as I made my way across the hall and through the dining room. I couldn't believe he'd finally decided to do something special. Guilt about Sonny flashed in my head for a second, but I pushed it away, deciding that I needed to focus on Harry. Whether things were truly over or really just beginning for us was about to be seen, and I needed a clear head and a clear heart to make that decision. I knew this would be the moment to make it or break it. Maybe we deserved this second chance.

I swung open the kitchen door, expecting to find him, but there was no one there. I called out for him, but he didn't answer. I decided to go back outside, thinking somehow I had missed him and he was leaving to meet Dan. But when I got out front he wasn't outside. His car was in the driveway so I knew he must be around somewhere. I stepped down the porch steps and walked to the side gate that led to the backyard. I spotted another car in front of the house next door. Maybe Dan dropped by with him and they were sitting out back, I thought. I opened the side gate and headed down the side of the house. It was a tight walk along the path between the house and the hedges. Little squares of cement strewn unevenly like a rocky trail in front of me led to a gorgeous entertainment area complete with outdoor bar and fireplace. I was still in my office suit, a navy blue Michael Kors number, and my tallest black patent leather stilettos, which were sinking into the ground with each step. The bushes along the path were blooming and my hair was getting caught in the hydrangeas and crepe myrtles, pulling it out all over my face. It was a little overgrown and I made a note to myself to have the landscaping service come by. I finally got close enough to hear voices coming from the patio, but Dan was not the voice I heard. I'd recognize that limelight-suckin' reporter's delivery anywhere. What in hell was *Dallas* doing at *my* house? She must have gotten straight off the air and come right over. I decided I needed a better look, but I didn't want them to know I was there. I glanced around at my options, then slowly climbed up the rose trellis a couple of steps to peek over the hedges. I could hear Dallas now as clear as a bell, but I could only see the top of her big, blond head.

"Thanks so much for seeing me, Harry, especially on such short notice."

"No problem, Dallas. I know Blake gives you a hard time, but I really believe you have good intentions about helping us find Lewis."

Ugh! I felt my blood start to boil and my eyes bugged out, but as much as I wanted to storm back there, I knew it was best to stay hidden so I could hear their little chat. I lifted myself up another couple of inches, and now I could see them both clearly, though I was still disguised by the overgrown rose bush.

"Oh, I'm not worried about Blake, it's you I'm concerned about, Harry." She moved closer to him. "You know, if you agree to help me with this list of Lewis sightings, I can certainly pay you back." Dallas licked her lips seductively. Harry was pouring her a glass of bourbon and handed it to her while she pushed her scheme. He had a drink in hand, too, and they both took a sip and continued their little meeting. They were face-to-face when she said, "Oh, it is so warm out here!" She slowly unbuttoned the top two buttons of her hot-pink sleeveless blouse. Harry had moved face-to-face with her, removing his tie and unbuttoning his shirt.

"What did you have in mind?" he asked her, taking a swig of alcohol.

"Well," she said, taking the last gulp and setting the glass on the table, "I just thought you would like a little extra coverage of your, uhm, studs, I mean stumps," she giggled, gently biting her lower lip. She reached down and grabbed him inside his waistband of the front of his pants and pulled him into her. "I know how expensive TV advertising is, so I'll make sure I am right there with the cameras at every fundraiser."

"I like the sound of that," he said.

"I thought you would. You help me win this Emmy by leading me in the right direction on my Find Lewis campaign, and I'll be there for your campaign and… whatever else you need."

I could not believe my ears. Or my eyes!

"Sounds like a plan to me." He began pulling her blouse off her shoulders as she unbuttoned his pants. The trousers fell down around his ankles. She arched her head back as he kissed her neck and slid her bra strap over her shoulder and down her arm, freeing one breast and lowering his head toward it. Just then, my heel snapped off and the trellis broke with a loud crack. Down I slid with a thump into the crepe myrtles. Dallas screamed and grabbed her breast with one hand and her bra strap with the other, and Harry fell over when he tried to move because his pants were down around his ankles.

"Sorry for dropping in like this, but I was sorta looking for my husband," I shouted, anger just pouring out of me.

"Oh, my God! Blake! How long were you there?"

Oh, don't you ask all the right questions? What a politico you're gonna make, I thought.

"What the hell does it matter how long I was there, you ass? What I see right this second is enough," I shot back. A rage came over me like nothing I've ever felt. The adrenaline was unreal. "How dare you!" I screamed, limping over on my broken shoe. "At my own house—and look at you, you sorry bastard, flat on your face! With your pants down! Both of you disgust me!"

"Blake, wait." Harry kept stumbling, trying to stand up while Dallas was running around looking for her jacket. "Please, Blake, I can explain…" Harry continued. He was just embarrassing himself.

"Explain?" I shouted. "Oh, my God, Harry, seriously, what's to explain? You have your pants down and Dallas's bare breast was practically in your mouth. I just can't wait to hear you *explain* that," I hollered. "*Please,* do tell. Were you trying to lick off some spilled alcohol or help her breast back into the bra it *accidentally* popped out of? Please, I can't *wait* to hear your *explanation.*" I crossed my arms and stared at him as he managed to stand and zip his pants. He opened his mouth but nothing came out. I looked at Dallas as she began to sneak back through the house. "And *you,* don't even think I'm done with you yet," I screamed as she stepped inside to escape.

"Blake, really! It's not my fault if you can't keep your husband happy."

"Aaaagggggghhhhh!" I screamed and went chasing her out of my house through the kitchen and out the front door. She ran down the steps with her pink stilettos in one hand, trying to button her blouse with the other as she made her way to her car. I slammed the front door behind her and went back outside to Harry.

When I reached the backyard, I stood there staring at him, waiting for any kind of reaction. But he just stood there. Finally, he muttered, "It wasn't anything, really. Please, Blake."

I had nothing to say back. I shook my head. "You make me sick." I turned and ran out and jumped in my car and went straight to Mother's. I cried so hard all the way there, I could barely see to drive. When I pulled in, I saw Kitty's car in the driveway. I was still hysterical when I ran in the back door. I stepped up into the kitchen, and both Meridee and Kitty were sitting at the yellow table. It was such a relief to see these two women I depended on sitting there in front of me that I cried even louder.

"What happened, child?" Meridee said.

"Honey, what is it?" Kitty said.

"Sit down, sweetie. Let me get you a Coke and some cookies." Meridee jumped up to get the snacks and Kitty got up to hold me and push the hair back from my eyes. My mascara had run down to my chin. I looked like a prizefighter stepping out of the ring.

"Harry…" I sobbed. "Dallas…" I was choked up and just couldn't seem to get the words out. "…breast…on the patio…" I screamed before falling into a heap on the kitchen chair Meridee had pulled out for me.

"Oh, my God, I'm going to kill that son-of-a-bitch with my bare hands!" Kitty started for her purse, but Meridee grabbed her arm.

"Wait, just a minute, now. We don't need both of those Heart boys dead or missing or whatever the hell they are. So, Kitty, you just sit your round butt back down here and, Blake, you listen to me. We will get that good-for-nothin' bum, but first things first. You need to stay here and calm down for a while. You'll need some things from home so you can stay with me, but I'm not sending you back there. Now, Kitty, you've gotta go get her some clothes and whatever else she needs—but don't you dare lay a finger on Harry or Dallas while you're there. Focus on Blake and what she needs."

Kitty nodded, full of purpose, her face blazing with motherly rage and a fierce protectiveness. She grabbed her keys and purse and was out the door. Meridee pushed the Coke and Keeblers toward me.

"Okay, Blake. Tell me all about it."

I had calmed down some and had to talk it out.

"We've been having a little trouble," I said.

"A little?" She wasn't trying to be sarcastic, but it was true. *A little* was quite the understatement.

"He's been wrapped up in this campaign all spring, and with Lewis disappearing and my case on the Brooks Mansion, we have been distant forever. I just never thought…" I couldn't finish. And it only made it worse that it was Dallas.

"Let's call Vivi," Meridee suggested. "I think you need her."

Before I knew it, Vivi arrived with a bag full of Taco Casa delicacies. This was my comfort food and she knew it. She had run through the drive-through of the little Mexican restaurant nearby and grabbed my favorite things—a combo burrito, some frijoles, some sopapillas and an iced tea with lemon. She brought enough for all of us and spread it out on the kitchen table.

"Come on now, sugar," she said, opening the bags. "This'll make you feel better."

I love living in a place where food can solve almost all the world's ills. Vivi held me while I cried some more.

"That bastard," she said, stroking my hair. "What the hell is he thinking? Every time somebody runs for office, an affair seems to pop up like toast. And Dallas! Well, that girl is a giant skank." Vivi was infuriated.

Kitty returned and we sat together quietly eating and just being close to each other. I had a good support system. That's the way us Belles are. Got your back for life, no matter what.

An hour or so had passed when Vivi heard a car

through the kitchen window. She peered over the sink. It was Harry, finally realizing that he'd better make his apologies. I was sure he'd just talked the whole thing over with Dan. A scorned and angry wife would not be very good on the campaign trail.

"I'm not seeing him," I announced. I promptly left the table and locked myself in the bathroom down the hall. I have to say, Harry was brave, coming over there to face me and my reinforcements. He knew he might, literally, get the living hell beaten out of him.

Harry came rushing in as if from a fire. He didn't even have the sense to knock.

"Where's Blake?" he asked, out of breath.

"Young man, you sit your cheatin' ass down right now," Meridee ordered. "You aren't gonna talk to Blake, you're gonna talk to me."

"And me, too." Vivi stepped into the kitchen from the darkened hallway like a member of the mafia. Harry was forced into the chair and grilled for thirty minutes, his phone ringing incessantly the entire time—no doubt Dan was trying to figure out what the damage was.

By the time my girls were through with him, Harry was bawling like a baby. Mr. Perfect had fallen off his self-made pedestal.

"It was one time! I've never been unfaithful! Dallas and I were just talking about her search for Lewis… Blake and I haven't gotten along in months. Ever since the investigation started, she's been so distant."

Vivi broke in to the monologue.

"Blah, blah, blah, and that gives you permission to go bang somebody else?" Vivi did have a point. And a way of getting it across.

"We were only kissing," he said, defensively. I don't

think he had any idea how absolutely ridiculous that sounded, but he continued anyway. "Dallas called me this afternoon to see if we could go over the call list for her Search for Lewis campaign. She thought that since Lewis is my brother, I might be better able to tell which were real possibilities and which were was just crazy calls. I told her I would help her. I had to run home to grab some flyers for Dan and she said she'd swing by for a minute. I was supposed to meet Dan at the office to go to the meet-and-greet this evening." He was breathing fast, like he had been running. It seemed like he was desperate to be believed.

"Well, I guess you missed the campaign thing with Dan. Now it's obvious where your priorities are. In your pants. Typical politician." Vivi was disgusted and she had no skills to ever hide her feelings.

Harry went on. "Anyway, when she walked in, she mentioned she was stressing because this search had turned into such an overwhelming project. I offered her a drink and before we knew it, both of us had had a few bourbons. She went to the bathroom and when she came out, she had taken off her jacket. It was a warm day and both of us had had a little too much to drink. I swear, I never meant to…uhh…" He stopped, realizing no one was going to be on his side in *that* house. His usually composed, stoic face said it all.

"I don't think you can see Blake tonight," Vivi announced. "I don't think she wants to see you! Blake?" she yelled down the hall to me. "Wanna see Harry?"

"Hell, *no!*" I yelled from behind the bathroom door.

"See?" she said back to Harry. "Now go home and think about what you did, you sorry bastard."

He answered his phone as he made his way to the

front door. Dan the man was calling again. He would be earning his money big-time for next little while, working to keep this "dinnertime spread" out of the media.

Later that night, I was still at Meridee's. Vivi and I had decided to spend the night in the bedroom that had two twin beds. We had grown up together in that room. Meridee and Kitty were in the other two bedrooms. It felt like it used to when I was growing up, everybody under one roof as if it were Christmas. Even though Harry was a jerk and I hated him tonight, something about being here with all of us girls together felt nice. And there had finally been a break in the elephant in the room that had become my marriage. Now that I had settled down, I realized that this episode might be a blessing in disguise.

Around ten forty-five my cell phone rang. I promised myself that if it was Harry, I wouldn't answer. But it was Sonny.

"Blake, I need to see you and Harry. Bonita got some information on that spotting of Lewis in Birmingham. Can I swing by?"

I wasn't sure I was up to it but it would sure be nice to see him tonight. "Sonny, hey. Sure you can, but I'm not home. I'm at Mother's tonight."

"I'll be there in ten."

I hung up and got out of bed, and then went to wash my face. Vivi followed me into the bathroom. *Here it comes. I knew it.*

"Sweetie, be careful. You're very vulnerable tonight. Don't be vengeful. You don't want to wake up tomorrow full of regret."

I grabbed my makeup bag and looked in the mirror, pretending I hadn't heard her.

"Blake Elizabeth, you listen to me." She had obviously put her "Mother" hat on. "I know how you are with Sonny. Your guard is down tonight. You want to hurt Harry and I understand that. Believe you me, I wanna hurt him, too. But you really don't want the regrets, sweetie. Really. Stop a minute and think."

But when I did think, I got excited. Okay, maybe it was wrong. Maybe I'd been waiting for an excuse to take things to the next level with Sonny for a while now. What I knew for sure was that these feelings were genuine. And the urge was stronger than anything I had felt in years. He would be at Meridee's in just a few minutes. I brushed my hair and rinsed my mouth with mouthwash and decided I would think about this later. Right now, all I knew is how much I wanted to see him.

18

Sonny arrived around eleven and the house was totally dark. When he knocked at the door, Vivi gave me the "You'll be sorry" look and hugged me and closed her door. I opened the front door and slipped out onto the screened front porch.

The moonlight draped us in heavy shadows. Sonny's face was lit from the side.

"What is it?" Sonny asked, whispering.

"Everyone's asleep, I don't want to wake them," I said. He had no idea about me and Harry, but he knew something was up. We sat down on the glider.

"Bonita has found over twenty calls from different people, all saying that Lewis was seen at a Birmingham bank within two hours of Vivi reporting him missing."

"It only takes about an hour to get to Birmingham," I said.

"Exactly. And with twenty different reports confirming the same sighting, she decided to subpoena the bank records and they came in tonight."

"What did they say?" I asked. I was anxious already but this was sending me over the top.

"They showed it was him. And that he took out a large sum of cash."

"Oh, my God," I said.

"They even sent us the video and we know he was alive and at that bank in Birmingham *after* he was with Vivi. It's the biggest break we've had so far."

"Oh, Sonny, that's wonderful."

"It is wonderful. Except… Well, he's still missing. We don't know why he disappeared, whether it was his own doing or whether he was forced to leave. We don't know where he went or who he gave the money to, but we do know he was alive at the time and that's huge. I expect we will have more news tomorrow on this." He stopped and looked at me to gauge my reaction.

"That is such good news! Thank you!" I said, trying to hold my smile. I was so happy about this turn of events, but so much more played through my mind that night.

"I called Harry and couldn't get him," Sonny added. "Come to think of it, why are you here? It's so late. Shouldn't you be home?"

I hugged him. "Thanks for coming here and letting me know." I started to tear up before I knew it.

Sonny was holding me in his arms and I had my head on his broad chest. "Blake, baby, what's wrong?"

"Sonny, it's too much right now. I don't think I can talk about it. Just hold me." And he did.

The glider swing swayed back and forth, rocking us gently in the shadows. The moon was full and so bright that night. Sonny stroked my hair and kissed my forehead.

"Is this something about you and Harry?" he asked softly. "C'mon, Blake, you can talk to me."

"Yes," I admitted. "It was a really bad fight." I didn't want to tell him about Dallas. I certainly didn't want him to think that my being here with him was just to get even with Harry. No matter how it looked on the outside, in my heart I knew that wasn't the reason. But I'll admit it was a damn good excuse to explore things. Harry and I had been headed down the road to this mess for ages. And this moment with Sonny had been brewing ever since we kissed in the kitchen that night.

I snuggled into his neck and he squeezed me tighter into him.

"It will be okay, Blake," he assured me. "It will all get fixed up in the morning."

"No, Sonny. It won't. It was worse than you can imagine."

He smelled so good and I felt protected. I pressed my face into his neck and breathed on his skin. He pulled away. He looked down at me and studied my gaze. The next thing I remember was his mouth so gently resting on mine. His lips were so warm.

"Oh, Blake, I don't want to make things worse. I'm sorry," he said. But he spoke in a whisper. He wasn't that sorry. I looked up into his sweet brown eyes.

"Harry and I have been having problems for a while. I need to put some space between us. It's okay, Sonny."

I placed my fingertips on his face and pulled him into me. I kissed him softly and he opened his mouth. He kissed me back much more deeply, rolling his tongue over mine and pulling me into his body. His lips trailed all around my mouth and down my neck. He was starving for closeness.

A heat had crept over my entire body, and it flared as I felt his lips glide down to my breasts. He looked up at me playfully, full of mischief. "Cleavage and cavity search, ma'am. All part of the job."

He winked at me and I laughed—amazed by the man who could incite passion and protectiveness and warmth and humor in one moment, never missing a beat. He began unbuttoning my shirt and smiled as he got to my pale pink, lacy camisole hanging loosely over my breasts. Gazing at me, he slowly began kissing my chest, dropping down below the lace and dragging his tongue over the tender flesh that was aching for his attention.

He stopped suddenly. "Blake. Are you sure about this?"

I looked at him and lay back on the glider, closing my eyes and giving him the unspoken permission he needed. Without another word Sonny moved on top of me.

I felt his body relax over me, picking up where he left off, opening my blouse slowly, one button, one kiss, another button, another kiss, slipping my spaghetti straps over until I felt them fall off my shoulders.

I was mesmerized by him and his slow attention to detail. He pulled off his shirt, and the sight of his gorgeous, big shoulders stirred something deep inside me. I felt his mouth at the top of my pants. I felt the button open and the zipper slip down. He continued teasing me as he slipped my pants off. His mouth and tongue moved south over my pelvis and to my pink lace panties, and soon I felt those, too, being removed, sliding down my bare legs, slipping off and dropping to the floor of the front porch.

There was nothing now between Sonny and me. He

had removed his pants and all had fallen to a heap on the concrete. He was a gentle and careful lover. Slow and deliberate, devouring me for hours, just like I needed. Sonny looked at me and smiled as we discovered each other again. It had been a long time since high school. And we never took our clothes off back then.

It was such a comfortable place, beneath him. We had managed to slip off the day's armor and melt into each other, flesh into flesh, under cotton blankets that had draped the back of the glider. I had always been the good girl. My experience with a lover was limited to Harry. I had never been devoured and connected to someone like this. To be physical and emotional and understood all at the same time was new to me and I loved every second. It was as if we moved as one, writhing in the passion we had held back for so many years, our bodies fell into a comfortable pulse.

I felt his hand slide under my back, lifting me up to him, pressing my thighs and pelvis into his. I wrapped myself around him. His fingers were soft and tender, and I loved feeling them wander down my backside, slipping over my hips and down my thighs. His mouth wandered over my breasts, tasting me, touching me. He seemed to have a map to me. Understanding every inch of my skin, every strand of hair, he knew just what I needed, and he breathed me into him. He caressed my hair, pushing it away from my face.

Brushing his fingertips across my face, he whispered, "You are so beautiful." He was looking right into my eyes, dropping his mouth under my cheek and rolling his tongue around my neck, gently kissing the top of my shoulder and sliding his lips and tongue softly down the side of my breast. I had never been taken like this.

His fingertips slipped inside my thighs and he gently touched me. His muscular body was hard but so tender and I slipped my hand down his inner thigh, caressing him softly. I ran my fingers up his back and dragged them across his perfect broad shoulders.

I was sure I had never been this free with Harry. The pressure for perfection shut me down in some ways. But Sonny just made me feel like I was the only woman in the world. His woman. And that feeling set me free in ways I had never felt before. I would never be the same. I couldn't go back now. I had become connected to someone on all levels and it was the most amazing thing I had ever felt. I smiled at him, looking into those brown eyes I had first fallen in love with so many years ago. It felt good to see my past in his eyes, the boy I knew, now a man. And to have him as a woman. Finally.

"I can't believe we never did this in high school," Sonny said when we were both sated and exhausted.

"I know," I said. "You should have definitely been my first." I was looking up at him still lying over me. I liked feeling his weight on me.

"Well, I sure tried to be," he said. "No, I think I may have begged. But you were the good girl. I always respected that."

"What about now?" I asked.

"I really respect you now." We both laughed.

"I don't regret this," I said. And I really didn't.

"I sure as hell don't," he said. "I feel bad for Harry, though. I mean, I've been working with him for weeks, but I can't help it if something is wrong with him and he can't realize what he's got here and take better care of it."

Sonny was so right. It felt good to be physical with

someone that I had such an emotional and mental bond with. I knew he understood me and I understood him. We get each other in a way that was different than what I had ever experienced with anyone. I was finally in his arms, one with him, after all these years of waiting. I breathed in deeply, just living in this moment, quiet and still. Sonny continued to kiss me.

I was filled with conflicting emotions. I wanted this, yet I was sad, too. Elated and sad. I wanted to lie in Sonny's arms a little longer, he made me so happy. And I knew my marriage with Harry was ending, which still hurt to accept.

The Southern night air grew damp and we played until dew-drops began to shimmer on the rose petals. I could see them outside the screened porch over his naked, big shoulders.

"Want some coffee?" I said, looking at the watch still on Sonny's wrist. It was 5:00 a.m.

"Won't Harry be looking for you?"

"He knows better than to come here, Sonny." I wasn't sure if I should tell him about Dallas, but I couldn't stop myself.

"Sonny," I said.

"What, beautiful?"

"I caught Harry with Dallas." There it was. I'd said it. It was out there, ruining the moment. "They were half-naked on my backyard patio and I sorta stumbled onto them."

"What?" He sat up. The blanket fell off his body and draped over his lap. "What was he thinking? Why? Why her?"

"I don't know, Sonny. But really, it's been a mess lately. It's been ending for a while, actually."

"Just the thought of them…"

"I know. But I'm dealing with it."

Then he looked up at me with hurt feelings in his sweet brown eyes. "Was this revenge sex?" He suddenly looked like a young boy again.

"Aw, no, baby." I kissed him softly. "No way. This has been coming since I was fourteen. The timing was just never on our side until now. I feel so good with you." Sonny pulled me into him.

"I have never been like this with any woman, Blake. You were worth the wait," he said, placing his hands on either side of my face, his fingertips sliding over my cheeks. "No other woman I have ever known has ever made me feel the way you do, Blake. No woman can glance at me from across a room and get my heart pumping. You still do that to me. And you see the best in me, too. That makes a man feel real good. My marriage never stood a chance. That poor girl could never even live up to the memory of you." Sonny leaned in and kissed my eyelids softly and then my nose and then each cheek, finally resting on my mouth.

As he talked, I was lost in his words, and then lost in his kisses. I needed to hear this. The good girl inside kept taunting me, though. *Oh, my, Blake O'Hara Heart, you ought to be ashamed, you unfaithful heifer. You're just as bad as Harry.* But then the stronger, braver Blake would think, *Harry, my big ass! That sorry pig! He just went for a Dumpster dive with your ex-stepsister and number one enemy on this planet!*

"Sonny," I said, half laughing, "being a good girl is *so* overrated."

He smiled and kissed my forehead. "Blake, I will never regret this. I hope you won't."

"Never, Sonny. You were the first boy that stole my heart. There's always been an easiness about us."

"There's something about your softness," he added. "I can rest my head against you and the world goes away. A man needs that. And God knows, no body excites this body like you do…always did." He exhaled and I felt his breath on my shoulder. "Blake, I'm okay with whatever you want now. You just need to tell me what that is."

"I know, Sonny. I've just got so much on my mind. So much to decipher. Let's just sit with this awhile."

"That's okay, beautiful. I will never, ever be done with you. I'll sit as long as you want."

He kissed me on the nose, then pressed his lips on mine and got up from the glider. I watched him get dressed in the light of the sunrise.

19

I ran the hot water till it steamed the bathroom into a fog. It was early in the morning now, the sun was rising and Sonny had just left. Wanda Jo would take all the calls today. I had called the office and left her a message that I was going to work from home. I needed some time to think and try to get my head around the evening's adventures and not have to run into Harry at the office. I wiped the bathroom mirror off just enough to catch my reflection. I stared at myself as flashes of what I had just done popped in and out of my head. I could still feel his weight on me, smell his cologne, taste his mouth on mine. Was I the skank now? I knew who would tell me whether I asked her or not.

"Oh, Miss Blaaaakeeee… Is that my new skanky friend comin' out of the shower?" Vivi teased from the kitchen as I was drying off. I smiled at myself in the mirror. *What's done is done. No regrets.* Yes, I had feelings for Sonny. They'd never gone away. They never would. I had no idea what I would do from here, so I decided not to worry about it.

"I'm coming," I said as I wrapped myself in a towel.

"Yes, I bet." She laughed at herself. Her red frizz preceded her as she popped her head into the bathroom door.

"Well, lady of the night...how was our detective? Did he hold a 'discovery of new evidence' session with you last night?" I smiled at her as I combed my wet hair. Vivi continued with the teasing.

"And did my attorney in this matter take good notes, or did she reenact the events?"

"Ha-ha. Very funny." I laughed.

"Okay, finish up and get out here and tell me everything."

I put my pink silky robe on and rubbed the towel in my hair. I started thinking about what Sonny had said. Was it revenge sex? No, this was makeup sex. Making up for the last twenty years of not making love with him. I finally just did what I wanted to do, not what was expected of me. Not what I was supposed to do. And it felt damn good.

Vivi and I sat in Meridee's kitchen talking lovers and marriage and the past. We never got dressed. It was a robes and coffee all day kind of day. Rainy and warm, we never noticed that the day had worn into evening. Meridee and Kitty hadn't come back from wherever they'd gone for the day. I left my phone on silent so I didn't hear from Sonny or Harry.

Along about 4:45, Vivi looked over the kitchen table at me. "You know, where is everybody today? Just too damn quiet for me," she said. I checked my phone and had two missed calls. One from Harry and one from Wanda Jo. I called the office and Wanda Jo answered.

"Well, well, are we on vacation?" she asked sarcastically. "I haven't even heard from you or Mr. Heart all damn day. Those Myrnas are driving me batty and now the Jennings have called three times about their son's car wreck. He needs to know if he's gonna be charged for hittin' Mr. Neighbor's mule since the mule had escaped to a city street. I told him that mule had no right of way…the street is for cars, but hey, I'm no lawyer."

By this time I was laughing to myself on the other end. "I'll take care of it, Wanda Jo. Don't worry. Why don't you go on home for the day?"

"Okay, that works for me," she said. "It's poker night with my sister so I need to straighten up my house. Thanks, I'll see y'all in the mornin'."

I checked the kitchen clock—five o'clock. I could not believe the day was gone. All I knew was Kitty better be getting all of our info from Meridee on those strange letters. If my grandmother was involved with Lewis on some old financial venture, I wanted to know about it and Kitty was the only one who could frame it just right. Those women were two of a kind—smart as whips and suspicious of everyone. But Kitty was more of a nag than Meridee and my money was on her. I'd have my answers tonight.

I had purposely avoided telling Vivi about the bank information and that they knew Lewis was alive after she reported him missing. We still didn't know why he'd disappeared or if anything had happened to him since he'd been seen at the bank. If the worst happened and they found he wasn't alive anymore, it would just be so unfair to get her hopes so high. So I left it alone until we had something certain to tell her.

I wanted to call Sonny so bad. The flashes of the night before kept popping in and out of my head. My stomach dropped a hundred times, remembering the feeling of Sonny kissing me, touching me, filling me. I had been toying with my cell phone and glancing at the screen all day. I couldn't stand it anymore.

"Go ahead." Vivi broke into my thoughts. "You've been looking at that damn screen like it holds the book of secrets. Just do it."

"What?" I said, all innocent.

"Don't play with me, girlie," she said with a wink. "Call your lover."

I smiled at her and hit Sonny's name on my cell. The deep baritone answered. "Baby?" he said. "Hey."

"I would have never pegged you for the love 'em and leave 'em type," I teased.

"Blake, I'm sorry, honey. We got a big break today. I've been with Harry all day and haven't had a moment alone to call you."

I could not speak. My breath was stuck in my throat.

"Blake?" he said. "Blake, baby, everything's just fine. And, no, next question, I did not tell him about the cavity search last night."

I laughed, breaking my stuck-together throat into a heavy relief. "What was the big break today?" I asked. "Do you need to see me?"

"Oh, I have seen you, and I like what I saw," he said.

"Look, big boy, I need to know what happened."

"Well, technically, Harry is supposed to talk to you. He was here and is your co-counsel, but due to the ex-

tenuating circumstances, I'll be glad to fill you in…
ahem…been there done that…."

"You just cannot help yourself, can you?" I said with
a smile.

He cleared his throat playfully. I could tell he was
happy. He had a lighter tone in his voice. He also
sounded like things were finally going well on this case.

"There were no matches for anyone we tested against
that hot-pink lipstick, so the good news is that Vivi is
definitely off the hook on that front—not that we imagined it would go any other way. I'm still runnin' one
more test…." A pause.

"What is it, Sonny? You sound like you've got something more to tell me."

"Well, thing is, Harry decided that we needed to
bring Dallas in for questioning."

"What?" I nearly dropped my cell phone. "Let me
get this all straight. I catch my skanky ex-stepsister with
her breast in the mouth of my two-faced husband, and
then I have the best sex of my life with my sexy old high
school boyfriend, and then both of them spend the day
with the skanky stepsister? Do I have this right? I'm
just trying to get this straight."

"That's pretty much it, babe," he said. "Especially
the best sex of your life with your sexy high school
boyfriend part. But, Blake, more importantly, we got
a break today, and it suggests even more than the evidence from the bank that Lewis is still alive somewhere."

"Oh, my God. Vivi!" I yelled. "Get in here! Sonny,
do you want us to get dressed and come there?"

"Let's get this clear—I never want you dressed. But,
yes, I want y'all to come here. We have a lot to discuss."

Even in a crisis, Sonny could make me smile...and always make me feel so sexy.

"Is Harry gonna be there?"

"Yes," he said.

I took a deep breath and blew it out. "Okay. Be there in a few."

Vivi came running in just as I hung up. "What is it, honey?" she asked. "Did Sonny and Harry fight it out?"

"Vivi, sit down," I said. I knew that I had to spill everything about Lewis now. If I didn't, and she heard it from Harry and Sonny at the station, she'd never forgive me for keeping the news from her. Regardless of what happened to Lewis from here on out, I had to bring her up to date on the fact that we were pretty sure he was alive. "Honey, there's something serious I need to talk to you about."

"What? Oh, my God, Lewis is dead! They found him!" She began to hyperventilate. "Oh, Lord. Oh, no..."

"Vivi!" I yelled at her. "Snap out of it! No, sweetie, no! They think he's alive."

"Oh, my God, oh, my God!" Now she was hyperventilating over the good news, so I just kept on talking.

"Yes, they believe they have evidence to show that he's alive."

I walked over to the drawer of plastic sandwich bags as I explained. "Sonny said they had a big break in the case today." I walked back over to Vivi with a Ziploc. She grabbed it from me and put it over her blue lips and breathed in, like we had done this a hundred times before. (We had.) The bag collapsed. I helped her hold it in place as I talked.

"Slow down, honey," I said. "Now, we gotta go down

to the station. Everyone—Harry, Dallas and Sonny—
will be there and you are going with me."

She breathed deeply into the bag a few more times
until her heart rate slowed and she could think again.
"Will you be okay?" she asked.

"Don't worry about me. There are bigger things
going on right now than Harry and Dallas. I am your
attorney. I have to be there. Now, c'mon. We need to
get dressed."

We left the kitchen and hurried to get ready. I went
into the bathroom and washed my face and brushed the
coffee off my breath. We threw on our clothes. *Okay,*
I thought to myself, *here I go. I can do this.* I took in
a deep breath and turned off the bedroom light. I was
fixin' to be standing with my cheatin' husband, his
lover and my lover, in the same room—all while trying to solve the case of my missing brother-in-law. *This
should be good.*

20

Vivi and I left for the station just as dusk was falling into a pink haze over the Warrior River. Vivi had squirmed and bitten her nails to the quick all the way over.

"I sure hope I don't have to look at Dallas in the eyes," she said with her trademark attitude. "I want to pull her hair out. What the hell was Harry thinking? She's been all around town already—I can't even imagine what he saw in her."

"Her easiness?" I joked. "But, Vivi, I slept with Sonny last night, too," I said. I was trying to show her I was just as guilty, thinking this would calm her down so we could hear the break in the case and do the hair pulling later.

"I know," she said, "but Sonny is a good man and he's loved you forever. Dallas doesn't care about Harry—I think she's just out to get whatever will help her career."

"That sounds just like Harry, too, doesn't it? Two of a kind, maybe?" She was quiet for a moment as we thought about that. Then her thoughts returned to Lewis.

"Blake, do you think Lewis ran away? I mean, if they think he is alive, why would he leave me like that? I really thought he loved me. I mean, I know Lewis is Lewis but he and I...we...had a thing."

"Oh, honey. He does love you. I know there must be a good explanation."

"If he's out there, I'd be so happy, Blake. This baby may get to know her father."

"Yeah, but we still need to find him and bring him home," I said.

I looked ahead and the station was just in sight. I knew everything was about to change. We needed answers before I could even think of where to sleep tonight. So I looked at Vivi. "You ready?"

Vivi reached over and squeezed my hand. "Blake, I am ready for anything that lets me know my Lewis is alive. I have to say something before we see these boys. Please don't take this the wrong way. I am only sayin' this 'cause you need to hear it before you look at these two men together."

Vivi was disarming. I was listening with a warning in the pit of my stomach.

"Something happened to you last night," Vivi began.

"It sure did," I said with a sly grin.

"No, really. I mean...Sonny has an effect on you. He brought you back to yourself. I saw it in you all day while we were sittin' at Meridee's table. Since you married Harry, little pieces of my Blake are being lost, year after year. You have become who Harry needs you to be. Not who you really are. You've had a blanket of sadness over you that I couldn't quite put my finger on. But Sonny brought you back last night. He took the blanket off…so to speak. I see that happiness comin' back. That sparkle."

Tears fell as I pulled into a spot outside the station and listened to her. Vivi knew me better than anyone, and deep down, I knew she was right.

"I'm sorry, sweetie," she said.

"No, it's okay. I know what you're saying. I haven't felt that good and that real in forever."

"Listen to me," she continued. "Your neck is nearly as red as the rest of us. You always had that little touch of class that the rest of us didn't, but underneath all those beauty crowns, education, worldliness and debate trophies, you love a good honky-tonk and a cold longneck just as much as we do. When you married Harry, he wanted to change you…squash out that little bit of red, and he barely let the Southern Belle show. Blake, you gotta be true to yourself or you'll die. Nothin' about you ever needed changin'."

I was fully engulfed now. She had opened the dam. Everything she said was true, and it left me more confused than I could deal with. Not only was I questioning who I really loved…but now I had to ask myself who I really *was*. Vivi handed me a tissue out of the glove box and I opened my purse and fumbled for my makeup bag.

Vivi had made me think. How could I not compare the two of them? I had loved Harry. I loved how he dressed and his preppy-boy good looks. I loved his ambitious nature. But now those ambitions were running me over like a bulldozer. I felt like I didn't matter. I felt invisible. I was sad inside. But Sonny saw me and made me see *myself* again. And he made me like what I saw. I was me again, after a long absence. The sheer joy in that was indescribable. Sonny was quite the opposite of Harry in terms of looks. But deeper than that he was rugged and real and more emotional. He didn't mind sharing his feelings with me. He was passionate and masculine and so confident. Harry acted confident, he loved the mirror all right, but it was just that— the constant checking on himself—that made him look insecure to me. Harry was ice to Sonny's fire. And I knew I got that fire going. I loved that. Maybe most of all. A Belle loves to feel alluring and beautiful. It's the Scarlett O'Hara in us. Most important, I felt like myself with Sonny. The best of me came out. He encouraged it and wasn't challenged by it…or jealous of it. I could shine. And breathe.

"I'm sorry," Vivi said again. "I had this on my mind all day and I just needed you to hear it."

"Now?" I said, and swiped some powder across my red cheeks. "I hear you. I have felt sad. For a very long time. And Sonny makes me feel like me again. The two of them are so different. I will need to talk to Harry when the dust settles. But right now, we've got business in front of us and I am your counsel. Not the other way around."

"And I need you," she said, smiling.

We climbed out of the car and entered the station through the back door and walked down the hall to Sonny's office. Vivi clutched my hand before we entered and we looked at each other. We were in this together. Like everything else.

Sonny was alone in his office. He had his back to us when we tapped on his door.

"Hey, ladies, have a seat." I wanted to kiss him and

hug him, but we just sat down in the overstuffed leather chairs. I scooted my chair up close to his desk.

Vivi spoke right up. "So, tell me, is my Lewis alive? Please tell me you think so."

I looked nervously at Sonny. He glanced at me and in that instant, I knew it was okay.

"Vivi, as you probably know, we have had many calls and leads and have even followed some of Dallas's leads from her TV campaign. But one in particular kept croppin' up, over and over," Sonny explained. "Seems many people think they saw Lewis at a bank in Birmingham not too long after you reported him dead at the motel and we realized he'd gone missing. I had Bonita check things out and the videotape and bank records do show it was him."

"Oh, my God!" Vivi jumped up. "That is just the news I was hoping for!" Vivi was full of relief and hope.

"We are checking on a couple more things at the moment, but we expect the answers will be in shortly." Sonny gave her a confident smile. He knew more than he was saying.

"Do you have any idea where he is? I mean, is he still okay? You said you know he was at the bank but that was ages ago. Where is he now? Is he still alive?" Vivi sat back down and began to look worried.

"We will know more in just a little bit."

"We will sit right here till we have our answers," I told her, grabbing her hand. I blew out a big breath and looked at Sonny.

"Is Harry here?" I asked.

Sonny looked at me with that look, eyebrow up. "Missing him?"

"Hell, no, she isn't," Vivi answered for me.

"No, just asking." Preparing, more like it.

"He went for coffee and Krispy Kremes."

"Oh, God, is it gonna be a long night?" I asked. Anytime somebody breaks out the Krispy Kremes at night, you just knew it was gonna be a long one.

"It could be," Sonny said.

My cell rang. Kitty. "Not now, Mother," I said out loud as I answered the phone anyway.

But that didn't stop her, and she started talking a mile a minute. She always did, but this was even faster than usual. Her words whooshing by, I caught the word "letters" and then "Meridee."

"Slow down," I said.

"Wait," Sonny interrupted. "Is that Kitty? Is she with your grandmother?"

"Are you still with Meridee?" I asked her, then nodded to Sonny.

"Tell her we need to see them. Tell them to come on down to the station right away."

I relayed the messages and hung up, becoming more confused by the second.

"What the hell is going on?" Vivi couldn't take it anymore. "Is Lewis alive—I mean right this minute? I just need to know the answer to that one question. Can anyone tell me that?" She was losing it, heading for an all-night conniption, and we just didn't want that.

"Sonny," I chimed in over Vivi's escalating shrill, "can we just answer that?"

"Definitely, Lewis is alive," he said. "Well, not definitely, but we are pretty sure we know who has the answers."

"Lemme guess," Vivi said, "Dallas?"

"No, not her," he said with a laugh. "Let's just wait till everyone gets here."

"Sonny, can I see you in the hall a sec?" I said, getting up from my seat. We walked down the hall and out of earshot of Vivi, Sonny leading the way. He turned to me and didn't speak. His presence was commanding, yet such a comfort. He looked down at me, smiling.

I had on thin, charcoal-gray yoga pants that tied with a drawstring at the waist, a white, low-scooped tank top and a long, gray cashmere, hooded sweater. My hair was wavy from air drying on the way over, and I had only mascara and lip gloss for makeup. We had left in such a hurry, no time for the usual pageant-hair and full face.

"God, you look good enough to eat," he said. Images of Little Red Riding Hood and the big bad wolf entered my head for just a quick second, enticing me with excitement, then I relaxed and grinned at him.

"Sonny, that is not what I brought you out here for…."

"Okay," he said, "I'll keep that thought for later. We think Lewis is alive. All the evidence is pointing that way. Just this afternoon, we got a positive ID on the cigarette."

"Dallas, huh?" I said. "She seems to be making the rounds on the Heart men."

Sonny's face turned serious.

"Actually, Blake…" His voice deepened and his eyes widened.

"What's going on, Sonny?"

"Blake, when I was with you last night—well, *after* I was with you… When I went to the bathroom just before I left, I took some of Meridee's hair from her hairbrush to just see…well, you know, if there was any connection. I mean we both knew she did have this secret communication with Lewis. And we'd already tested the rest of us, so it just seemed like the logical next step."

"And?" I prompted. My heart felt like it was choking me.

"Blake, the hot-pink lipstick came back positive for Meridee."

"What? Are you kiddin' me?"

"This is no joke, Blake. Your grandmother was in Lewis's condo twelve hours before he disappeared."

"Oh, my God!" It finally hit me. "All this time… Well, what in hell was she thinking? Does this mean she's known where Lewis was all along?"

"Well, that's why we wanted to see both your mother and grandmother," Sonny explained. "You told me last night that Kitty would get the answers from her. I'm just hoping she did."

21

I slipped into the vending room and Sonny followed me. I was in shock. I fumbled around in the bottom of my sweater pocket for change. I felt Sonny behind me. He kissed the back of my head and placed both of his hands on my shoulders.

"What's your poison, beautiful?" he whispered in my ear. "Still Diet Coke?"

I nodded.

"And Miss Vivi…Dr Pepper?"

I nodded again.

"I got it." I stepped aside and let Sonny take care of it. He handed me the ice-cold can and Vivi's Dr Pepper.

"Thanks," I said.

"Anytime, sweetheart," he said. "It will be okay, Blake."

I smiled at him. I popped the top and sipped the Diet Coke. I knew Sonny was right. Eventually it would work itself out. Sonny was facing me and I looked up at him, Just as I was about to say something, Harry appeared in the doorway. The sight of him took my breath away. It startled Sonny, too, since he was just holding me and calling me sweetheart.

"Hi, Blake," he said quietly. This was the first time I'd seen him since I caught him giving Dallas a breast exam.

"Hi," I said, looking at him—no, glaring at him—and not sure exactly what I was feeling. I had done my own deed, I knew that, but the situation with Dallas made me feel like I had lost. Blake O'Hara does not share. I didn't even like sharing my clothes with her, let alone my husband! Even if I thought I was through with him, some jealous, girl-who-gets-everything part of me was sad. Sonny interrupted my thinking.

"I was just telling Blake about the cigarette and Meridee and that we both believe Lewis is alive."

Back to business.

"Wait a second, Sonny. I got the whole DNA, letters, Meridee connection," I said. "But why does all of this make you think Lewis is alive?" I looked at them both. I knew those looks—they had not told me everything.

"C'mon, you two. What is it?"

"Let's go back to my office," Sonny suggested.

Vivi was up and pacing when we all walked in.

"Well, look what the cat dragged in," she said, looking straight at Harry.

"Vivi." Harry acknowledged her, then stared straight at her belly. Vivi was beginning to show and she was dressed in a too-tight navy tank top and a light white sweater hanging open in the front. The little baby bump was now just barely visible and the look on Harry's face almost made me laugh.

"Yes, Harry. I am pregnant. It's time I said it out loud

for everyone," Vivi said. "And, yes, it's your missing brother's baby. Now somebody better damn well tell me right now, is my Lewis alive or not?" Vivi was understandably upset. *"Now!"* she demanded.

Harry and Sonny both stopped and stared for a minute. They both looked like this just added another fly in the ointment.

"Okay, well, I believe a congratulations is in order here," Sonny said, leaning over to Vivi and giving her a kiss on the cheek. All Harry could manage was a smile and a nod.

"Yes, congratulations," he said.

Sonny picked right back up on the business at hand. "We brought Dallas in for questioning today," he said.

"Oh! How convenient for you, Harry. Was she just as easy to talk to as she was to—"

"Vivi!" I cut her off. "We have to remember we are here for Lewis."

"We had known for quite a while about that interesting phone call she got the day Lewis disappeared," Harry said. "It was one of the first things she told Blake the day of the press conference."

"I remember," Vivi said.

"So," Sonny broke in, "we questioned her. She told us that the day that Lewis met you at the Fountain Mist, someone, her source, had called with some strange information. A tip," he explained.

"A tip that Lewis would go missing?" she asked.

"No, actually," he answered. "But that he was seen at the bank and withdrew a large sum of money."

"Well, what do *we* believe?" Vivi asked, becoming impatient.

"We believe Lewis may have owed someone some

money," Sonny began to explain. "We believe he had to pay someone by the end of the day. He met you for your…uhh, meeting, and couldn't bring himself to tell you. So he made the snap decision to just go ahead and get outta Dodge. Get the money and get it delivered. We think someone was helping him. We don't have any idea why he owed the money. We are hoping Kitty or Meridee can fill in the blanks."

Harry took over. "We do know now for a fact that Meridee was the smoker in the condo the night before Lewis went missing."

"What?" Vivi jumped up again. "You mean to tell me that Mother was the woman with Lewis the night before? Oh, my good God, why? Somebody explain that one to me."

I shook my head at Sonny. Harry's sense of timing had always been off. Sonny jumped in. "She's on her way here and she is going to be the one to explain it to all of us."

"So let me get this straight," I said. "The night before Lewis disappears, Meridee is at his condo. Is this a fact?"

"We think so, based on the cigarette evidence. We can place her there between 11:00 and 11:30 p.m."

"Okay," I continued. "Then the next day, Lewis meets with Vivi, disappears then later that day Dallas gets what will be the first of many phone calls saying someone saw Lewis at a bank in Birmingham a couple of hours after Vivi had reported him missing. The bank records show it was in fact Lewis, and that he withdrew a large sum of money and no one has seen him since. Do I have this straight so far?" I said like I was in a trial.

"Yes, so far, unless you count all those sightings

at Walmart and the Piggly Wiggly, I think that's what we've got," Sonny answered.

"So, where is Lewis? Who does he owe the money to?" I asked.

"Well, why don't we ask Miss Meridee herself," Sonny suggested.

And in the doorway of Sonny's office stood Meridee and Kitty with a look on their faces I will never forget. They looked like two little girls who had been caught stealing from the candy store and were in a huge heap of trouble. I looked directly at Kitty. She looked exhausted but raised an eyebrow at me that told me she got everything we were after. I nodded and looked at tiny little Meridee. She'd be eighty in a week and she was still causing trouble. She looked at me and made no gestures. She looked full of both guilt and pleasure at the same time. She seemed to almost relish in the confusion that surrounded her. Vivi approached her and placed both hands on Meridee's shoulders.

"Look at me, Mother. Please, please, tell me." Tears fell from her cheeks. "Is my Lewis…is he alive?"

Meridee, all five feet of her, looked at Vivi straight in her eyes and nodded. "Yes, he is."

Vivi lost it. "Well, why in hell didn't you tell me? You knew I was losing my mind! I can't believe you let me go through that for all this time! Meridee, why?"

Sonny moved over to Vivi to steady her.

"Why don't we all step down the hall to the vending room. We can sit at the big table in there and get all this out in the open," Sonny said.

I looked at Sonny and he lifted his drink as if in a toast. I got it. He was telling me not to worry. But I had to. It's what I do.

I walked between Vivi and Sonny. Harry walked between Meridee and Kitty. We all found seats at the big table and the questions began flying. Everybody was talking at once and voices were escalating. Harry and I avoided even making eye contact. Vivi was crying and mumbling over and over, "Where is my Lewis? Where is my Lewis?" It was completely out of control.

After a few minutes, Meridee stood.

"If y'all would hush for one damn minute, I could just tell y'all what ya wanna know."

The room fell into silence. The tiny woman with the face of an aging beauty queen commanded the group. She was fixin' to have her say.

"Okay, Meridee, the floor is all yours," Sonny said. Meridee looked slowly at each of us with her ocean-blue eyes, which squinted now as she studied us. No one dared speak or even breathe loudly. Mother was about to talk.

"Harry, several years ago, you and Lewis had that damn family-splitting fight…and all over money. I thought, my God, your daddy and granddaddy both would turn over in their graves. You ought to be ashamed," she said.

Harry was silent.

"That stormy night, your poor, drunk-ass brother showed up soakin' wet at my door. I put him to bed with some coffee and hoped he would sleep it off and that everybody would come to their senses and fix it in the morning. Little did I know, he would wind up in jail.

"While he was in jail, he wrote to me. He knew I took him in before, and he knew I was still behind him. I believed in him. I always did. He loved that microphone and that Crimson Tide like my sweet Frank did."

She walked around the table and stopped again at Harry, just over his shoulder. He looked down.

"You know, I always liked your brother," she went on. "He had a lot of potential, but you were an arrogant SOB to him. I never liked that. Anyway, he needed my help to repay some bad loans, and then he needed someone to invest in a dream of his. So he wrote to me. Couldn't come to you now, could he, Harry? I have my own money. I decided to help him. Frank would have greatly approved. And I didn't need anyone else's approval. So we've been working on something and it has finally started comin' to a head. He needed to put it to bed. And it was nobody's damn business, 'cause nobody else would have supported him anyway."

Again, she was staring at Harry, but she had a choice look for me, as well. I was clearly enjoying this verbal beating of Harry, but I knew I had to accept some of the blame myself. I'd followed Harry blindly, after all. And that was no one's fault but mine.

"Lewis had to do what he had to do," Meridee continued. "And he had to do it totally alone, 'cause y'all would have tried to stop him. So he left."

"Where did he go?" Vivi asked. "I am carrying his little one now and wherever he is, he will be a daddy soon."

Meridee walked over to Vivi. She bent down to look her in the eyes. She kissed her cheek and said, "I am so happy for you and I know Lewis will be ecstatic. He's very much alive, baby girl, and I am so sorry I had you worryin' this whole time. He's coming home to you soon. He is wrapping up something important."

"What the hell has he gone and done now?" Harry stood up, boiling over at all the accusation he'd faced in Meridee's eyes. "You think you've got Lewis under control—but you've just been naive! He's taken you for a ride, just like he did to me and my mother."

Meridee stood up straight and shot Harry a look that could knock the breath out of you. She was so good. The original Sassy Belle.

"You know what?" she said firmly, "I really appreciate your underwhelming concern for me and my money, but that boy came to me for a reason. You'll just have to wait and see what that is. Not one damn bit of this concerns you."

She wasn't finished. "And Dallas is another one y'all disrespect. That girl is rough around the edges for sure. Having a damn lunatic for a mother who was a no-show most of her life sure as hell didn't help, either. But she's got balls, that girl. And she knows how to get that story. It's high time all of you quit your snobby lookin' down at her and give her some respect."

"Nanny!" I stood and shot back. "How dare you? She made out with Harry! Yesterday! Right in my own backyard!"

"Well, Harry made out with her, too, don't you forget. And last I checked, she's not the one who's married."

I sat back down and strictly avoided eye contact with Sonny.

"So yes, everybody, make your judgments. It was me at Lewis's apartment before he took off. And, yes, Kitty—I was smokin'."

"What about the clothes? The ones that washed up in the river? I know they were his," Vivi said.

Sonny broke in. "We think he may have thrown those in the day he disappeared."

"He was doing whatever he had to do to make this work and keep Harry off his trail," Meridee explained. "He wanted—no, he *knew* this would work if he just could do it without interference. No law against throwin' your clothes in the river."

I took a big swig and finished off my drink.

Meridee went over and spoke to Vivi quietly.

"Vivi, listen to me. You know Lewis. He is doing a good thing. Don't you worry. He'll come back to you soon and he'll have you a story to tell. You'll be proud of him. It's all he ever wanted. Someone to be proud of him. I know I am."

"Why would he not want me to know about this?" Vivi asked.

"I know he meant to tell you. That's why he called you to meet that morning. But he was worried it would put you in an awful spot with the media and all. And especially with Blake. Both of them, Blake and Harry, would have hounded it outta you till they got what they needed to stop him from doing this deal. He just needed to get gone and put it all to bed. I'm sure when he sees you he will tell you everything."

"Well, I may be proud of him later but right now that really makes me mad," Vivi said. "I'm so mad I could cry, but I'm so happy he's alive, too. I'll have to beat the livin' crap outta him when he gets back."

I touched Meridee's old hand that still held her wedding rings, slipping around on old bony fingers. "Nanny," I said, looking over at her. "I understand, I think. Is that why you left to go gambling? Were you helping him somewhere?"

"Hell, no—" she laughed "—I was gambling just like I said. I just decided to get the heck outta town when he left. It's been hard enough to hold my tongue. I didn't want to have to lie, too. Besides, nobody would suspect the little old lady, would they? Especially if I was gone." She laughed. "Y'all trust me. I have never been wrong about a person in my life, and I'm not about to start at eighty years old."

Sonny spoke up. "Meridee, we also found a set of keys in Lewis's apartment. I matched it with the bank. But no box is registered to Lewis."

"That's 'cause they're my damn keys," Meridee said. "I gave Lewis a copy of the keys just in case."

"In case what?" I asked.

"In case I died! I am nearly eighty, and as hard as I was plannin' on partyin' on the gamblin' boat, well, you just never know, so I wanted him to have a copy of everything."

"Of what?" Kitty asked. She'd been well-behaved until now, but she just couldn't sit still any longer without jumping in.

"Of all of our hard work. I wanted to protect Lewis. This was all my doing and I wanted everybody to know the truth. I offered to help him on this venture. So I wrote it all down, every single thing and put it in my old box at the bank, and I gave Lewis a copy of my keys. I had it signed and notarized so nobody could ever call him a liar! So we'll just have to wait till he gets back to open the box."

"What in the world did South America have to do with all of this?" Kitty asked.

"Lewis found some pretty sound investors down there. They invest in projects like ours and we found them to be very credible. But now he has finished up with everything and I am certain he has paid them off."

"I want to know how the hell he got to Birmingham since we had his car pulled here for an evidence search," Sonny said, looking at Meridee. She looked at him,

"Damn, y'all don't miss a beat do ya?" she said. "He took my car and left it there in Birmingham while he did what he went to do. And I left it there for him at the motel."

"So, your car hasn't really been in the shop this whole time?" I asked, smirking at her.

"If it's the only little white lie I had to tell, then so be it." She smirked back at me.

Everyone sat silently, looking at each other, not sure of what to say or whom to say it to until Kitty broke the silence.

"Well, it's almost eleven. Y'all wanna go to the Waffle House?" Count on Kitty to be thinkin' of food in the middle of all this drama. "I think we have some celebratin' to do with this precious baby on the way and Lewis coming home soon."

Actually, it was a good idea since all the arguing and crying and stress had worked up everyone's appetite. We went for waffles and grits in the middle of the night, like one big, happy, dysfunctional family. But there was still one thought on everyone's mind: Would Lewis make it back to Tuscaloosa in time for kickoff? It was three months away, but with a baby on the way and so much to iron out with his job at the university, not to mention explaining himself to the whole city of Tuscaloosa, our plates were more than full. To get it all done in time would take a miracle, and that all depended on when Lewis would finally make his way back home.

22

With the dripping hot and humid days of May gone, the summer was crashing in with an incessant flurry of activity, but the excitement of fall and the buzz of Bama football were already in the air. The season, football of course, is all anyone talked about. That, and Lewis. Newspaper headlines, internet, radio and TV were all asking the same thing: Where is Lewis Heart? The Tide was missing its voice. Everyone had questions, but relief had fallen over Vivi like a blanket. "Lewis is alive," she said over and over. Sometimes it was like a mantra. Sometimes it was like an announcement.

The campus would be full of students again once summer ended, so Vivi and I decided to enjoy the quiet and go over to the strip for some ice cream a few days after Meridee had put us all squarely in our places at the police station.

We parked behind the Bryany-Denny football stadium, which seemed to be growing larger and larger every season. Higher and higher up they built it, so the

Tide could pack in more fans. They had won so many national championships, the fans were coming in from everywhere these days. Football season was the very best time to be in Tuscaloosa. And Tuscaloosa was the very best place to be during football season. The tailgating and the famous Dreamland ribs, I could get excited just thinking of it. And this year, Arthur's Moonwinx BBQ would be added to the mix! We still had summer in front of us, but we were all excited for the arrival of fall and football.

We made our way down the sidewalk to the quad and stopped at Denny Chimes, where we sat down on the steps at the base. The concrete was warm under us. Vivi was just over four months along now. She swore she and Lewis had been careful back in February, during one of their now-famous "meetings," but I guess some things are just meant to be. The early June sun baked us as we stopped to sit on the steps of Denny Chimes where only a month before we had the press conference about Lewis's disappearance.

"Blake, what do you think it's gonna be?" Vivi asked, rubbing her tummy, which was just starting to show its telling roundness. "I feel a girl is coming, but that may be just because I want to have more excuses for spa days," she said. We both giggled.

"I think it might be a boy," I said. "I've been doing a lot of thinkin' on this and Lewis would just love a boy."

She stopped and looked out over the huge expanse of the quad up toward the massive steps and entrance to the library. "You do think he'll be back, don't you, Blake?" I put my arm around her and pulled her to me. She dropped her head on my shoulder.

"Of course I do. Meridee said so. I just hope he has

one damn good story. I, myself, am a tad mad at him. I mean, he has put you through absolute hell. I know, Meridee said he had to, but I still want to question him," I said.

"I know, Blake, but I kinda get it, I think. I truly believe he was gonna tell me everything that morning, but he didn't want me to have to lie to you and Harry and say I had no idea where he went, when I would know. He also knows I tell you everything and he totally knows that you and Harry have no faith in him and would go to the ends of the Earth to stop him from doin' whatever he is doin'. I get it."

"I know, but he has put you through hell," I said.

"Yeah, I guess you can look at it that way, but I love him and I know he was protecting me."

"From what?"

"From you and Harry."

Instantly, I felt bad. I sat there in the warm sun under the protective shade of Denny Chimes and wondered if all these years since I had been married to Harry, Vivi had thought I was as pompous as he was. I guess I had been, and she had put up with me anyway.

"Why didn't you tell me that?" I asked her.

"What? That you had joined the head-up-your-ass club of which your dear husband is the president? You know how he loves to hold office."

I laughed in an embarrassed kind of way. Vivi was right. "I just wish you had said something," I said.

"Blake, how could I? I mean, really. I saw the changes comin' right after you started datin' Harry. But, you're my best friend. Really, you're more of a sister. And sisters stick together no matter what. Sassy Belles, remember?" She leaned into me, reminding me of our childhood club. "And, Blake, I know you. There are some things that a stubborn Belle like you needs to see for herself, even if it takes a little time. I didn't want to tell you and risk losing our friendship if you felt forced to choose. So I just had to wait and trust that you'd find your way back to yourself eventually. And you did—with a little help from our sexy cop...."

"Was I really that awful?" I asked

"Honey, you were the vice president of the club," she said.

I took Vivi home and went back to the office. The big showdown with the Myrnas was that afternoon and I needed to prep. Ms. Crabtree was on her way over to meet with us, too. This was the day I hoped to be rid of them once and for all. I arrived to find Wanda Jo sitting fanning herself with an old church fan.

"Hey, Wanda Jo, isn't the air conditioner working?" I asked her, going over to check the thermostat.

"Yeah, I think it is. I hear it anyway, but it's hotter than doughnut grease at a fat man's convention today and I'm 'bout to die. Probably the menopause." She was smiling, anticipating my next question. "And, yes, everyone has called and confirmed."

"Thanks," I said, "I'll call the repairman and see if he can come take a look." I walked down the hall to my office.

I felt ready to get this Myrna file closed and put to bed. We had been fighting them for months. I had finally written them and told them that the dates were perfectly clear, and the old place was fixin' to be placed on the Alabama Places in Peril list and it was time for them to find another spot for their mall. I thought we were done until I got a call from them yesterday and they said they had new information to present. *Fine. I'm ready,* I told myself. After what we had been through the last month with Lewis, I felt ready for anything. The Myrnas and Ms. Crabtree arrived at the same time and Wanda Jo set us all up in the conference room as usual.

"Good afternoon. Y'all have a seat," I said as everyone shuffled to a spot at the table. "Thanks for coming by today. I understand there has been a significant new development?"

"Yes, and we felt it was best to come in person and present it so we could all be on the same page," the younger Mr. Myrna explained. "As you stated, Ms. Heart, in your recent correspondence with us, the old Brooks Mansion is still zoned as a residence and no matter what, as you pointed out, we could not build a shopping center in that location. Years ago, before the zoning board was created, the structure could serve as anything, but these days it does need zoning approval. Well, we presented our proposal to the zoning commission this week and we are happy to report, the Brooks Mansion and the land it sits on *has* been zoned commercial by the Tuscaloosa zoning board." He smiled as he spoke.

My mouth suddenly felt like cotton and my chest tightened like I had had the wind knocked out of me. All I could manage was, "May I see the paperwork, please?" I looked at Ms. Crabtree and she was tearing up, certainly imagining that grand old place falling to the ground. I took a deep breath as I looked at the new zoning of the area. I was shocked and sickened.

"I know this must come as a surprise, but we intend to begin demolition in the next two weeks once the property offer is final." The old Mr. Myrna had a smirk on his face I wanted to slap right off of him. I swallowed hard as I looked at the new developments.

"Okay," I said, "we still have a couple of weeks. I will research this and get right back to you. I know we can still file an injunction. So this is not quite over yet, I assure you." I stood and said, "Thank you for coming, Wanda Jo will see you out."

Ms. Crabtree and I retreated to my office and shut the door.

"Oh, Blake, what will we do now?" she said as soon as we were safe from earshot.

"I am fixin' to march straight down to City Hall and get those damn meeting minutes and just see who voted on this. Then I'm going to wring their necks." I grabbed my bag and flew down the hall. Wanda Jo had just shut the door behind the Myrnas. I was on fire.

"See Ms. Crabtree out, too, please, and ask her if she needs a drink first. I've got a zoning board member I may need to kill. I'll be at City Hall if you need me."

"Well, for heaven's sakes, don't kill anyone in front of City Hall, they'll catch you for sure," she said, heading up the hall to Ms. Crabtree. I shut the door behind me and jumped in my car. I tried to call Harry several times but he never picked up. *Why hasn't he told me about this? He's on the zoning board for God's sakes. Surely he knows about this.* I arrived at City Hall and parked in front and ran up the steps like it was a hospital and someone I loved was in the emergency room. In fact it was just like that. I loved that old Brooks Mansion like it was a member of the family. I was rushing in to save her.

I ran straight to the zoning office, my high heels

clicking all the way down the hall like corn popping. After a brief discussion, the clerk handed me the minutes from the last vote, with one abstention. It was just last week. I stared at the minutes until I saw the Brooks Mansion listed. It was a three-to-two vote. I scanned down the page and there it was: *Should the Brooks Mansion be zoned for commercial business?* Attorney Harry Heart—*YES.* Harry had voted to zone the property commercial! My whole world was spinning out of control and my blood boiled into a rage. His name was listed right next to Judge Shamblin, the judge he saw at the University Club a couple of weeks ago. *Abstain.* The Judge hadn't voted on this issue. I couldn't make sense of it—and I was too absorbed by my fury to try to put it together. Harry knew I was working on this place! It was all I'd talked about now for months. He knew how much I loved it and how much I was invested. *That son-of-a-bitch!* It was even worse than finding him with Dallas. This was a betrayal of the worst kind. He had taken something I loved, something he knew was important to me and he'd used it to stab me in the back. Sadness swept over me. I felt sick. Defeated. It was over. My marriage was officially over in my heart at that second. I had a copy of the file made by the clerk and went back to my car and drove straight home.

I sent Harry a text: Emergency, meet me at home.

He was waiting for me when I got there, sitting at the dining room table putting finishing touches on a speech. I threw the file down on the table in front of him.

"Wanna explain this?" I said, glaring at him.

"What?" he said as he wrote, barely looking up.

"These are the minutes from the most recent zoning

meeting. You know, the one where you voted to have the Brooks Mansion zoned for commercial use?"

"So?" He really didn't get it. But he was about to.

"Harry, you voted yes and now the estate will be torn down. I have been working against that for months. You knew that. I told you the Myrnas and their silent partners were badgering the hell outta me and I was fighting them tooth and nail. Then you go behind my back and with one swish of your pen you undo all my sweat and hard work. Why, Harry, why? That place means so much to me, you knew that." I was shouting and my heart was racing. It was all I could do not to hit him. "I told you just a couple of weeks ago how important the place was to me. What the hell is wrong with you? Don't you ever hear me? Just tell me why."

He stood and walked over to the credenza and poured himself a glass of ice water. He was cool and matter-of-fact—like nothing I said had registered.

"Blake, it's business," he finally said. "I had to vote that way. I had no choice. You really can't take it personally."

"Of course you did. I'm sure no one was holding a gun to your head were they?"

"No, but it was a matter of election support, campaign support."

I stood there trying to put the pieces together. "What are you saying, Harry? Is that what you were talking to Judge Shamblin about at the University Club a couple of weeks ago?"

Silence.

"Was it? Answer me, Harry, *was* it?"

"Judge Shamblin has an interest in the property. She is invested financially."

"Oh, my God. *She* is the Myrnas' silent partner?" I stopped and stood in shock for a moment. "So she couldn't vote because it would be a conflict of interest, and she needed you to vote yes as a favor! And *now* she's gonna swing all her support and money your way for your campaign. Do I have this straight, Harry?"

"Blake, you wouldn't understand."

"That infuriates me, Harry. I get it, but you're right, I don't understand. I don't understand how I could be married to such a complete ass. Who are you? At one time, I had hoped we would try to figure things out, but as of right this second, we're officially done. I don't know you anymore. I can't trust you."

"Blake, as usual, you're taking this too far. Overreacting, as usual. Do you like being this dramatic all the time?"

"Okay, you want me calm and rational? I am exhausted from trying to be whoever it is you need me to be. I don't even know who that is. Lawyer's wife, politician's wife, perfect wife? Why wasn't I good enough being just me, Harry? You needed to marry someone that you could outshine, not someone who is your equal, your partner. You wanted someone who could be the little wifey and stay hidden behind you."

Harry broke in. "Blake, you know I have always supported you."

"Yes, as long as it didn't mean I would be in front, doing something amazing, like saving the Brooks Mansion. What in the world would you do if I ever decided to run for office? Would you campaign for me, be the political husband?"

"Oh, Blake, like you could ever hold an office. Come on, we all have the things we are good at."

"So, we can't both be good at the same thing?"

Silence. Harry had been pushed into a corner.

"Thanks for making my point. We're not really partners, then, in your mind. That's why you think you can do things like this. You truly believe I come second, behind the almighty Harry. You are the biggest ass I have ever known." I swallowed hard and choked back the lump in my throat. I didn't recognize the man in front of me. Or maybe I had just removed my rose-colored glasses.

"Just so I understand the *Harry Rules of Marriage,* I can do or be whatever I want as long as I stay in my box and never be good at anything *you* are also good at—especially if I might be better than you at it? Is that right? Do I have it straight?"

In that second, he looked at me, knowing I had uncovered the deadly fissure in our marriage, the kernel that had led to the destruction of us. I was married to an egomaniac. And my place would always be behind him, nodding like a bobblehead. How could I ever reach my own potential as a woman, as a lawyer, when my husband would only be able to cheer for me until I caught up to him? Then, in order to make sure he stayed ahead, he would do whatever it took to hold me back, including selling out on my dream for the beloved Brooks Mansion. I knew I could never be his bobblehead wife. No way. Not me.

Although I was exhausted from fighting with a husband who had betrayed me so deeply, I actually felt stronger. I had realized a truth and it felt like a cleansing. Harry would never be my partner, not in anything. His ego wouldn't let him. It was time to acknowledge and accept that fact.

"I want you out tonight," I told him calmly. "I'll stay at Mother's while you get out of here. And Harry, I hope you're happy. You've traded in our happily-ever-after for your own selfish political dreams, for your own ego. You're just out to see what favors you can cash in, from Dallas to Judge Shamblin, regardless of who you hurt in the process. You really are a piece of work. You disappoint me." With that, I headed back to my car and called Vivi and Sonny to meet me at Mother's.

Everyone was sitting at the yellow table when I walked in through the back door. Even Kitty was there. I got everyone up to speed and Meridee served us coffee and made us spaghetti.

"We still have two weeks," Sonny said.

"Yeah," Vivi jumped in. "The deal isn't final with the Myrnas yet, so maybe we can come up with something to stop them in time. We'll need money. A lot of money—then we could buy it ourselves."

"That's a brilliant idea," Kitty said. "The only problem with that is it's been zoned commercial now and so in order to finalize a purchase, even to make a bid, we'd need to be a commercial entity." Kitty did know her stuff.

"Well, we've got to think of something. I can't imagine the place being torn down," I said.

"Blake, I'm sure nobody else can, either," Vivi agreed. "We'll put our heads together and come up with something. Tonight I think we all need some rest. It's been a crazy week. Don't worry. You never go down without a fight and you've got the cavalry behind you here."

Meridee looked up from her supper and said, "Look,

I am not the least bit worried about this. When you get to be my age, you know everything's gonna be just fine. Things have a way of taking care of themselves. It always works out like it's s'pose to."

"Hey, that reminds me," Kitty said, "your big day is this weekend. Are you ready?"

"Ready as I can be," Meridee said with a smile. "It's gonna be a big party, so y'all hold on to your hats."

Meridee's birthday was the upcoming weekend, just a couple of days away and she had already booked the place and done the preliminary planning. She didn't want any of us in charge. She made it clear it was her damn party, as she liked to say, and she would be running the show. It was time to think about something happy.

I had known my marriage was over weeks ago. It was true. The minute Sonny kissed me that night right here in this kitchen, I had no idea how I would ever manage to stay married to Harry. But between my feelings for Sonny, his escapades with Dallas and now the zoning vote, we had nothing left. It seemed crazy, but I felt lighter. As though a burden had been lifted and now I could move on to the next chapter in my life. I had dreaded the big separation talk with Harry, but now it was over. It was *all* over. All in one swoop.

There was an easiness about this night at Meridee's supper table with Sonny there and Vivi and Kitty. It felt good between all of us. I relaxed into it and let the night wash over me. Meridee was right. Things do have a way of working out.

We finished supper and Kitty said good-night first and then Vivi went up the hall to her room at Meridee's. She and I planned to stay with Meridee until the party that weekend was over. Sonny and I cleaned up the dishes after we told Meridee good-night.

"Blake," he said, handing me a dish from the table, "I know you. And you'll figure something out. I have never seen you take no for an answer."

"This one is beyond me, Sonny. I have no idea what to do. I guess I could launch a fundraiser and try to out-bid the Myrnas, but I don't think I have enough time."

"No matter what, I'm right here. Just use me as you see fit." He smiled—hoping I would.

"Go home, big boy. I'm so tired tonight, I would fall asleep before we even got started."

"Sounds good," he said, "you sleepin' on me." He leaned down and kissed me good-night, long and soft and tender. He felt good all the way down to my soul. *This is what the real thing feels like,* I thought.

My sleep that night was restless as I tried to come up with ways to stop the Myrnas. When I finally did fall into a deep slumber, the ghosts of the Brooks Mansion invaded my dreams.

23

I spent the next couple of days at Mother's. All of the women kinda moved in till the big party was over. It just seemed right for us to stick close together while we waited out this storm of events. Apart from everything else, I wanted to make sure Harry got himself well and truly out of our house before returning.

Meridee cooked for us. She loved to make a big breakfast with biscuits and gravy and grits. I could hear her deep, rolling laughter all over the house. The scent of her perfume, the smell of coffee and bacon, it all made me feel so warm. We were safe here, no matter what was going on in our world. It kept me from having to deal with my own reality. I never wanted to leave the safety of those walls.

The plans were under way now for Meridee's big birthday party, and the phone rang off the hook all day long. She was loving it. The party would be her celebration, with her signature all over it. Meridee might have been turning eighty, but in her mind she was about to be twenty-one and Prohibition had just been lifted.

She wanted to have her party at the local karaoke bar, though Kitty had argued for the much tamer and more dignified Cypress Inn.

"A sunset ride down the river on the *Bama Belle,* followed by dinner on the banks of the Cypress Inn. That would be lovely," Kitty kept saying.

Meridee would answer in her truest voice, putting Kitty in her place. "Lovely for who? Queen Elizabeth? Or maybe you, for that matter? It's my damn party and I wanna dance and sing and throw back a few. No. The Catfish Bayou is my kinda place. I'm catering us a feast! Fried green tomatoes, fried okra, corn bread, turnip greens, boiled cabbage, black-eyed peas and lots of fried catfish! And I expect to dance all night! Now that's my kinda party!"

"Okay, Mother," Kitty would say, always pulling at her too-tight suit of the day. "Have it your way."

"Why, thank you so much. I believe I will," Meridee would answer. And she'd Charleston off.

The morning of the party, I awoke to what sounded like a circus. The phone ringing, Meridee and Kitty laughing, bacon frying and Meridee singing and dancing her way over to answer the phone. "Fletcher's Madhouse. May I help you?" I heard Meridee say into the phone from the other room. Vivi and I hadn't even left our beds yet, but Meridee seemed wide awake. "Great, Clara! Yes, you are RSVP'd, my dear. See you tonight!" She hung up. "Okay. That's 102!"

Vivi opened her eyes and looked over at me.

"I hope I can be like her when I'm eighty. I sure as hell don't have that kinda energy now." She laughed.

I rolled out of bed. We walked down to the kitchen

and Meridee was sitting at the table holding the news-paper. Lewis wasn't back yet, but Meridee seemed re-laxed about it. Excited even. Maybe because her big day was finally here. Maybe because she knew things we didn't—which seemed to be par for the course these days. She turned the paper around, laid it down and pushed it across the table under my nose in front of me just as I sat down. There it was, the headline: BROOKS MANSION SAVED! WEALTHY ANNONYMOUS BUYER SAYS THEY WILL RESTORE IT AND NOT TEAR IT DOWN.

"Oh, my God!" I felt the weight of the world lift from my shoulders. I felt like I was floating.

"I thought that might make your day," she said. "See, it all works itself out in the end." Meridee was smil-ing as she reached over and patted my hand. "Quite a birthday present, don't cha think?"

"Vivi!" I yelled down the hall. "Come here quick! The Brooks Mansion is saved!" Vivi was in the bath-room and stepped out with a toothbrush in her hand just as I called her name.

"What a miracle!" She was as excited as I was.

My cell was ringing in the bedroom. I ran down the hall and grabbed it. It was Sonny.

"Mornin', beautiful. See the paper? What about that?"

"Oh, Sonny! I am thrilled. Any word on who it is and what they're gonna do with it?"

"I guess it must be a business since the property is commercial, but no one's breathin' a peep about it. Guess it'll be a surprise."

"Oh, my Lord, it's the best surprise I've had in a while. The weight is off me and—oh, I've gotta call Ms. Crabtree! She's gotta be crazy with excitement."

"Talk to you in a few, baby." And he hung up.

I immediately called Ms. Crabtree. She said she was at the Preservation Society with the morning paper in hand. She said they were just thrilled that whoever it was wasn't planning to tear it down but to restore it.

"It's right here in the paper, Blake. It says *restore*. Oh, thank God for whoever it is. They are tuned in to Tuscaloosa and doin' the right thing. I am gonna personally hug whoever it is, that's for sure!"

"I'm so happy, Ms. Crabtree," I said. "Now I've gotta go help my grandmother turn eighty today and I couldn't be in a better mood to celebrate."

"Blake," she said, "thanks again for all your hard work. We are proud you are one of our members."

"Thanks, Ms. Crabtree, talk to you soon." I hung up and was literally skipping back to the kitchen where Vivi and Meridee were eating breakfast.

"I wonder who it is," I said as I sat down at the table.

"Whoever it is, it is an angel in disguise," Vivi said.

We finished up and cleared the table and made our plans for the day. We decided to start with shopping for gifts.

"C'mon, let's get going. Meridee's gonna need us. We'll be her assistants."

"Yes, the Assistants to the Queen!" Vivi said with a laugh.

"You need anything?" Vivi asked Meridee as we were stepping out the door. "We'll be right near the Piggly Wiggly."

"No, but if y'all are near Winn Dixie, I can use some more silver streamers. It's where I got all my decorations for the party," Meridee answered.

"Will do," Vivi said.

While we were out we bought Vivi a fantastic new

maternity outfit, a really sexy, clingy little navy pant-suit and new flat shoes. Her feet were already swelling.

We arrived back at the house in the early afternoon to find Kitty and Meridee visiting with the boys—Jack, Jim and Mr. Bailey for the dessert chaser.

"You girls don't get too sauced before the cake cuttin'," Vivi said playfully to them as we walked in the back door.

They sat at the kitchen table laughing and drinking their whisky. I had to stop a minute and just take this in. I wanted to remember them just like this: the clank of the glasses, the sound of their laughter and the smell of their perfume and alcohol floating throughout the house.

We got to the Catfish Bayou around five. The catering trucks were already there. Meridee had rented the karaoke bar out and it was being fully decked out in a "Hollywood Nights" theme from the disco years.

"She is so crazy!" Vivi said as we arrived. "This is gonna be awesome. This baby better be ready to dance the night away."

Kitty and Meridee got out of Kitty's white Lexus and walked across the parking lot to the entrance. A red carpet had been rolled out and red velvet ropes lined each side. A banner swung over the door. It read, WELCOME MISS MEREDITH, OUR STAR, ON YOUR 21ST BIRTHDAY. Meridee was so excited.

"Mother, I am assuming that you were in charge of signage?" Kitty said, full of sarcasm and a little laughter.

"Why, yes, is something wrong with it? I'll be over at the bar directing traffic if y'all need me. I'll be making a grand entrance, so somebody come get me when it's time."

Meridee walked over to the outdoor bar set up in the parking lot for the pre-party reception.

Vivi walked over to the table full of appetizers and I followed. There was really nothing left for us to do but greet everyone. Meridee had ordered all the food and decorations. The place was buzzing with workers and excitement inside and out.

The party would start at seven, with drinks, and hors d'oeuvres were beginning in just a few minutes. I pulled a chair over for Vivi and she sat down. I stood next to her, greeting and hugging everyone as they began to arrive.

Meridee's guest list was long and filled with memories held warmly in her heart. Seeing everyone reminded me of who I was and where I had come from.

Until guest #74 walked in.

"Hi, Harry," I said politely, "glad you could come." It wasn't public knowledge that we were breaking up so Dan thought it would be best if he at least made an appearance. Dan, the man, was right next to him— If he was going to get Harry to the Senate, he needed to protect his assets, so to speak. *Babysit* is the word that popped into my head, but I kept it to myself. Harry really had no idea how terrible he had been. He was blinded by his political ambitions and thought it was just all in a day's work. Politics was his new world, but I knew it wouldn't be mine. I was content to stay right here in Tuscaloosa taking care of my family and friends and being part of a community that I cared so much about. I certainly couldn't imagine a life anywhere else but here. I suddenly realized I was the happiest I had been in years.

I smiled at Harry and bumped Vivi on the shoulder. She glanced up at him.

"Hey." That's all she could muster. Vivi was never good at hiding her feelings and Harry had been awful to the two people she loved the most: me and Lewis.

He tried to compliment her. "You look nice," he said. But his comments hit like a rubber ball on glass. He walked on by.

"Hey, Blake, Vivi." Dan leaned in and hugged us and we both shot him air kisses.

"Good to see you, Dan. Harry's keeping you busy, I hear," Vivi said as I shoved her on the shoulder. It was so hard for her to keep it quiet. Especially when she really wanted to let it all out.

"I do love my job." Dan kept it going with a smile.

"Good thing," I said. He was smooth, there was no denying that. He walked on into the party, shaking hands with everyone and following closely behind Harry.

Not too far behind, I caught a glimpse of the bottle-blonde mouth of the South.

"Heads up," Vivi warned. "The entertainment has arrived."

Oh, God. How to greet her? "Thanks for coming." *No, that's not quite it. She may take that as an invitation to come again. What do I say?* "Nice to see you without your breast in my husband's mouth." *No, that wouldn't be right. Get a hold of yourself, this is Meridee's party.* So I simply said, "Dallas," as I nodded. Vivi did exactly the same.

She barely stopped to acknowledge us, and she said

nothing. Finally, near the end of the line, as I was hugging an old judge friend of Meridee, my eye caught on a welcome sight and I felt my shoulders literally drop in relief. Like the knight riding in on the white horse—well, maybe the cowboy sheriff on his stallion.

"Sonny," I said when he approached, and I reached out my hand to his. He grabbed it and I pulled him to me.

"Hey, beautiful." He kissed my cheek. "And Miss Vivi, you look stunning and you do have that glow."

He leaned down and kissed her cheek, too.

"Save me all the slow dances, baby, that's why I'm here," he said to me and winked.

I glanced over my shoulder and saw Arthur and Bonita arriving in style, both of them dressed up and stunning. Bonita was smiling like it was her party instead of Meridee's.

"Hey, darlin'. You and Vivi look maaavelous," she said in a playful tone. "I told you all of this would get solved before we knew it. I had every confidence in Sonny and myself. Now, we will see you all later. Arthur owes me a dance."

"Ain't she just something?" Arthur said, smiling ear to ear.

Sonny made his way up to the front near the door to the restaurant. People were already gathering around the open bar Meridee had ordered. When most everyone had arrived, Vivi and I left our posts near the door. Meridee had asked Sonny to announce her arrival. The guests, all milling around in the parking lot, were instructed to take their places for the grand entrance on either side of the long red carpet that stretched from the entryway to the dance floor. Sonny grabbed the karaoke mic, and we all gathered around the red carpet. The bar was darkened and someone turned on the spotlights and disco ball, lighting the place up like a movie premier. One spotlight was aimed at the center of the red carpet and my Stetson man stepped right into it.

"Ladies and gentlemen, tonight is like no other. We are here not only as guests, but as witnesses to a fantastic, once-in-a-lifetime event. May I present to you the woman of the hour, on the occasion of her twenty-first birthday, Miss Meredith Fletcher!"

All of a sudden, the spotlight swung around toward the end of the red carpet, and there in its glow was Meridee, perched upon a Persian cot held up by four shirtless men of pure muscle who were squeezed into tight Wranglers and cowboy boots.

Meridee had a drink with an umbrella in one hand and a fan in the other. She waved and blew kisses at the crowd. She had even hired a photographer.

The DJ started the song "It's Raining Men," and it could probably be heard for miles. Everyone along the velvet ropes was toasting her and laughing. And Meridee just kept waving to her adoring public and blowing kisses.

Kitty came over and stood next to me as she cried and laughed at the same time.

"God, I love that old woman," she said. "My birthday's next month, remember? There's still time to throw me a shindig like this."

"I thought you wanted a classier affair at the Cypress Inn," I reminded her.

"I do, but I just love the idea of being the center of attention with all these gorgeous men and their washboard abs. Delicious!" She was smiling and picturing herself in the middle of it all.

As the buff men carried Meridee up the red carpet to her premier, the crowd followed her to the dance floor where the party took off. Meridee was at the center table wearing a tiara and signing autographs. Everyone was laughing and the Buff Boys were waiting on her like boy toys.

Harry was working the room like it was a political fundraiser. He split his time between glancing at me and smiling at Dallas. I think he was just watching me to see if I was looking at him and not Sonny. I was looking at Sonny.

As I glanced in a mirror to check that my makeup was still in place, my eyes caught the reflection of a man in silver, wire-framed glasses just behind me. I formed my mouth to scream when he caught me and pressed his index finger to his lips. "Shhhh," he insisted, shaking his head. "No."

It was Lewis.

My stomach had dropped. I turned to look at Vivi, then darted my eyes quickly back at Lewis. He was gone. The spot where he stood held other faces. Bodies moving about. *Was he really ever there?* My cell phone buzzed with a text. It read: TAKE VIVI OUTSIDE. I did not even think. I immediately leaned into Vivi and said over the loud music, "Hey, I need some air. Come outside with me a sec."

"Oh, Blake, the party is just starting! Really?"

"Vivi Ann McFadden, if I have to carry you on my back, you are going out now!"

"Okay! My God! You must be 'bout to suffocate! I'm comin', I'm comin'."

We followed the red carpet outside. Little trees had been set all around the parking lot covered in little white lights. In the now darkened lot, the lights cast an amber glow.

"It's so pretty, isn't it?" she said.

"Yeah," I answered, barely paying attention, looking for Lewis. My breath had not come back from thinking I had seen him. *Okay, Lewis,* I thought, *where the hell are you?*

Just then I saw him. He was larger than life after all this time. He was in perfect blue jeans and a whiter-than-white starched oxford shirt, untucked—a gentler, more relaxed version of his older brother. He was behind one of the lighted trees.

Lewis walked over to me, quietly gesturing for me to be silent. He moved up behind Vivi, who was staring up at the bright moon and wispy clouds. I smiled and stepped back and we traded places. Her back was to him and so I knew he hadn't yet seen the telltale roundness that was starting to show under her clingy pantsuit. They were both about to give each other the shock of a lifetime. I realized in that flash of a second that I was going to get to witness this unbelievable moment firsthand. I had front-row tickets to the event of the year!

Lewis moved right up to Vivi. Then, pushing gently, he pressed his mouth to her ear from behind.

"Hey, Red," he whispered.

Vivi turned around and for one moment she was speechless.

Lewis saw her belly as she faced him and was also silent.

It took about three full seconds before both of them

began hollering, "Oh, my God! Oh, my good God in heaven!" simultaneously.

All the screaming was followed by a huge embrace. Then more oh-my-Gods and then another long embrace.

"You!" she said.

"Yes! You?" he said back to her, looking at her belly.

"Us! Ours!" she exclaimed, laughing and crying at the same time.

"Well, my God!" she said. They held each other tightly, talking in one-word sentences.

I felt so lucky as I watched them bubbling over with emotion and couldn't help a few tears of my own.

"Come over here, Blake. Can you freakin' believe this shit?"

Lewis was laughing and crying, too.

"No, I can't," I said, wiping tears and walking over to them. "Now, Lewis!" I said, grabbing him and hugging him tight. "What the hell!"

"I know, Blake. I am so sorry."

God, I had to admit, it was really good hearing that deep voice. I breathed for the first time in minutes.

Lewis was home. It was all gonna be okay.

"What in the hell has been going on? Where have you been?" Vivi said.

"I'm so sorry, baby," he said to Vivi as he hugged me. "I didn't know what else to do. I was gonna tell you that day at the Fountain Mist. That's what I met you there to do. But I lost all train of thought just knowing I was gonna see you. You make me so crazy. So then I thought I would tell you afterward. But then I realized that if you knew everything, Harry would browbeat you till you told him. I thought he'd use Blake against you and I just couldn't put you in that position. The more I thought about it the more I…"

Vivi put her finger to his lips. "Shh," she said. "It's okay. You're here now. I already cussed your name and had several hissy fits. Blake and Meridee helped me see why there was no other way. I know you did what you thought you had to at the time. Just don't you ever freakin' do it again!"

"I'm so sorry," he said. "I will make it up to you. I promise you. I have a big surprise for you, Vivi." He was holding her face in his hands.

"I think I had one for you, too," she said, laughing.

"You sure did! I'm gonna tell you my secret, baby, and you'll see there really may be such a thing as Happily Ever After."

"What?" Vivi asked, her face growing more curious.

Just as he began to speak, Meridee appeared at the front door of the bar.

"Hey," she yelled, "get over here and give your partner a hug. This is my damn party, after all."

Lewis walked over to her at a clip and enveloped her in a bear hug that lifted her off the ground.

"You get her all put to bed?" Meridee asked.

Clearly she knew more than we did.

"And tucked in with a kiss." He winked at her.

"Good for you, honey! Now, let's go spread the news." With that, Meridee held Lewis's hand and reached back for Vivi with the other hand. "Here we go," she announced.

"I guess we'll all find out together," I said, looking at Vivi with a shrug.

We headed inside the Bayou. The music hit us as we walked inside. People were everywhere and the drinks were flowing. Sonny was standing at the door. I slipped my hand into his. He looked over and his eyes caught Lewis.

"Oh, my God!" he said. "Finally. This should be good. We're gonna get our answers."

"Yes," I said. "I think right now."

Meridee took the mic from the DJ and interrupted the music and dancing. She tapped the microphone and it made the usual popping noises.

"Excuse this interruption of your fabulous time, but the Disco Queen has a very important announcement. Y'all please make room for the media."

Dallas made her way to the front, her camera crew following her. Meridee was always for the underdog and no one could argue that Dallas and Lewis weren't the underdogs. While I still just hated her on so many levels, I was starting to see Dallas through Meridee's eyes. Scrappy, trying to better herself. I still knew I would never be friends with her.

That's what Lewis was doing, too. Trying to be better. Meridee was just drawn to dedicated people like them. She knew she could help them. And that made her happy. That was at the core of who Meridee was, a helper, a problem solver. Kitty was like that, too, to a point. And so was I. I had to help Vivi. And she had to help me. I smiled and realized that it wasn't really our attitude that defined us, but our love and dedication to each other—that's what made us real Sassy Belles.

Lewis was behind Meridee, with Vivi holding on to him for dear life, as though she'd never let him out of her sight ever again.

Meridee began. "Do I have your undivided attention? I'd like to introduce someone to you. Y'all have known him for years, but not in this capacity. I'd like to introduce to you the new owner and CEO of WCTR, Tuscaloosa's brand-new radio station, the Crimson Tide Roll. Everyone, please give a warm welcome to Lewis Heart, the brand-new 50,000-watt Voice of the Crimson Tide. *All Tide, All The Time.*"

Gasps, oh-my-Gods and applause and mumbling filled the entire bar.

"Yes," little Meridee interrupted. "A shock, I know. WCTR's virgin broadcast will premier just in time as the Tide kicks off their season. Lewis, take the floor, baby." She handed the mic to Lewis and silence quickly muffled the room.

"Hi, y'all," he said. "I guess you've been wondering where I've been. Well, I have been a little busy."

Everyone laughed.

"I know, it wasn't right of me to take off without a word of warning. But I had to handle this with no interference so we could hit the broadcast in time for the Tide's kickoff. And I couldn't have done it without the help of my partner here." Lewis draped his arm over Meridee's shoulder.

Everyone gasped again. Meridee spoke into the mic, grabbing it from Lewis. "Yes! I damn well helped him. It's my birthday present to myself!" Then she handed the mic back to Lewis.

"I have always, for as long as I can remember, dreamed of owning my own radio station. This time, with Miss Meridee by my side, it will be a huge success. I want to say a very public thank-you to Miss Meridee, especially for believing in me when no one else would. Thank you for seeing my dream and knowing it could be a reality. For knowing it could be successful.

We are partners for life on this. The station is going to be located in a place near and dear to our hearts right in the center of town so everyone can come and visit and take tours. Did anyone see this morning's paper? Well, I am very proud to announce I am the new owner of the Brooks Mansion."

Spontaneous applause broke out at this amazing announcement.

"Oh, my Lord have mercy!" Vivi said.

"Lewis is wonderful! You were right all along. Oh, my God, I could kiss him," I said to her.

"I have always wanted to make everyone proud and give back to the city and its citizens who have done so much for me," Lewis continued. "Y'all stood behind me no matter what—and you kicked up a search when you thought I was missing—and this makes me very proud. The mansion is being restored and will be ready by the end of summer, just in time for kickoff."

More applause broke out and whistles and everyone was chanting Crimson Tide cheers.

Then he turned to Sonny and continued. "To the police and the citizens of Tuscaloosa, I am prepared to pay any fines or answer any charges for faking my disappearance. But it's the only way this station could ever become a reality, and I wanted to give it to the city I love and the team that I adore."

Lewis was emotional and there wasn't a dry eye in the room. It was what he'd always dreamed of, to do something wonderful, respectable. To be better than Harry. He had outdone himself and had come up the hero for all of us, saving the beloved old mansion and giving us all a radio station to be proud of. He wanted people to know his heart. And now they did. Lewis showed an integrity and a substance that only Vivi could see before. Well, Vivi and of course, Meridee. He was really something unexpected. I was so proud of him and for him. He turned to Vivi next.

"To Vivi Ann McFadden, I love you. I always have. I'm sorry for all the incredible hell I put you through."

"I understand completely now," Vivi answered and tiptoed up to kiss his cheek.

Lewis looked down at her. "I wanted to save this for later, but now really is the best moment." Lewis dropped to one knee and pulled out a sparkling square-cut diamond in an antique silver filigreed setting.

"Vivi Ann McFadden, I have loved you for as long as I can remember. You make me happy like no one else ever has. You are the spice in my life, all my fun and my whole heart. I want to share my life with you forever. Please do me the honor of sharing my life with me. It will be all the gift I will ever need. I love you and will always love you—till I am done in this life and then forever after that. Will you marry me?" Lewis was smiling that dimpled grin and his eyes were misty as he looked softly at Vivi.

"I absolutely will! Yes! Yes! Yes!" Vivi squealed.

Sonny squeezed me into him. It was such a beautiful, happy, romantic moment. Vivi had found the perfect man for her, and I knew Sonny was the man I wanted. I had wanted him for as long as I could remember.

Vivi thinks I saved her but actually I think she saved me. I really had been saved by a belle. A belle named Vivi. And my cop? I guess Harry *had* always been right. He always said I should have just married my cop. I smiled to myself at the thought. I had changed so much in a month's time—or maybe I had just simply come back home. Vivi was a new woman herself, a mother-and wife-to-be. She was calmer, maybe even a tad less needy. Being pregnant was already bringing out the best in her. It was the Vivi I had always known was there. And it was so good to see her like this.

Lewis rose and held Vivi's face and kissed her long and soft and sweetly in front of everyone—including the media, who went wild snapping pictures and rolling tape. Dallas stood front and center with her film crew getting footage for the ten o'clock news.

Mic in hand, she gave one of her trademark smiles to the camera as she announced, "The town of Tuscaloosa has three whole months before the kickoff of the new season, and it looks like the Voice of the Crimson Tide has a busy summer ahead."

* * * * *

Acknowledgments

I am so grateful to:

My fairy godmother and beloved agent, Elizabeth Pomada, for believing in me and always saying the right thing, my favorite of which is, "Don't worry, Beth. Just write." Much more than my agent, you are also one of my dearest friends.

Everyone at Larsen-Pomada Literary Agents: Michael Larsen, you are the best coach! Clare Cavanaugh, for providing me a gentle crash course on writing.

My family at Harlequin MIRA: the design team of Michael Rehder and Quinn Banting, for making my cover sexy, fun and oh-so-Southern. Sheree Yoon, Melanie Dulos, I am so lucky to have you both in my corner. Michelle Venditti, for fantastic ideas and for being the binding that keeps us all on the same page. My editor, Valerie Gray, for believing in me and helping my story blossom like a magnolia. Underneath, I am sure you're wearing a cape. You are my superhero.

My mother, Betty, an original Sassy Belle, for being the most stubborn person I know and never letting me quit—pushing me over the finish line.

Brooks, my son, for giving me constant love and support and a shoulder to cry on (which I did a lot), for your patience and for helping me make my computer work when I was ready to toss it. I love you more than life itself. You are forever my sweetheart and the center of my universe.

Ted, my husband, best friend and source of the passionate love scene. You are the most patient soul on the planet. You always make it all better.

My brother, Bruce. I am so lucky to have a former tackle-football player running block for me. My stepfather, Richard, for supporting me unconditionally. My in-laws, Dr. Margaret Bosse and Dr. Richard Ishler, Dr. Ann Ishler and Dr. Richard Bosse, for all of the encouragement.

My Sassy Belle sisters, Lynn Watts Zegarelli, Susan Sexton DePappa and Joyce Albright. For providing me with so much laughter and "bless her heart" moments. Joyce, for the suitcase full of green tomatoes you brought with you to L.A.! Susan, for providing the margarita slumber parties every time I was home. Lynn, for all the best ideas and for reading the book as many times as I did. Full of Southern sass, a part of each of you lives on these pages.

My "brother" Steve Philips, for suffering through the first draft and encouraging me with gentle statements like, "How does this make any sense? Maybe it's just 'cause I'm a guy."

Connie Hunnicutt Stringer for helping me spread the word in social media. Trace Neighbors, for so much inspiration. Greg Dawson, for making me believe I really could. David Thompson, my high school debate coach, for pushing me on so many levels. I am the best me because of you.

My family in heaven: Daddy, for being my guardian angel and for parenting me from the other side. My grandfather, Frank, former play-by-play announcer for the Alabama Crimson Tide, for all the inspiration. My Grandma Albright and my grandmother, Nanny, two very Sassy Belles. Nanny, your yellow kitchen table was the center of my childhood happiness. I felt you on my shoulder every single day as I wrote this.

And to all my friends and family in my precious hometown of Tuscaloosa, Alabama. I love Tuscaloosa like no place else. I hope I have made y'all proud.

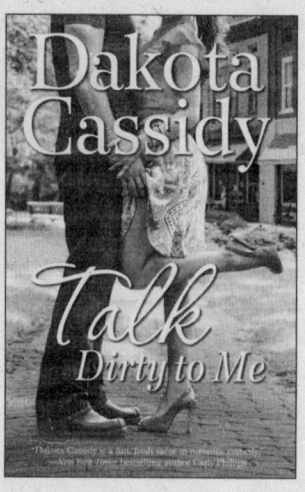